DEADLY DANCE

A David Vogel mystery

Hilary Bonner

This first world edition published 2017
in Great Britain and the USA by
SEVERN HOUSE PUBLISHERS LTD of
Eardley House, 4 Uxbridge Street, London W8 7SY.
Trade paperback edition first published
in Great Britain and the USA 2018 by
SEVERN HOUSE PUBLISHERS LTD

British Library Cataloguing in Publication Data
A CIP catalogue record for this title is available from the British Library.

ISBN-13: 978-0-7278-8734-4 (cased)
ISBN-13: 978-1-84751-852-1 (trade paper)
ISBN-13: 978-1-78010-912-1 (e-book)

Typeset by Palimpsest Book Production Ltd.,
Falkirk, Stirlingshire, Scotland.

For Chris Clarke
Who planted the seed...

I glimpsed him in the twilight
I lost him in the night.
I thought I had him in the daylight.
There he was before me surely
In all his twisted might,
But I never saw him really.
With a pirouette and a prance,
He led me such a deadly dance
I didn't stand a chance.

PROLOGUE

The water cascading over my head was cold as the ice in my veins. Only my tears were warm.

I did not deserve the comfort of hot water.

With what I had done.

I scrubbed at my shivering body until my skin hurt. I needed to make myself clean. I deserved pain.

With what I had done.

I was still dirty when I eventually switched off the flow from the shower. Of course I was. Filthy. I doubted I would ever be clean again. Not really.

My right shoulder hurt at the top.

I reached to touch it. My fingers came away stained with my own blood. I had rubbed myself raw.

The sight of the blood turned my stomach. I reached the lavatory just in time. I fell to my knees retching and was sick into the bowl again and again and again. It was as if my body were purging itself. I stood up and stared into the mirror above the basin.

In order to survive, I had to regain control of myself.

The eyes staring back at me were rimmed red because of my tears.

Were they frightening eyes?

They seemed to be expressionless. After all, I was now a frightening man. I had committed an act of pure evil. For the first time? I wasn't even sure of that.

I hadn't meant to, of course. Or had I?

I barely knew myself any more.

PART ONE

ONE

The girl had been reported missing by her mother at 2 a.m. when she'd failed to return home. Her body was found three and a half hours later, in the heart of Bristol's red light district by refuse collectors on the early shift picking up the rubbish put out by the bars and clubs and restaurants.

It was jammed into a boarded-up doorway, behind two wheelie bins towards the top end of Stone Lane, a cobbled cul-de-sac leading from West Street to a row of commercial warehouses and goods depots, all of which would have been empty of people after daytime hours.

There were CCTV cameras protecting the commercial premises and more outside a pair of incongruous, run-down, Edwardian villas set back to the left; but none covering the stretch of cobbled street where the dead girl lay and where she had almost certainly met her death.

There could be no doubt that she had been murdered. Detective Inspector Vogel wondered if the perpetrator had known where the CCTV cameras were positioned and had calculatedly avoided his violent crime being recorded.

Little attempt had been made at concealment. The wheelie bins provided only a partial screen. It was reasonable to assume that the body could not have remained unnoticed, had she lain there during daylight hours the previous day.

The girl had almost certainly been strangled. That seemed clear enough to Vogel before even a preliminary medical examination had been conducted.

The Detective Inspector stood looking down at the skinny little body lying before him. She was the same age as his own daughter. He already knew that she was fourteen.

Her tongue protruded from blackened lips showing the vestiges of vermillion lipstick. Her face was swollen and her neck bruised. Her unseeing eyes were wide open, their dead emptiness emphasised by the dark eyeliner that encircled them and the black fringe of lashes heavy with mascara.

There was dried blood on her face, spattered on her clothes, exposed flesh, on the raised step beneath her and over part of the cobbled street.

She looked only tragic now. And so very young. Vogel tried to imagine how she had been the previous evening. She would have appeared considerably older than her years, he thought, which no doubt had been her intention. She'd been wearing a sparkly black top over a denim micro-skirt, black lacy tights and silver shoes with platform soles and very high heels.

Vogel imagined her teetering off on those heels, excited, perhaps just a bit nervous, embarking on what was to be her last adventure.

Her mother had thought she was visiting a school friend for a homework-sharing evening. As time passed and her daughter did not return home, the anxious mother had telephoned the school friend, who'd confessed that she hadn't seen the girl at all.

The girl surely wasn't wearing the sort of clothes she would have chosen for an evening at home with a chum. She'd had some other plan. An arranged meeting more than likely. Perhaps with someone she had met on the internet, some pervert who had groomed her and persuaded her to meet him.

Vogel couldn't know that, of course. He was already aware that no computer had been found at her home. Neither her mother nor her husband, the girl's stepfather were computer people, apparently. That meant they might not be fully aware of the dangers vulnerable, young people faced from the internet, and the ease with which they could be tempted into high-risk and often out-of-character behaviour. The girl had a laptop, the mother had said, but she'd taken it with her, in the little, pink ruck sack that served as her schoolbag.

Now the rucksack lay on the ground a few feet away from her body. It had her name stencilled on it, at the centre of an elaborate doodle of vibrant, multicoloured butterflies. Mel Cooke. Short for Melanie. That was how the preliminary identification had been made so quickly.

Vogel glanced at his watch. It was 7.05 a.m. on an unseasonably cool, mid-May day. The second Friday of the month. He shivered in the chilly, early-morning air; though the heartbreaking sight of the dead body was probably the cause of that every bit as much as the cold.

His nose was beginning to run and he feared he might be about to have a sneezing fit; something to be avoided at a crime scene. After taking a couple of steps away from the body, he pulled down the zipper of his Tyvek suit (worn to protect the integrity of the scene) and reached into the pocket of his inadequate, corduroy jacket in search of a handkerchief. His fingers brushed against the envelope he had been carrying around with him for over a week. Even now, being reminded of its presence unsettled him. He couldn't just ignore it, but neither could he think about it at such a moment.

He turned his attention back to the dead girl. Even in the condition she was in he could see that she must have been exceptionally pretty. Her hair was only gently wavy but very black and her skin just dark enough to indicate that she was probably of mixed race.

He wondered if she would have been allowed to go out on a school night if it had not been for her homework sharing story. A lot of parents didn't insist on that sort of thing any more, of course. But as she had bothered to lie, the indication was that she might otherwise have been kept at home. Not for the first time Vogel reflected on the fine thread from which all human life was suspended.

He stepped carefully towards the pink rucksack. He thought the butterfly drawing was rather well done. Assuming that Mel Cooke herself was responsible for it, maybe she would have grown to be an artist of some kind, like Bristol's own Banksy, or another Tracey Emin. Banksy's influence was ever present in Bristol, where those seeking to emulate him plastered the city with graffiti, including on the walls of Stone Lane.

When confronted by murder victims, Vogel could rarely stop himself wondering about their lost lives. What the future may have held for them. What they may have become.

With the fingers of one gloved hand he unzipped the rucksack and peered inside. He could see no laptop, only what appeared to be a change of clothes. He called over a Crime Scene

Investigator to empty the rucksack. It contained a pair of jeans, a tee-shirt and a sweater and a pair of trainers.

Vogel had half expected to find those clothes, or some that were similar. The girl's mother had given a description which indicated that when she'd left home she had not been wearing anything like the provocative outfit in which she'd been dressed when she met her death. He assumed that the skirt and the glitzy top and shoes had been in her rucksack ready for her to change into as soon as she got the chance. Her mother would have taken it for granted that the bag contained schoolbooks for her daughter's homework session. And her laptop, of course.

Would they never learn, Vogel wondered? He knew the answer, of course. At that age you didn't see danger. Only the thrill of a new experience. That was how it had always been. Vogel suspected that was how it always would be. Parents could make rules, the police and the media could issue warnings and publicise the dire consequences of rash behaviour. It made no difference, and it never would.

With a heavy heart he glanced back at the dead girl. It was such a damned waste.

Her top had been ripped open, exposing slightly paler skin and one, barely-formed breast. The little skirt had been pushed up around her waist. Her tights and panties, both black, had been torn from her. They lay in shreds alongside her body. Vogel wondered vaguely if the tights had been torn before the attack. He was an observant man. And, in any case, it was impossible not to notice the modern fashion for ripped clothing – jeans as well as tights – favoured by the young. Vogel did not find it attractive and was glad that his own daughter had not shown any tendency towards that particular fashion. Not yet anyway. But he supposed both Rosamund and this poor, dead girl would consider his attitude to be that of a boring, old fogey.

The girl had barely any pubic hair. Vogel blinked rapidly behind his thick, horn-rimmed spectacles. His hands were trembling and he was sweating now, even though the morning air was so cool. He had lost count of the number of murders he had investigated. It never got any easier. And this was a bad one.

Melanie Cooke was just a child to Vogel. He didn't want to look at that part of her. He felt like a voyeur. With the camouflage of her street-wise attire half removed, she was so very vulnerable.

Her thin legs were covered in scratches from her assailant's finger nails perhaps as he ripped at her clothing. But wouldn't he have worn gloves? Vogel wasn't sure. It would, he supposed, depend on whether or not the attack was premeditated.

Even if a meeting had been arranged with some pervert, even if Vogel was right about that, it did not mean the bastard had meant to kill. It did not even mean that he had meant to assault the girl. Men of that ilk often thought of themselves only as seducers; they believed they were capable of getting their way by persuasion. And sometimes they so captivated and confused their young victims that they were able to do just that.

Not in this case, though, that was clear.

SAUL

I wanted to get married. No, it was more than that. I *needed* to get married. I'd been married before. But that was when I was little more than a kid and it was just a distant hazy memory. I felt if I had a wife now, the right wife, that would solve everything.

I wanted the security of it. Somebody once wrote that marriage was the deep peace of the double bed after the hurly-burly of the chaise lounge. I'd never known peace. Not in my entire life. Surely I was entitled to some peace? Just like other people. That was all I wanted really, to be like other people.

But I couldn't quite trust myself, because I never knew when the demons were going to get hold of me. So I didn't feel able to court a woman in the normal way. Internet dating seemed to be the solution. I liked the anonymity. You can hold back as much of the truth about yourself as you like. Indeed, tell no truth at all, if you wish.

It wasn't that I was ashamed of myself, what I did, what I was. Far from it, really. But I wanted to be sure that I hadn't made some dreadful mistake, before I revealed too much about myself. There were things about me which were difficult to share. I wasn't a straightforward man. I had certain personal difficulties. I needed to protect myself.

And I wasn't just secretive. I was also shy.

I googled dating sites first, but most of them were not what I wanted at all. They were all about sex. Sex was incidental to me. I wanted a wife, one who had the same ideals and priorities that I had.

So I signed up to *Marryme.com*

It was pretty easy. I just had to supply an email address, a picture and write something about myself. And pay a fee, of course. Photo-shop is a wonderful tool; I used a real picture of me and then doctored it. I changed my hair colour, gave myself tinted spectacles and some facial hair, altered the shape of my chin and nose – just a bit. The idea was that, if I ever got to meet a woman this way, she would be able to accept that the picture was one of me – with a different look. After all it's not just women who do different looks nowadays, is it? But if anyone who knew me happened to log onto the site and call up my details, they wouldn't recognise me at all. That was what I hoped for, anyway.

Then came the personal details and the message to prospective brides. Clearly the idea is that you should sell yourself or, at least, make an attempt to. I wasn't very good at that sort of thing. I might not be ashamed of myself, but I suppose I don't have very high self-esteem. So I'd tried to be brief and factual, whilst making it very clear how serious I was about the outcome of any internet-based liaison. After all, there was no point in not doing so, was there? I certainly wasn't seeking 'a bit of fun', as a lot of would-be internet daters seemed to call any kind of sexual encounter. Indeed, I had never been very good at 'fun'. The various sexual encounters I'd experienced over the years had, more than anything else, been stressful to me.

I suppose people might regard me as a dull sort of man. I'm certainly awkward socially, which doesn't help when you are trying to find yourself a wife. So there was no point in trying to portray myself as being a dashing, charismatic sort of chap. I could only hope that I might somehow come across a woman who was like me. She didn't have to be beautiful or clever or anything special. Just someone who wanted what I wanted.

'My name is Saul and I am a 33-year-old supply teacher,' I wrote. 'I live in a village near Swindon and I would like to meet a young woman of around my age whose intentions are as serious as mine. I can easily travel anywhere in that region or to London or the West of England. I want to share my life with someone. I want a family, so I'm looking for someone who would have a child with me. I don't care what that someone looks like, what she does or doesn't do for a living, or anything like that. I don't mind whether or not she already has a child or children. I just want someone to care for, who will care for me. I've never really had that, not as an adult. I want the same sort of marriage my parents had: long, loving and complete. But I never seem to meet anyone with the same values and ambition that I have. My interests are simple and quiet. I like to read and go to the cinema. If you are out there, please get in touch. I need you.'

It was true. I needed her. I really did. Even though I did not yet know who she was. In fact, there was a lot of truth in what I wrote for my profile on that website.

Not all of it, of course. But I was confident that, when I finally met my someone, she would understand my reluctance both to post an accurate photograph of myself and to plaster the intimate details of my personal life all over the net.

I would save that for the right person. For the one who would become my wife. Until then I would keep my secrets.

TWO

Vogel was still standing, quietly looking at the sad scene before him, when the rest of his team began to arrive.

One high-heeled, silver shoe lay close to the body. Totally unsuitable footwear for a 14-year-old in any circumstances, Vogel thought. He knew his colleagues (and sometimes even his own wife) considered him old fashioned and behind the times, but he was too old and set in his ways to change now. In days gone by – before the age of political correctness – police, judges, and lawyers alike might well have referred to a victim, dressed up the way this one was, as having asked for it. Vogel would never even think that. He was a compassionate man. He felt deeply for the victims he encountered, sometimes rather too much. He just wished that young girls would think a little more about how they presented themselves and the effect that might have on the wrong sort of man. They shouldn't have to, of course, he didn't disagree with that. But there was no shortage of evil perverted bastards out there and this poor kid had been unlucky enough to meet up with one.

Vogel couldn't see the second shoe. The CSIs might find it. The girl could even be lying on it. It was also possible that her murderer had taken it as a souvenir, such things were not unusual.

'Morning boss.'

Vogel swung on his heels. DC Dawn Saslow, newly transferred from uniform, sounded as bright and cheery as she always did.

Vogel grunted.

Saslow's eyes dropped to the body at his feet. Her whole demeanour changed.

'Sorry boss,' she said, her voice quiet now.

Saslow, an attractive young woman, fresh-faced with shiny dark hair fashioned into a geometric bob, had already proven herself to be an officer with considerable promise.

'You've nothing to be sorry for,' said Vogel. 'Not yet anyway.'

The DC half smiled.

Not for the first time did Vogel wonder at the way they all behaved when confronted with such horrible sights. The coppers, the doctors, the CSI team. There was always banter. It was the only way they could get through it, he supposed.

Detective Sergeant John Willis was right behind Saslow, still fastening his protective polyethylene suit as he hurried towards the crime scene.

He and Vogel had been working together for six months now. Vogel found Willis to be intelligent and often, he thought, more sensitive than a lot of police officers. At 35 the DS would be hoping for promotion soon. Vogel would be sorry to lose him. The two men had already gained something of a rapport, although neither of them were prone to giving away a great deal about themselves.

Vogel nodded towards Willis, who inclined his head very

slightly, his watchful, grey eyes taking in the scene before him. Vogel saw the sergeant wince. But, in common with his superior officer, it was not Willis's way to show the emotion he was undoubtedly feeling. Not if he could help it anyway. He glanced back at Vogel and waited for instructions.

Unlike Saslow, Willis didn't speak. He didn't make it necessary for Vogel to say something banal. Nor indeed to pass any comment about the wretched nature of this inquiry, which the Avon and Somerset Constabulary's Major Crime Investigation Team were about to embark on. DCI Reg Hemmings – the head of MCIT – was Senior Investigating Officer, as usual in a case of this severity. Vogel had already been appointed deputy SIO, a more flexible and hands-on role. He began to issue the instructions now required.

'Right Willis, let's see if we can find someone, anyone, who saw or heard something,' Vogel began. 'There must have been some noise. Screaming, I would say. There are flats over a lot of those shops and bars in West Street and presumably people living in the two houses just up the lane. Get a team together to knock on doors.'

Willis spoke for the first time.

'Yes boss,' he said quietly.

The DS was always a man of few words; something else Vogel liked about him.

Vogel turned to Saslow.

'OK Dawn, you're with me,' he said. 'The poor kid's mother hasn't been told yet.'

Vogel watched the shadow flit across Dawn Saslow's face. He would have been disappointed if she hadn't reacted like that. He hated this side of the job too. They all hated making death calls.

The district Home Office Pathologist arrived just as Vogel and Saslow were about to leave. Karen Crow had been the first woman in the country to gain such an appointment. She was nearing retirement now and inclined to give the impression that she had seen it all before.

None the less she shook her head sorrowfully at the sight of the young body spread-eagled before her and glanced curiously around.

Even now that day had broken, Stone Lane remained shadowy

and somehow forbidding. The entire network of insalubrious alleyways and cul-de-sacs, which led off West Street and Old Market Street, was inhabited only by rats and the occasional prowling cat after dark.

'What the heck was she doing here on her own at night?' Karen Crow muttered vaguely in the direction of Vogel.

'She wasn't on her own,' said Vogel grimly. 'And I've no idea what she was doing here.'

The whole Old Market area was certainly no place for a schoolgirl, not once night had fallen. There was The Stag and Hounds on the corner; Bristol's oldest pub and looking its age. A number of bars better known for late night brawls than anything else. Sex shops catering for every possible inclination, one was little more than camouflage for a brothel and several other brothels in the neighbourhood were making no pretence of being anything other.

'I suppose it's possible the body could have been moved,' Vogel continued.

The pathologist was staring at the dead girl, as if willing her to come to life and tell her story.

'I don't think so, do you?' she muttered. 'Not from the way she's lying.'

Vogel shrugged his agreement.

'We can approximate a time of death from what the girl's mother has already told us and from the time her body was found,' he continued. 'It's unlikely she would have been killed here until quite late in the evening. Too many people about, even on a Thursday night, and it's mid May. Doesn't get dark until nearly nine. But you'll let us know as soon as you've got anything more concrete, indeed anything at all, won't you, Karen?'

'Oh no, I was planning to keep it all to myself.'

Vogel stretched his lips into an apology for a smile. He just meant he didn't want to have to wait for a written report. And Karen Crow knew that perfectly well.

'My mobile, yeah?' he said.

'Naturally, Detective Inspector,' the pathologist countered.

'Right we're just off to . . .'

Vogel didn't finish the sentence. He didn't need to. Karen Crow knew exactly where he and Saslow were off to.

'Good luck,' the pathologist said quietly.

Vogel smiled wryly. A genuine smile this time. He actually liked Karen Crow because he knew how good she was at her job. Nothing else about the people he worked with really mattered to Vogel.

LEO

I sat in a corner of the Bakerloo line tube trying to make myself invisible. It was always like that. As usual on these occasions, I was convinced that everybody around me would know at once what I was. Not that I was entirely sure myself, of course, nor ever had been. I would be all right, well just about, once I'd completed my transformation. But a bag of nerves until then.

I'd hurried home to get ready as soon as I'd finished work and now I was on my way to Soho, to the heart of London's gay scene.

I wasn't a frequent visitor, but there were days when I just couldn't keep away. This was one of them. And I had a special reason for returning rather sooner than usual after my last visit.

As the tube I'd taken from my railway station approached Piccadilly Circus, I began to think about what might lie ahead that evening. It wasn't straightforward for me. It never had been. I wasn't just out to get laid, like so many men, straight or gay, of my age.

Or maybe I was. I wasn't entirely sure about anything connected with my sexuality.

Certainly I was aware of a degree of excitement rising within me as I rode the escalator to street level, followed the shuffling queue of other passengers through the ticket barriers and headed for the exit closest to Leicester Square.

There is something about coming to terms with what you are. And I rarely did. I wasn't like most gay men I'd encountered. I wasn't glad to be gay. I didn't have the slightest desire to be gay.

I didn't even like the word. I've never liked euphemisms, and surely that's what 'gay' is.

When you called yourself a homosexual, it didn't sound quite so modern and attractive. And what about queer? Is that what I was, queer?

I had a 1969 edition of Pears Cyclopaedia at home that had belonged to my mother. Homosexuality is listed in it as a mental illness. In my blackest moments that was how I thought of myself. I was mentally ill. Irreparably so. And nobody could help me.

It wasn't about other people's perception of me, because nobody in my life knew. I hadn't been given a bad time for it by my parents, or anything like that. Neither my father, my mother, or my stepfather ever had a clue about my secret sexual leanings. Why would they have done? I wasn't the slightest bit camp in my everyday life. I made damned sure of that. I wore the most conventional of clothes. I joined in with all the usual sexist, and sexual, banter you get among a group of men at work and in the pub. I was one of the lads, wasn't I?

I had an invented love life. With women, of course. Nothing too extravagant. I left most of it to the conveniently disreputable minds of others. Occasionally, I made sure that I was seen with an appropriately attractive, young woman in a bar or at a party. Indeed, I dated them. That wasn't difficult for me. I enjoyed female company and women always had liked me. Perhaps because they instinctively knew that I wasn't really one of the lads. That I was actually as uncomfortable as they were with some of the near-the-knuckle jokes and innuendo. Make no mistake about it, even in this the age of political correctness, such jokes were still the staple conversational diet of the majority of men of all ages when no thought-police are present. Particularly after a drink or two. Usually when women were out of earshot, but not always even that.

I rarely dated a woman twice, and there was never an attempt at anything sexual, of course. I couldn't cope with that.

I live alone now, so I don't have to pretend in my own home. But I'm alone deep inside myself, too. That's the problem. Terribly alone. Sometimes the urge to share what I am, or what I think I am, with another, similar human being becomes too much for me. It's more than a sexual urge. Human beings are like all animal species, aren't we? We have a need to be with our own kind. Birds of a feather flock together. Hyenas run with hyenas. Wolves hunt in packs. Rabbits interbreed in their burrows.

So, every so often, I can no longer keep up the pretence of being an uncomplicated, heterosexual man, with little more than one thing on his mind. It's then that I venture out into the gay world. Even though it frightens me to do so. I seek camouflage. I transform myself, or try to anyway. I have a small separate wardrobe of clothes set aside for these occasions: my favourite clothes.

For my trip to Soho, I'd chosen the pale blue skinny Levis I called my pulling jeans. Also a tight-fitting, light-weight, black leather jacket, with studs on the collar and cuffs, which I always wore with the sleeves rolled up to just below the elbow. On top I had a black T-shirt, with a V-neck that showed off my pecs and my six-pack. I was, after all, pretty fit.

I wasn't wearing any of those on my journey of course. I couldn't take the risk of being seen dressed like that as I left my house or anywhere en route. They were tucked away in the rucksack I carried over one shoulder.

Once I'd arrived in Soho, I always felt safe somehow. I believed I could be myself. Indeed, anything I wanted to be. I knew a pub in an alleyway off Leicester Square, where the gents' toilet was conveniently situated down a flight of stairs right by the door. It was there that I habitually changed out of my straight clothes.

As usual, I scurried in with my head down. I would look totally different when I left. The cubicles were of a generous size and fairly clean. I slipped quickly out of what I was wearing and into what I regarded as my gay-man gear.Then I took the jar of styling gel from my bag and smeared it over my hair, combing it through and pressing it flat to my head – except for a small quiff to one side at the front.

I carried with me a little mirror, which I hung from the hook on the cubicle door so that I could check my appearance.

My pièce de résistance was the snake tattoo, which wound itself around my deliberately exposed right forearm. Only, it wasn't a real tattoo, of course. Just a clever transfer, which I would be able to remove before returning to work after the weekend.

It always gave me a tremendous sense of forbidden pleasure

to apply that fake tattoo. I had done so before I left home and also liberally applied fake tan – almost everywhere except my face, much of which was covered in designer stubble. I'd deliberately missed shaving that morning, so that by the time I arrived in central London my naturally heavy facial hair would provide a certain camouflage.

A close shave before I returned to work would get rid of that, but the fake tan would take a few days to fade away. Until it did, I would have to be careful to keep the sleeves of my shirt down and my cuffs buttoned.

It would not be hard for me, though. I was used to being careful.

I ran up the stairs and left the pub as swiftly as I'd entered it. I hurried back towards Piccadilly Circus again, turned right into Shaftesbury Avenue then left into Greek Street and left again into Old Compton Street. This was it. The heart of gay Soho. I passed The G-A-Y Club and The Admiral Duncan without pausing. The former was too stereotyped for me; the first stop for gay men who had just got off the train from the provinces. The latter held too much history. Unlike many of its clientele, I was old enough to remember the night the place was bombed by anti-gay activists in 1999. Three men were killed and upwards of 70 injured. I'd not long left school and was struggling to come to terms with the nature of my sexual feelings. I had already come to despise myself for them; something that has never really changed. A part of me, in those days, thought the Admiral Duncan atrocity would, in my case, have been justifiable retribution. It was possible that a part of me still did.

I crossed the road to Clone Zone, one of a chain of sex shops, which proudly promoted itself as having 'the UK's largest selection of top-quality, gay sex toys, aromas, fashion, underwear and jock straps.' It also boasted that all its merchandise was 'processed through our own fulfilment centre.'

I don't have much of a sense of humour. Neither the gay nor the straight me. But even I couldn't imagine how anyone could pronounce something like that and keep a straight face. They had to be joking, surely.

The Clone Zone sold Poppers, a drug widely used by gays which enhances sexual arousal and performance. That's why I went to Clone Zone. I could buy them on the internet. But I prefer to purchase what I need while I am in Soho and discard it, just as I do my gay self, before returning to my other life.

Poppers is a slang term for a group of chemicals also known as club drugs. Composed of alkyl nitrates or isopropyl nitrates, they have been popular since the 1970s disco scene and, more recently, widely used amongst gay men as a way to enhance sexual pleasure.

The drug opens up blood vessels, increasing blood flow and reducing blood pressure, while increasing the user's heart rate and producing, literally, a rush of blood to the head.

It is legal to sell them in the UK, in bottles with labels like Liquid Gold, Rush and Xtreme Power, as long as they are not advertised for human consumption. I don't do the harder drugs popular in the gay community, like mephedrone or crystal meth. I need to remain in control of my head, even if not other parts of my body. I continued on my way, turning right off Old Compton Street into Wardour Street. A bottle of Xtreme was tucked into my jacket pocket, which I, one way or another, was quite determined to find a use for later.

I was beginning to feel the spirit of 'anything goes' all around me. I began to walk with more of a spring in my step. I held my head higher and started to look around me, taking it all in. There was a drag queen standing in a doorway to my right, smoking a cigarette through a long, black, Bakelite holder, twenties or thirties style. She smiled at me. I smiled back.

This was fantasy land, I reminded myself, I could do what I liked here and with whom I liked. I could be whoever I wanted to be whilst I was here.

I felt almost happy as I approached The Freedom Bar. This was a cool place. A gay cocktail bar with style and panache. I peered through a window. Even the waiters were gorgeous, muscles bulging through tight white shirts. The clientele looked relaxed, at ease. Like any group of people in any bar.

I'd never been to the bar before. After all, I wasn't worthy of this sort of place or these sort of people. I was the hole in the corner sort. I didn't have the courage of my own convictions. Not in anything. How could I ever aspire to be accepted by the likes of them, when I couldn't even accept myself?

I had met men like me before. Well, perhaps not quite like me, but men who were not entirely sure of themselves. Decent ordinary men who had another life, one they were not yet ready to share with the world, even in these allegedly enlightened days.

There was one in particular I hoped I might meet again. Here, in this bar. Not that I could really expect him to have anything to do with me, though, not after the last time.

There were no empty tables. In any case, I told the greeter, a woman wearing a tuxedo over tights and a bow tie, that I preferred to be at the bar. She escorted me to a vacant stool. I ordered myself a Cosmopolitan. I'd never drunk one before, but I knew it was popular amongst gay men. It was pink after all. I found that I quite liked the drink. It was certainly more to my taste than the beer I usually downed, as part of my straight camouflage. I glanced casually around, in such a way that I did not seem to be looking. Nonchalant. Cool. Or that's what I hoped, anyway.

The truth was that I was well aware that I wouldn't be cool if I lived to be 100. I am the living breathing walking epitome of not cool. Dressed the way I was that night, complete with gelled hair and tattoo, I might almost have looked the part. Amongst those gathered in this bar I may even have overdone the 'gay look.' But I wasn't truly it, and never would be.

Also, this was all too open, too ordinary. I was not comfortable.

My spirits fell again. Perhaps I should just go. I didn't belong here.

I downed the rest of my Cosmo in one gulp, and was about to stand up and leave when I felt a hand on my shoulder. I heard the voice at the same time.

'Leo,' he said.

I turned to him. He was even more gorgeous than I remembered. Fresh-faced and boyish. He made me feel even less confident of my own appearance. But then, he was thirteen years my junior. A little more than that actually, because I'd fibbed, just a bit, about my age. I hoped I didn't look like some of the older guys I'd seen around Soho, trying so desperately to be hip.

But at least I was fit, I told myself.

He had tousled dark blonde hair and gentle brown eyes. The haircut was different to when I'd met him before, even though that was just a few days ago. It was shaven at the sides and spiky on top. I took in the already familiar smattering of freckles on his forehead and along the top of each cheek. His lips twitched into half a smile.

'Tim,' I responded. 'I was hoping you might be here.'

He looked at me quizzically, his head slightly on one side.

'You remembered?'

'Of course. You said you'd heard about this place, that it was hot on Friday nights and that you might try it the next weekend.'

'Only might,' he said.

I shrugged.

'I was hoping you would remember too,' I said.

His smile broadened, fleetingly. Then his face clouded over and he removed his hand from my shoulder.

'I didn't understand what happened the last time, though,' he said. 'Why did you just go off like that?'

I stared at him. Unsure what to say. After all, how could I explain? But I so didn't want to lose him again.

THREE

T he family lived in a small but clearly well-cared-for terraced house, one in several lines of similar properties forming a modest, residential district on the southern outskirts of Bristol. 16, Carraby Street. Dawn Saslow knew she would remember that house and that address for the rest of her life. Her heart was beating fast as she pulled the patrol car to a halt outside.

She glanced towards her senior officer. Vogel's face was impassive as usual. But she noticed he was blinking rapidly behind his thick spectacles. She'd quickly become aware, in the brief time that she had worked with Vogel, that this was what happened if ever he were uncomfortable, ill at ease or nervous. There was rarely any other indication that Vogel was emotionally affected by anything. He was a self-contained man, who sometimes gave the impression of being quite detached from the rest of the world. It had become known within MCIT that Vogel's principle interests, apart from his work and his family, were compiling crosswords for an undisclosed specialist publication and playing Backgammon. Usually with his computer, Dawn suspected. The DI not infrequently gave the impression he was more comfortable with computers than people. Naturally, he was known as The Geek.

On the drive Vogel had told Dawn what he knew so far about the dead girl and her family.

Melanie Cook lived with her mother and stepfather, Sarah and Jim Fisher.

Vogel, sticking to the facts as usual, passed no comment about that, but Dawn had known he would be thinking what she was thinking. Parents were always going to be among the suspects in a case like this. A stepfather was a far greater one.

Melanie's father, Terry Cooke, was a lorry driver. Her stepfather was a jobbing brickie. Her mother worked in Marks and Spencer on the till.

A younger half-sister, Petra, also lived at Carraby Street.

Vogel opened the door on his side of his car.

'C'mon,' he said.

Dawn nodded. She stepped outside the vehicle and began to follow him to the house. A smattering of tulips, the last of the UK's spring bulbs to flower every year, were still in bloom in the little front garden, which was surrounded by a manicured privet hedge just two feet or so tall. From the moment the front door was opened the family waiting inside would know. They always did. Nothing would ever be the same for them after that.

This was not Dawn Saslow's first death call. Even though she was young, relatively inexperienced and brand new to CID, she'd already had more than her share of them. The women always did. Alleged equality had done nothing to shift the notion that women were best at that sort of thing. And that the bereaved liked having a female officer around. Nobody ever used the term 'it's a job for a woman' any more. But that's what most of them thought.

Dawn Saslow wasn't sure she was any good at all at death calls. Not only were you passing on the worst news in the world, but all too often you were required to treat those to whom you were delivering it as suspects. That was certainly going to be so in this case.

Dawn hated it, and she already knew that it would never get any easier.

The woman who opened the door to number 16 looked disconcertingly like an older version of the dead girl, though rather darker skinned. She was small, with glossy black curls framing an unbearably anxious face. Even at this time of unbearable stress, she was as neat as her front garden and the outside of the house. Dawn was pretty sure the inside would be the same, but she wondered if it would stay so well-kept after the news she and Vogel were about to deliver.

Sarah Fisher raised one hand to her mouth as soon as she saw them standing there. They could have been making a routine follow-up call, surely, concerning the progress of the investigation. A uniformed team had been dispatched to interview the family straight after Sarah had reported her daughter missing. So the family would probably have been expecting another police visit. Yet Sarah Fisher knew. Before either Dawn or Vogel said a word. Just as Dawn had been so certain she would.

'Oh my God,' she said.

'I'm so very sorry,' murmured Vogel.

It said everything of course. Sarah Fisher took a step backwards, then another. She swayed. Her knees buckled. Dawn was afraid the woman might fall. She glanced at Vogel. He was standing very still. Deadpan, as usual. He certainly didn't look as if he were ready to make a move to assist the woman. Sarah Fisher's eyes glazed. Dawn was about to push past Vogel to get to the woman, at least to stop her from falling, when a man stepped into the hall behind Mrs Fisher and, after just a moment's hesitation, wrapped one supportive arm around her.

He too seemed to know what was happening, but he glanced enquiringly at Vogel.

'Could we come in please?' asked Vogel.

The man, who had a world-weary, careworn look about him that Dawn thought was permanent, rather than a result of the terrible news he was now expecting, nodded and stepped backwards. He still held on to the stricken Sarah Fisher, who no longer looked as if she was going to faint at least. Indeed, she suddenly shook herself free of the man and half ran back into the house.

The man followed. He was a thin, bony individual, probably of above average height, but appearing shorter because he walked with his shoulders slumped, which Dawn thought was also probably a permanent tendency. He was white, with dull, pale eyes and hair of a nondescript brown, flecked with grey, which had been cropped short. In turn, Vogel and Saslow followed the man, entering a small but well-decorated and well-appointed sitting room.

'I'm so very sorry,' said Vogel again, speaking very deliberately and without expression.

He looked directly at Sarah Fisher.

'The body of a young woman has been found, Mrs Fisher, and we have reason to believe she may be your daughter.'

Sarah Fisher sat down with a bump and uttered a small cry of anguish.

Then she did a sort of double take, '*May?*' she queried, grasping at this tiniest straw of hope. '*May be my daughter?* You mean you are not sure?'

'I cannot be entirely sure until she has been officially identified,' said Vogel formally. 'But the victim answers the description you gave us, although she was wearing different clothes at the time of her death. I am afraid I have to tell you that the distinctive pink rucksack you said Melanie had with her, with her name on it, was found by the victim's side.'

Mrs Fisher gasped, then uttered a small, low cry, like an animal in pain. Vogel glanced towards the thin man, whose shoulders had drooped even more. Now, he seemed to be in almost as great a state of shock as Sarah was.

'We need someone to do that. Perhaps your husband . . .'

'This is Terry. My ex. Mel's dad. I called him last night, when she didn't come home. He came straight over. Jim, my husband, he's away working. Over in Kent. He's on his way back now.'

Well that, presumably, was one less suspect, thought Dawn Saslow. Not the stepfather after all.

'I'll do it,' said Terry Cooke. 'I'll identify her. Maybe it's not Mel. I'll do it.'

For a second Sarah looked as if she were going to protest, but she didn't.

Her face was distorted by her anguish. Her hands, clasped tightly in her lap, were shaking. Terry Cooke, meanwhile, was clearly fighting back tears, and seemed to be losing the battle.

'Well, I'll let you both know as soon as an identification can be arranged,' said Vogel.

Vogel didn't mention what would have to happen first. Dawn knew that was for the best. What indeed was happening at that very moment was the preliminary examination by the home office pathologist. The poking about amongst Mel Cooke's belongings. The removal of her clothes and anything else that might become evidence. And then the post-mortem examination itself. Something relatives invariably found additionally upsetting.

'Meanwhile I need to ask you both some questions,' Vogel continued.

He went over again the chronology of Melanie's disappearance, asking particularly about the manner and circumstances of her leaving the house.

Sarah made no protest. She seemed to answer everything quite mechanically. She spoke in the present tense about her daughter and Dawn suspected she may not yet have fully taken everything in.

'Everything was just normal, ordinary. No, I wasn't a bit suspicious when she said she wanted to go to her friend's home to do homework. Why would I be? They do that quite often. Sometimes Sally comes here. They're good girls. They work hard, but it's less boring for them, I suppose.'

Sarah Fisher paused before speaking again.

'You think I should have known, don't you? I should have guessed she was up to something. I should have stopped her, but I didn't, I didn't. She's only 14 . . .'

Suddenly reality seemed to hit the woman.

'She was only 14,' she corrected herself.

Then she began to weep quietly. Terry Cooke was already in floods. He had said little since offering to identify his daughter, and had ultimately just broken down and wept.

Dawn noticed that Cooke was peering at his ex-wife through his tears, with what seemed to be distaste. Totally without compassion anyway. He may have stepped forward in the hallway to physically support Sarah, but he blamed her, thought Dawn, that must be what it was. He blamed his ex-wife for what he probably saw as negligence leading to Melanie's murder.

It almost certainly wasn't fair, but perhaps that was what we all did in these situations, tried to find somebody to blame. The mother had custody too. In her father's eyes that would make her responsible for their daughter's safety. He probably believed he would have behaved differently, he would have known what was going on and he would have stopped Melanie going out. He would have saved her.

'Mrs Fisher, I know this is going to be a terribly painful time for you and we want to do all we can to help,' said Vogel gently. 'I will arrange for a family liaison officer to come over to be with you.'

A thought occurred to him.

'You have a younger daughter, don't you, Mrs Fisher? Is she here, in the house?'

Sarah Fisher shook her head.

'I sent her to school, I didn't want her upset, her gran's picking her up later . . .'

Her voice tailed off.

'More than anything, Mrs Fisher, I promise you I will find whoever did this,' said Vogel.

Sarah Fisher looked at him with blank eyes.

AL

They get what they deserve, these young girls in their skimpy skirts and the little shorts they call hot pants. They're hot all right. Everything about them is hot. Burning hot.

Surely their mothers must realise they're asking for it. And their fathers, assuming they have fathers in their lives. So many of them don't any more. Any father would know what men are like. *All men*. I have always been quite sure that it really is all men.

Can there be a man who hasn't looked longingly at the legs of a schoolgirl in a gymslip? I know they don't usually wear gymslips any more, unfortunately. But that's the ultimate fantasy isn't it? A long-legged girl reaching puberty, the skirt of her gymslip only just covering her pert, little bum and her hidden, secret, as yet untouched, little fanny.

Any man, any man alive, *really alive*, who says he doesn't want to touch that bum – and explore that other hidden, secret place – is a liar, I say.

However much we try to deny it, that is the truth. My truth, certainly. I have tried to get rid of the urges. God knows, I have tried. Once I even booked a series of therapy sessions. Oh yes, they do exist. But in the end, I cancelled the lot, because I reckoned the therapist was likely to be as mixed up as I was. They would have to be, if they wanted to hear – in gruesome detail – the shameful thoughts which dominated my every waking hour, and my dreams too. What sort of person would want to see into the mind of a pervert?

Then there was the fear of what might be revealed, even though such sessions are supposed to be confidential. Yes, I was afraid of being exposed. Perhaps I was even more afraid of the inevitable realisation that nothing could be done.

I'd say I am how God made me, if I believed in God. I don't, of course. I don't believe in anything. How could I? I don't care for or about anybody else, either. Why should I? There's nobody out there who cares a jot about me.

Maybe I believe, somewhere deep inside me, in the devil. Because I am surely his creature.

I tell myself that perhaps we all are. Men if not women. I respect women, truly I do. I just can't cope with the turmoil they unleash inside me, that's all. Particularly the young ones, the girls blossoming into puberty.

I've always supposed that most men, who also lust after the fruits of youth, do nothing about it. They look but don't touch. Recent revelations seem to indicate that I've been wrong. Far more men than I ever realised are unable to control their innermost, secret longings and, eventually, allow the monster of their desire to take over.

It now seems, beyond all reasonable doubt, that Jimmy Savile assaulted hundreds of young girls and also a number of boys, over a 50-year period. Some were under five. Many were disabled, mentally and physically, or in hospital. And yet, for so long, he was feted and lauded to the extent where the world came to regard him as some sort of saint. They even made him a knight of the realm. Sir Jim of 'Jim'll Fix It'. He fixed it all right. I heard an interview with one of his victims. She said she reckoned he wore tracksuit bottoms in order to more easily remove his trousers.

I was shocked by that. Oh yes, I can be shocked.

As I am indeed shocked by what I do. I really do not mean to hurt anyone.

I remember, all too clearly, hurting someone by mistake; someone very young. Maybe a second time too, I can barely remember. It was several lifetimes ago. I have come to believe that I'd been too young to know any better, which I honestly think is true.

I'd got away with it. Scot-free. Nobody even suspected me. Indeed, I'd almost convinced myself that I did not mean to do anything wrong and hadn't done anything wrong, as if I wasn't guilty at all.

Funny how you can do that sometimes, isn't it?

I look on the internet of course. There's so much stuff out there. Child porn, they call it. I don't. It's not porn to me. It's perfectly natural to me. What can be unnatural about looking at beautiful, little bodies? The youngsters appear happy enough in the pictures and videos on the sites I use. Why wouldn't they? At that age they accept anything, as long as they're treated kindly.

I would never be unkind to a child. Well, not deliberately, anyway. I love children.

I've also dabbled with those sites where you can chat to young girls and boys. Not that I'm interested in boys; I'm not that way inclined. That is unnatural to me.

Grooming, they call it. But it's just a way of getting to know them, isn't it? I've always been cautious about carrying anything through, afraid even. Setting up meetings is something to be extremely careful about. It can be so dangerous in so many different ways.

However, internet pictures don't satisfy me. I like to look in the flesh, not at celluloid images. I may be cautious but, thankfully, there are lots of places you can go where that is possible: playgrounds, swimming pools, beaches. Look but don't touch. Just sit back and enjoy the innocent frolicking of little girls.

Merely thinking about it gives me an erection.

I can't help it. It's the way I am made. It's not my fault. None of it is my fault.

FOUR

Vogel thought they'd done enough for the first visit. He was about to indicate to DC Saslow that they should take their leave, when he heard the front door open and close loudly, as if it had been slammed. Within a second or two the door to the sitting room burst open.

A short, stocky, pale man, with prematurely white curly hair strode into the room. He had a thick neck, burly shoulders and an ample belly, all of which contributed significantly to making him look almost as wide as he was tall. The morning was still cool and there did not seem to be any heating on in the little sitting room, but he was red-faced and sweating profusely.

'Sarah, I got here as soon as I could,' he said.

Then he stopped speaking. Vogel guessed this was Jim Fisher, the husband and stepfather. He could see that Fisher had suddenly taken in the expression on his wife's face, the presence of her tearful ex-husband and two strangers.

'Oh my God, oh no!' he said. 'She isn't? She can't be. Tell me she's not . . . is she?'

He couldn't get the words out.

He didn't need to. Vogel knew what he meant.

'I am afraid we have found the body of a young woman we fear might be Melanie,' he said.

Jim Fisher sat down next to his wife. The sofa slumped slightly under his weight.

'Oh darlin', I'm so sorry I wasn't with you last night,' he said.

'You didn't answer your phone, Jim,' said Sarah Fisher accusatively. 'You always answer your phone.'

'Sweetheart, it was the middle of the night when you called, gone two anyway. I've been getting these damned junk calls at all hours. I switched my phone off so I could get some sleep.

You know the kind of schedule we're on. I was knackered. Don't forget I was driving back today anyway, after a day's work. As soon as I picked up your message this morning, I called you and then I just got in the car. I'm so sorry.'

Sarah Fisher nodded distractedly, Vogel didn't think any of that mattered to her any more. It might to Vogel, though, and to his investigation.

'Mr Fisher, at what time this morning did you speak to your wife?' he asked.

Fisher hesitated. Vogel thought he had the look of a man who was considering whether or not to risk a lie. He knew that look. He had seen it often enough over the years.

'Uh, about six,' he said. 'Maybe a little later.'

Vogel nodded and looked pointedly at his watch. It was still only 9 a.m.

'And where were you in Kent?' he asked.

'Just outside Deal,' said Jim Fisher. 'Big construction job. Two hundred houses. Everybody's gambling on the new, high-speed rail link. I'm lucky to have got hired. Months of work. Good money too. I stay up there through the week, get home every other weekend . . .'

Fisher's voice tailed off, as if he realised he was rambling.

Vogel inclined his head and assumed his most thoughtful expression, the one that made him look so much more like an old-fashioned school teacher, than a modern policeman.

'So you got here in under three hours,' he remarked mildly. 'You made very good time then.'

'Yes, I did.' Fisher looked and sounded extremely uncomfortable. As well he might, thought Vogel. Both he and Jim Fisher knew damned well it was practically impossible to get from Deal to Bristol in under three hours at the best of times. If Fisher really had left Deal soon after six, he would have hit the southern outskirts of London and the M25 as the morning rush hour was beginning to peak.

Vogel glanced at Sarah Fisher. She was still weeping, quite silently now, consumed by her own dreadful misery. She didn't seem to have noticed the significance of the exchange between Vogel and her husband, let alone reacted to it.

Vogel saw no reason to add to her distress. Not yet, anyway.

'Mr Fisher, I wonder if you'd be kind enough to step outside with me,' he said. 'I need to ask you some more questions and I think your wife would appreciate a little peace and quiet.'

Vogel moved towards the door which led into the hall. He indicated to Dawn Saslow that she should remain with the bereaved woman and the dead girl's father, who had finally stopped weeping and was perched awkwardly on a hard chair as far away as possible from the sofa his ex-wife and her current husband were sharing. Wordlessly, Jim Fisher stood up and followed Vogel. Sarah Fisher, even though she had been so eager to have her husband home with her, barely seemed to notice that either.

Once in the hall, Vogel confronted Fisher directly. He didn't bother to point out the impossibility of the logistics of Fisher's alleged journey. He was pretty sure from the other man's uneasy demeanour that he didn't need to.

'So where were you last night, Mr Fisher?' Vogel asked. 'You sure as heck weren't anywhere near Deal, were you? That much we both know.'

Fisher avoided the DI's gaze. He looked down at his feet.

'I was in Bath,' he muttered, almost inaudibly.

'And what were you doing in Bath?' asked Vogel.

'I was with a friend,' replied Fisher, still mumbling.

'A female friend by any chance?' Vogel enquired.

Fisher nodded.

'I'm afraid I need a proper answer from you,' said Vogel. 'I need to know exactly where you were last night, with whom and what you were doing. That includes the name of your female friend. And will you please speak up? I want to be quite clear on this.'

'Her name's Daisy, Daisy Wilkins,' said Fisher, glancing anxiously towards the living room door and speaking only a little louder than before. 'I was, well, I was visiting her. I'm working all hours on this job. I have three days off every other weekend: Saturday, Sunday, and Monday. But sometimes I manage to sneak a Friday off, so I can spend Thursday night with Daisy. Then I come back here Friday evening as usual.'

Fisher paused.

'Look, Mr Vogel, my wife doesn't have to know, does she? I mean, you saw the state of her. I can't believe what's happened. It'll destroy her, I know it will. I don't want her even more hurt.'

'Perhaps you should have thought of that possibility before you spent the night with Daisy Wilkins,' murmured Vogel. 'Now, I assume from what you have said that Ms Wilkins is some sort of regular fixture in your life, even though your wife doesn't know about her. Is that the case?'

'Yes, but it's not what it sounds like, Detective Inspector, honestly it isn't.'

'And what exactly does it sound like, Mr Fisher, may I ask?'

'Well, it sounds sort of sordid, doesn't it? You know, the usual thing. Man having bit on the side, not telling the missus. But you see, Daisy's a lot more to me than that. Sarah and me, well, we've not been happy for years. We never were really, except in the beginning. I've been planning to leave her, to do right by Daisy, but it's never seemed to be the right time. I thought I'd do it when the kids were a bit older, particularly our Petra, she's only seven. Sarah, she has trouble with her nerves, you see. God knows what she's going to be like now . . .'

Vogel was unimpressed. He'd heard it all before.

'Mr Fisher, it's not my job to stand in moral judgment. The rights and wrongs of your behaviour are none of my business. What is my business, is that you were not here with your wife and family last night. You've admitted that, at the time we think your stepdaughter died, you were actually not at all far from where her body was found. Therefore, I want to know every detail of your exact whereabouts throughout the night.' Vogel raised his voice slightly as he spoke.

He was aware of the other man taking a step back, eyes wide open as if in disbelief.

'My God, you think I killed her, don't you? That's it, you think I bloody killed our Mel. I loved that kid like she was my own. I'd never have hurt her. You *have* to believe me.' There was shock and fear in Jim Fisher's voice. He was sweating more than ever and his face had turned vividly red.

Vogel did not reply for several seconds. He wanted Fisher to be fully aware of how serious his situation was.

'We just want to eliminate you from our inquiries, sir,' the DI said eventually, keeping his voice level. 'It would help if you'd come with us to the station to be fingerprinted and have a DNA swab taken.'

'*Are you bloody arresting me?*' Jim Fisher almost screamed the question.

In the sitting room, behind the closed door, Sarah Fisher called out. Her voice quavering.

'Jim? Jim, are you all right?'

Fisher did not respond. He lowered his head into plump, pink hands and began to rock to and fro on the spot.

Vogel assessed the other man's reactions. Fisher's histrionic response to his line of questioning did not influence the detective in any particular direction. Vogel, as ever, began with the assumption that Fisher was innocent and would only allow careful assimilation and evaluation of fact to govern his opinion. That was the basis of British law, was it not? Innocent until proven guilty.

'No, sir, I am not arresting you,' Vogel replied in the same level tone. 'I'm asking for your cooperation in order to find your stepdaughter's murderer and, if you have told us the truth, to eliminate you from our inquiries. I am asking you to come to the station with me to swiftly facilitate that.'

SAUL

T he first reply I had that interested me was from Sonia. I liked the name. It sounded solid and old-fashioned. It even seemed to go rather well with my name. Saul and Sonia, Sonia and Saul, sounded like a couple straight away, I thought.

At once I began to fantasise about the life Sonia and Saul could have together. I'm inclined to do that. I know I should rein myself in, proceed with caution, refrain from dreaming but I can't help it. I quickly began to believe that Sonia would prove to be the woman I'd been seeking for so long.

I read her reply over and over again.

'Hi, Saul,' she wrote. 'I was a little surprised to spot your entry. Most people are not quite as direct as you. Certainly not in regard to marriage and children. Not even on this

website. I like it though. If that's what you want, why not say
it? After all, it could save a great deal of time-wasting for all
concerned.

'I'm a little older than you, so I thought I should make that
clear straightaway. I'm 38. I've never been married and I'm
childless, but I would very much like to have children before it
is too late. I am looking for somebody who wants that too and is
prepared to be as direct as you have been about it. I no longer
have unlimited time. I know women nowadays seem to have
children much later in life, but I do feel that my body clock is
running out.

'I am a qualified nurse and I work in a residential care home,
not far from where I live in Cheltenham. This was a natural
progression for me. I looked after my mother full-time, until her
death three years ago. When I was twenty-five she had a stroke
which left her helpless. Perhaps it's unusual nowadays for a
daughter to do what I did. Perhaps you think it stupid, I know
some people do, but I decided that I would care for her and did
so for ten years. I couldn't get out much, so there's never really
been a man in my life.

'I am only telling you, so that you can understand why I've
joined this site and why I would very much like to get to know
you better.'

Obviously that was what I wanted too, but I wasn't at all sure
how to go about it. I liked the sound of Sonia, I really did. And
if I was serious about marriage, which I really thought I was, in
spite of the difficulties which would almost certainly arise, then
surely the sooner I met her and her ticking body clock the better.

However, I wasn't ready to meet her yet. Fortunately, I learned
through doing a little research that there was a kind of etiquette
on a site like this. It seemed that considerably more email correspondence was called for, before you actually met. This suited
me well enough.

So began our internet courtship. Sonia was shy too, which
helped me. It was, after all, my shyness which had somewhat
conversely driven me to this most extraordinarily open way of
getting to know someone.

She sent me pictures of her family. Of herself at work. Of her
pet cat.

I decided I would be a cat person too. Well, it was only barely a lie. I'd always liked cats. They were lazy, indolent and fiercely independent. They did exactly what they wanted. They were probably the kind of creature I wished I was. But I was more like a dog. I wagged my tail. I sought approval. Unless I felt threatened or abused, then I'd lash out and attack, just the way dogs do. I had gone out of my way to please those around me. However, unlike most dogs, I wasn't very successful at that either.

I sent Sonia a picture of a large, black cat I found somewhere on the web and pretended he was mine. I hoped she would forgive me that too. I said his name was Tigger. I've come across cats called Tigger before, named after the creature in 'Winnie-the-Pooh', I suppose; although I think the original Tigger looked more like a comic book tiger.

I was getting really good at Photoshop. I took a selfie of myself outside Swindon comprehensive, then amended it as I had my original *Marryme.com* picture, adding the facial hair, changing my hair colour and the shape of my chin.

'Got lucky this term with six weeks at a school right on my doorstep,' I told her.

Of course, Swindon comp was nowhere near my doorstep. I'd never taught anywhere, and had no qualifications to do so. But I started collecting stories about teaching from newspapers and off the net, changed them slightly, added a personal slant and sent them to her as anecdotes from my own daily life.

There were good stories, like the pupil I managed to motivate by encouraging him to expand on graffiti he'd scrawled all over the walls of a classroom and he'd turned out to be a natural poet. Then there were bad ones, like the girl I'd felt to be no threat to anyone, who'd suddenly launched herself at a co-pupil using a biro as a dagger. I made myself a bit of a hero, relating how I'd managed to step in before anyone was badly hurt, thus negating the need for calling the police or any other emergency services.

Sonia lapped it all up, expressing her admiration of what she called my 'selfless courage.'

'What happened to the girl?' she asked.

'She was excluded I'm afraid,' I told her. 'What we used to call expelled. A shame, but apparently there'd been other incidents and it was agreed our school wasn't the place for her. She was obviously seriously disturbed and needed special treatment. I was disappointed by the outcome but couldn't argue against it.'

Sonia took everything I said absolutely seriously and totally at face value. I found myself fantasising a little. Using more and more poetic licence about myself. Once I realised how much she liked my stories I began to embellish them quite extravagantly, far more than I'd ever intended.

But Sonia never demurred. She never questioned anything.

I knew I was reeling her in most effectively and I liked it. I very quickly became more than a little afraid of losing her.

In spite of my original good intentions to portray myself as honestly as I could, I became desperate to seem more interesting. I built up a most unlikely scenario, surprising myself with the extent of my own inventiveness. It was as if, once I started making things up, I couldn't stop.

'I had an unhappy childhood and as soon as I was old enough I ran away to join the French Foreign Legion,' I told her. 'Actually I lied about my age. I was only 15, but either they didn't know or didn't care. I turned out to be a rather good soldier. I don't know why, but I never seemed to have any fear. Once in Algeria, I ran straight into enemy fire to drag a wounded comrade to safety and escaped without a scratch. My comrades said they thought I was blessed by God. They called me Saint Saul.'

It was more than unlikely. It was errant nonsense, but Sonia didn't seem to find it so.

'It should have been King Saul, like your biblical namesake,' she said.

Then she asked: 'Are you Jewish? It's an unusual name.'

I said that my grandfather had been Jewish. She took that at face value too.

She eulogised about my every ridiculous exploit, asking few relevant questions, except how I made the quantum leap from my adventurous life in the Legion to becoming a school teacher.

I rambled on about a desperately unhappy love affair ruined by my soldier lifestyle. How I'd decided I needed a new, more settled career, in order to become the family man I so desired to be. And how I'd studied on the net, via the Open University, until finally gaining a place at a teachers' training college, using the savings acquired during my mercenary career to tide me over until I qualified.

I began to get to know Sonia. Every crazy tale I told her was something I was convinced she would want to hear. And I suppose that was why I eventually told her that I was falling in love with her. Sonia responded with the level of unbridled enthusiasm that I had come to expect.

'I'm thrilled,' she wrote. 'I've realised for some time that I am in love with you. To know that this love is reciprocated is probably the best thing that has ever happened to me. When can we meet? Please can it be very soon.'

'Of course,' I replied.

And therein lay the problem.

FIVE

By the time Vogel and Saslow were leaving the Fisher home, DCI Reg Hemmings had already set up a dedicated incident room at Kenneth Steele House, the Bristol headquarters of MCIT. Hemmings had also appointed his favourite administrator, DI Margo Hartley, as joint deputy SIO, along with Vogel. She would be operations manager, overseeing the mechanics and logistics of the investigation.

Fisher was to be taken to The Patchway Police Centre on Gloucester Road, Bristol's most modern station incorporating a state of the art custody suite and forty-eight police cells.

Terry Cooke, Melanie's father, would make the formal identification at the morgue later that morning, as soon as the pathology team was ready. Cooke would be accompanied by a family liaison officer, PC Kelly King, who was on her way to the family home. He had also agreed to come into Patchway in the afternoon for DNA testing and fingerprinting.

Whilst Saslow was loading Fisher into the back of the squad car, Vogel took a step away and made a quick call to Willis.

'The father's second wife, Mrs Susan Cooke, is on her own, or I think she is anyway,' he said. 'Pop round will you? Better find a woman PC to take with you. Let's see what she's got to say about her old man and what he might have been up to last night. Melanie's father seems genuine enough to me, but you never know. Just a preliminary chat. Might help build a picture.'

At Patchway, Vogel quickly handed Fisher over to the custody boys and told them not to hurry with processing him.

Back in the car, Vogel called DCI Hemmings to report what was happening. It was still not 10 a.m. yet.

'Seems Jim Fisher's been playing away from home,' he began.

'A dodgy stepfather, eh?' muttered Hemmings. 'What do you think? How likely a candidate is he?'

'I don't know,' replied Vogel. 'The DNA tests should sort things out. Forensic say they found some hair, with follicles of skin attached, under Melanie Cooke's fingernails. Presumably torn out of her assailant's head whilst she was fighting for her life, poor kid.' Vogel paused, trying not to think about that too much. He kept seeing his own daughter's face.

'He lived with the girl, Vogel,' Hemmings interjected. 'Any decent brief would argue that of course we're likely to find his DNA on her.'

'Not strands of hair under her fingernails, though, surely boss? That's a classic result of lashing out in self-defence. There might be more forensic evidence too, that's what I'm hoping for. We don't know enough yet and, as you know, it will be days before we get the DNA results. So Saslow and I are on our way now to check out Fisher's alibi. I didn't like the man but . . .'

'Vogel, you don't like anyone!'

'That's not fair,' said Vogel, who, in spite of appearances to the contrary, was not averse to occasionally indulging his lurking sense of humour. 'I'm very fond of you, sir.'

Hemmings grunted and made no direct response. Vogel knew the form well enough. A bit of banter made the day go by more easily, on investigations as disturbing as this one, but enough was enough.

'Look, boss,' he continued. 'Fisher claims he spent last night with his mistress, if that's what she is. This Daisy from Bath is certainly someone he's serious about, he insists. I'd like to get her version of events before he has time to prime her . . .'

'OK,' interrupted Hemmings. 'But on the way back, will the

pair of you stop by the girl's school? The North Bristol Academy. It's the right side of town. We need to officially inform the head-mistress and it'll be an opportunity to chat to Melanie Cooke's chums.'

'Right, boss.'

'And, by the way, I've given Willis all the backup I can spare on the door-to-door. Nothing yet though.'

'I know,' said Vogel. 'I've just been talking to him. They're still hard at it, but I've asked him to break off for an hour or so and do some checking on the father, Terry Cooke. He seems a less likely suspect than the stepdad, however Willis is going to have a chat with his second wife. She may paint a different picture. Particularly if she's caught alone and on the hop. Cooke said he was going to stay with his ex for a bit.'

'OK, but tell Willis not to take too long about it. We need some hard evidence. Some kind of witness would be handy. You know how it is, Vogel. People don't always realise the importance of things they have seen or heard.'

'Yes sir,' said Vogel. 'I'll get Willis back on it as soon as I can. You're dead right, boss. Those boys out there door-stepping really do have to keep plugging away. And it's been such a damned thankless task so far they may well need someone cracking the whip a bit.' Vogel echoed what he had earlier said to Willis. 'A girl was assaulted and killed. She struggled and fought for her life. Someone must have seen or heard something, surely.'

LEO

All I knew was that I had to keep Tim. I wanted him. I needed him.

I said the first thing that came into my head. And it was very nearly the truth.

'I couldn't quite come to terms with what we were doing,' I replied. 'Or rather, where we were doing it. It was all so awful . . .'

'I didn't like it either,' he said. 'But I didn't run off. I couldn't have done that to you.'

His eyes were fixed on mine. Then he glanced away, blushing.

'I'm sorry,' I said.

He looked back towards me.

'Do you want a drink?' I asked.

'I have one,' he replied, gesturing at what looked like a glass of white wine on a table behind us.

I wondered how I hadn't seen him as soon as I walked in the place.

Maybe he read my mind.

'I spotted you when I came back from the gents,' he said.

'I'm very glad you did,' I responded lamely.

He asked if I wanted to sit with him.

'Are you on your own?' I asked.

'No, I'm with a group of trendy gay mates,' he said, the sarcasm heavy in his voice.

Of course he was on his own. He was like me. Not quite like me, obviously. But not out. Not glad to be gay. Or proud to be perverted, as one of my work colleagues called it.

Until recently my Soho haunt had been Larry's Bar, a throwback to another age. A place almost exclusively for those who, even in the modern world, were still not openly gay.

Most of the clientele, I'd always suspected, were married or in long-term relationships with women. There were still far more men in that situation than was generally realised. Some were probably in jobs where homosexuality continued to cause problems that no amount of legislation could fix.

There had also been, on the basis of supply and demand, a number of young men more or less on the game.

Larry's had finally closed down the previous year. Young Tim probably didn't know it had even existed. Although it might have suited him.

Instead, as he struggled to come to terms with his sexuality, he used more modern methods of seeking out kindred spirits. Notably Grindr, the gay app which brings sexual opportunity straight to your phone.

After Larry's had closed, I'd bought myself a pay-as-you-go iPhone and had also turned to Grindr. But only when I was well away from my home territory. I needed to cut down, as much as possible, any chance of coincidentally contacting someone who might recognise me.

It was through Grindr, albeit indirectly, that I'd met Tim, as I flicked my way through the list of available men, whose exact whereabouts was made known to me by Google tracker.

As in: 'John. 500 yards away. Come and give it to me hard.'

An approach of that sort was totally unnerving to me. And, like a lot of gay men, I'd become wary of the app since the case of Stephen Port. He's the serial killer and rapist who was convicted last year of the murder of four men he lured back to his East London flat after meeting them through Grindr. I might be fit and strong, but during the sex act I would be as vulnerable as anyone. I determined to stop using Grindr. I couldn't resist looking on the app though. It was there that I'd come across an invitation to a weekend sex party at a flat just off Endell Street in Covent Garden. I'd seen this sort of thing before but never succumbed to the temptation. That time I decided to take the risk. Just the once. After all, I convinced myself, surely there would be safety in numbers?

Before I rang the doorbell, I inhaled from the bottle of Xtreme I was carrying. I needed something just to get me inside. A number of men were lounging around a stylish sitting room. Some of them were wearing just their underpants. Mostly they looked pretty relaxed and were chatting away as if they were at a normal party. Of course, their relaxed states may have been partly caused by alcohol and drugs.

Champagne, wine and vodka appeared to be the drinks of choice and I could see bits of drug paraphernalia around the place: mostly Crystal Meths, the party drug version of meth, GHB or G, and, of course, bottles of poppers.

I sat down as far away from the others as possible. Nobody took any notice of me. I watched a couple slide into one of several, adjoining rooms, presumably bedrooms, as a group of three made their way out.

On the one hand, I found it distasteful and on the other hand, erotic – pretty much the story of my sex life. However, poppers work almost instantly. Their effect combined with the heady, sexual atmosphere meant that I badly needed release. There was only one person in the room I could imagine making a move on. A young man standing in the far corner, fully clothed and looking even more uncomfortable than I felt. I liked that and I liked the fact that he was so pretty. It was Tim, of course.

I moved across the room to him.

After a few minutes of largely forgettable small talk, during which we discussed Soho gay bars and he mentioned The Freedom Bar and his plan to check it out, we headed into one of the bedrooms.

It didn't take long. Not for me anyway. I inhaled deeply again from my bottle of Xtreme and offered it to Tim, so we were both high. Then I just let rip. But, predictably enough, once it was over the sordid nature of the ghastly event in this incongruously stylish apartment hit me, like an out-of-control juggernaut. Within seconds I was fully dressed again and out the door.

I heard Tim calling after me, but I didn't stop.

Now I had another chance, it seemed, to be with this beautiful boy whose face had haunted me ever since.

There we were, among the confident, cool, gay set of The Freedom Bar, two awkward, reluctantly gay men sitting at a table making small talk again over a Cosmopolitan, in my case, and a glass of New Zealand Sauvignon in his.

I wanted to tell him how ashamed I was now, of having been so desperate that I'd sought out that awful, sex party. I couldn't say that though, could I? Not to him. After all, he'd been there too. I certainly couldn't really explain my revulsion and the reasons for it. I wasn't repulsed by Tim, that was for sure. Indeed, looking at him again, even whilst feeling so awkward and stupid, I found my desire for him rising in me. And that was without the Poppers.

'Do you want to go somewhere?' I asked suddenly.

I saw him stiffen. I feared rejection.

Instead he said, 'I can't take you back to mine. I told you before, I'm a student, I still live with my parents.'

It made me smile that. It seemed so absurd, here amongst the cool ones.

But Tim wasn't awkward and secretive about his sexuality in the way that I was. He was only eighteen. It wasn't a habit of years, a way of life for a man who probably rather liked it this way, if the truth be told. A man who almost enjoyed the inherent sleaziness of his own behaviour, the hiding in corners and the lurking in shadows. Tim just didn't know how to do things differently. Not yet. If he was at all hole in the corner, it was simply because he had not yet found the courage to fully confront his own sexuality, to tell his parents and those around him. He had no gay friends, because he himself was still coming to terms with what he was. The sex party was just a part of his exploration. The truth was that he would have loathed Larry's Bar and everything it represented. I'd been kidding myself ever to think differently.

'I remember that you live with your parents,' I said.

And I certainly wasn't able to take him back to mine.

'There's a Premier Inn at Leicester Square,' I continued. 'We could get a room.'

'I don't have much money,' he said.

'Don't worry, I'll pay,' I told him.

So we ended up spending the night together. I paid cash in advance. The hotel was suitably anonymous. The room was basic, but clean and comfortable. And we were alone. It was certainly a vast improvement on that dreadful party.

I'd spent the night with men before, but not often. Over the years I'd mostly contented myself with sweaty fumbles in dark corners, cubicles in public conveniences late at night or the doorways of backstreet shops long after opening hours. My conviction that it was all I was good for remained ever with me, and Poppers made the surroundings irrelevant. Nothing mattered except the sex. Until it was over.

This was so different.

It felt good to lie on clean sheets. It felt good to hold Tim in my arms afterwards and watch him fall asleep, with his head resting on my chest.

For those few hours, I felt quite fulfilled. I felt complete, but I didn't sleep much. I knew, all too soon, it would have to end. I would have to walk away, back to my usual, daily state of self-denial.

Somewhere around six, I wriggled my way free of my young lover. It was still dark. I didn't switch on a light. I made my way quietly into the bathroom, where I washed the gel out of my hair and dressed. I was hoping to leave and disappear into the early morning, without having to face Tim. Particularly as I had put on my straight clothes.

But he woke as I re-entered the bedroom.

'Hey, you,' he said softly. 'Why are you moving around in the dark?'

He reached to switch on the bedside light. I could see that he was smiling at me.

'I have to go,' I said, trying not to look at him. 'I'm sorry. I have to be somewhere. I shouldn't have spent the night with you.'

His face fell.

'No,' I said quickly. 'I didn't mean it like that.'

Although I half did, of course.

He studied me, curious, frowning.

'You look different,' he said. 'Your hair, your clothes. Everything.'

'My work look,' I said, trying to sound casual. 'I have to go to work.'

'On a Saturday?' he asked, still frowning.

'Look, I just have to be somewhere,' I said, more sharply than I'd intended.

I tried to soften my response. 'Uh, it's personal stuff. You know. I really do have to be somewhere else.'

'Somewhere you can't go looking how you did last night?'

I nodded.

'Do you want to talk about it?' he asked.

Rather to my surprise, he seemed quite accepting. But then, he'd already told me he wasn't 'out'. Not yet. He always added 'not yet.'

I didn't want to talk about it, of course. *Bless him*, I thought, *if only he knew*. But he would never know. There was so much in my life that I would never be able to talk about.

'Not now,' I said. 'I'm sorry, I really don't have the time.'

He threw off the bed covers revealing his beautiful, naked, young body. He had an erection again.

'Stay just a bit longer,' he said.

I glanced away. I would not let myself look at him. I must not. I could not.

'I can't,' I said. 'I'm really sorry, I do have to go.'

He looked crestfallen. He climbed out of bed and wrapped his arms around me.

'Look, that wasn't just a quick one-night stand,' he said, 'Not for me, anyway.'

'Not for me either,' I lied.

Although it wasn't a lie that I had feelings for him, which had not necessarily been quenched by our sexual activity.

'Look,' I said. 'Give me your phone number. I'll call you, make a date to meet again.'

'OK,' he agreed, although he still looked disappointed. 'Where's your phone? You can put my number in it now and call me straightaway, then I'll have yours.'

'No,' I said. 'I'm really sorry, but I'm in a big hurry. Just write your number on this, it'll be quicker.'

I delved into the top pocket of my jacket, where I'd already placed the receipt for the hotel room alongside the pen I always carry with me and handed both to him.

He did as I'd asked, then passed the sheet of paper back to me.

'Don't I get yours?' he asked.

I scribbled a number on the bottom of the receipt, tore the piece off and handed it to him.

As I did so he leaned forward and kissed me on the lips. I couldn't let myself respond, not even a little. Our time together was over.

I pulled away.

'We will do this again,' I said.

'I hope so,' he replied quietly.

I was lying. I had no intention of seeing Tim again. Not then. The number I'd given him wasn't mine, merely a random jumble of digits, and I wouldn't be phoning him.

I would just have to find another Tim. I told myself it wouldn't be difficult. Grindr was a smorgasbord. I'd probably been over-reacting to the Stephen Port murders. Thousands of men used Grindr and encountering another lunatic like Port would probably be less likely than being struck by lightning. I wouldn't go to a sex party again, though. That was a step too far.

I was aware of Tim's eyes on me as I headed for the door, but I didn't look back. And, thankfully, he didn't say anything more.

I put on the baseball cap I always carried with me and hurried through reception with my head down, although there was just one disinterested man on night duty behind the desk, and a cleaner mopping the floor who did not look up from his duties.

I felt how I always did after these adventures; even worse than before them.

I told myself I must stop. That I did not need another Tim. That I could even do without the titillation of Grindr browsing. And I must stop now, because the risks were too great.

I told myself I could do it. I could end all this now. I told myself I could make it stop. That it was over. That I would make it be over.

But I was, of course, lying to myself.

SIX

D aisy Wilkins lived on one of those hills at the back of Bath, from which you get spectacular views.

Her home was a small, but rather exceptional, one-bedroomed apartment in a modern block. Virtually the whole of the front wall of the sitting room was glass, with ceiling-to-floor windows and big, double, glass doors leading onto a narrow balcony overlooking the famous Georgian spa town.

Daisy was a small slim woman with good skin and regular features, pleasantly pretty, but Vogel thought she was considerably older than he expected Fisher's mistress to be. Indeed, rather than the young floozy that the DI had been automatically expecting – a term Vogel would never use in public, but one which his mother had favoured and lurked resolutely inside his head in circumstances such as this – Daisy was a mature, modest-looking woman, who was probably ten or even twelve years older than Fisher.

Her fair hair, only lightly streaked with grey, was neatly styled. Her clothes: pale blue jeans with a crease in them, a pink, silky looking T-shirt and a cardigan just a touch darker pink, were also neat. As was her immaculately-presented and tastefully-furnished home.

Vogel thought about Fisher's wife and the well-cared-for home they shared. Although not noticeably careful about his personal appearance, Fisher was clearly a man who liked his surroundings and his women to be neat and tidy.

Daisy Wilkins's voice suggested she was well-educated and, once she'd recovered from the shock of two police officers arriving unexpectedly at her front door, she showed herself to be well-mannered and hospitable. She invited Vogel and Saslow into her sitting room and offered them tea or coffee.

Her expression registered alarm, along with more than a hint of embarrassment, when Vogel told her that they were there to speak to her about Jim Fisher. Her blushing response instantly indicated the respectable sort of woman she was, the DI thought.

'Is Jim all right?' she asked anxiously. 'Has something happened to him?'

Vogel assured her that nothing had happened to Fisher.

'We need to check on his whereabouts over the last twenty-four hours, that's all,' he said. 'He told us he was with you last night. Is that true?'

'Why are you checking on his whereabouts?' the woman responded, a sudden sharpness in her voice. 'I need to know why.'

'Could you please just answer the question?' repeated Vogel quietly.

He already did not think Daisy Wilkins was the sort of woman who would give a man a false alibi and certainly not in a murder inquiry, but Vogel believed in acquiring as much information as possible from interviewees, before giving them any at all.

Daisy Wilkins looked, for just a fleeting moment, as if she might protest further, then she gave a small sigh of resignation.

'Clearly you know about our . . .'

She hesitated again.

'Our relationship,' she continued, both her manner and her voice suggesting that she might not think it was much of one.

'Yes, Jim was with me last night. He's been staying over quite often on Thursday nights over the last few months. He's working away, so I suppose I'm a stopover on the way home. We don't talk about that side of things and I have no idea how he arranges it. To tell the truth, I don't want to know. He's been doing it for years. The whole thing has been going on for years. Too many years, not much doubt about that . . .'

Her voice tailed off and she sighed again, rather more heavily.

'Was Mr Fisher with you all night?' Vogel asked

'Yes, but he left suddenly, quite early. I think he checked his phone when he went to the bathroom. I know he does that. He said he had to go and he would explain later. I was still half asleep. Anyway, I'm used to sudden comings and goings. That's how it is if you have a married man in your life.'

Daisy Wilkins paused, switching her gaze from Vogel to Saslow and back again.

'Does that have something to do with your visit?' she asked. 'Won't you tell me what's happened? Please?'

'We have to ask you some more questions first, I'm afraid, Miss Wilkins,' said Vogel.

Dawn Saslow chipped in then.

'We need to know the time Mr Fisher arrived last night and the time he left this morning, as exactly as you can, Miss Wilkins,' she said.

'He got here just after ten. Then we had some late supper. So we didn't go to bed until after one. I think it was probably about seven when he actually left the flat.'

If that was so Vogel thought, Fisher would have had quite a lot of time to kill before he turned up at his home at 9 a.m. It was only forty-five minutes or so drive away. Presumably, even after learning that his stepdaughter was missing, the man had been protecting his cover story, trying to prevent his wife discovering that he had a mistress.

'Like I said, I was still half asleep,' Daisy Wilkins continued. 'We didn't get to bed until so late, and . . .'

She didn't finish the sentence. Vogel was grateful. He preferred not to contemplate what he suspected she had been about to say. After all, married men did not usually visit their mistresses in order to get a good night's sleep.

They hadn't gone out anywhere, Daisy asserted. There was nobody else who could confirm what she was telling Vogel, but it was the truth, she assured the detective.

'It's always been just the two of us and it's always been only ever here, at my flat, for more than six years now, Detective

Inspector,' she said. 'Jim wouldn't risk being seen out anywhere with me, you see. It's ridiculous really, I shouldn't have put up with it, not for this long. But you get fed up with being alone. I like having a man in my bed now and then and Jim is rather good in bed as it happens, surprisingly so, perhaps.'

She paused. Vogel had to make a conscious effort not to let his embarrassment show. He was a police officer of more than twenty years' experience yet, all too often, he continued to find himself embarrassed by personal revelation, particularly of a sexual nature. And he really couldn't come to terms with the picture her words presented, of this slim, rather elegant woman romping in bed with the barrel-shaped, red-faced and somewhat uncouth Jim Fisher.

Of course, few looking on would ever have guessed at Vogel's disconcertment. Only his rapid blinking, partially concealed by the thick lenses of his spectacles, might have given him away, usually just to those closest to him. The sharply observant Dawn Saslow had, however, already recognised the trait in him, but Vogel had no idea of that. The young DC suppressed a smile with difficulty. Vogel continued to stare at Daisy Wilkins.

'Well, I'm not going to find anyone else at my age, am I?' Daisy continued. 'So I just accept what he has to offer, even if it's not a lot, and his lies, of course.'

The words were bitter, but the manner of her delivery was merely resigned.

Vogel listened without immediate response.

'Detective Inspector, won't you tell me why you are here now? Something has obviously happened. Do you suspect Jim of having committed some sort of crime?'

Vogel still wasn't ready to answer Daisy's questions.

'What kind of lies?' he asked.

'The usual in this situation. That he would leave his wife when the kids were older. Isn't it almost a courtesy for a married man to say that to his mistress? Though I've barely been even that.'

She stared at Vogel quizzically.

'You think he may have lied to me about something more sinister, Detective Inspector, is that it?'

Vogel avoided her question.

'Just let me confirm again that you are absolutely sure Jim

Fisher was with you for all of last night?' he asked. 'Was it at all possible that he could have left during the night and returned without you knowing it? Whilst you were asleep, perhaps?'

'I'm a light sleeper, Mr Vogel. And, in any case, when he is here, Jim doesn't give me much time to sleep.'

Vogel winced. He felt himself blinking rapidly again. He could do without that sort of detail, even though it was only as he had expected. He didn't like the thought of someone, especially someone he regarded as an oaf of a man, taking advantage of this woman who was surely far too good for him. He found it hard to believe that Daisy Wilkins had needs that could be so well satisfied by the likes of Jim Fisher. She must be just kidding herself, surely? Although, she had already indicated that she'd come to settle for whatever was on offer.

Vogel rather liked to put women on pedestals. That sort of woman anyway. A woman who he could not imagine would deliberately give anyone a false alibi. If she was sure that Jim Fisher had not left her, at any time between his arrival around 10.00 p.m. and his departure at around 7.00 a.m., then the man seemed to be in the clear. Karen Crow, the pathologist, had yet to confirm time of death, but it was already believed to have been after ten, at the earliest.

Although the DNA results would not come through for several days, Vogel now felt pretty confident of the results. He didn't think Jim Fisher would be incriminated. This case was not going to be that simple.

He heard Daisy Wilkins's voice almost in the distance, it was pleading now.

'What is going on, Mr Vogel? Why are you asking me all this? Please, *please*, tell me.'

Vogel considered for just a split second. He could not see any advantage in further concealing the reason for his visit. Indeed, it might be counterproductive to do so. Vogel really didn't think Daisy was protecting Fisher from anything, nor that she was the type of person who would lie to the police. He was even more certain that she would not do so, once she knew about Melanie.

'I am afraid Mr Fisher's stepdaughter has been found dead,' he said bluntly, all the while watching Daisy carefully. 'She was murdered in Bristol last night.'

The woman gasped. Her hand went to her throat. Her jaw dropped.

'And you suspect Jim?' she blurted out eventually.

'We just need to eliminate him from our enquiries,' Vogel said in his most unexpressive voice.

'Well, you can certainly do that,' Daisy Wilkins responded swiftly. 'Even if he hadn't been with me all night, you could do that. Jim Fisher is a lying, manipulative bastard, but he doesn't have a violent bone in his body. He never speaks of his wife to me, but I know all about the children. He adored Melanie. Loved her as much as his own. I'm sure of it. Always telling me so. I find it rather irritating, actually. I have such a small slice of him, yet even when he's with me he talks about the children, their achievements, what they've been up to. Doesn't seem able to stop himself.'

'I see.'

Vogel was as satisfied as he could be with Daisy Wilkins's response to all of his questions. He had just one more for her. And he was honest enough to himself to be aware that, as he voiced it, his reason for asking was as much personal as professional.

'How did you meet Jim Fisher?' he asked.

Daisy smiled. Was it because she – quite rightly – suspected the motive behind Vogel's new line of questioning, or was she smiling at the memory of her first meeting with her secret lover? Her answer, when it came, rather indicated the former. It caused Vogel to once again blink; he hoped he looked disinterested rather than flustered.

'Yes, most of the people I have ever known would think we were an unlikely pair,' she said. 'He was involved in a renovation project on the old building next door. One afternoon, he carried in my shopping for me from the car. He was younger then, slimmer and fitter too. And so was I, of course. Well, younger anyway. I'd just been made redundant from the library. I'd been a librarian all my life. I'd never married. I thought I had good friends, but they were all connected with my job. When I lost that, I gradually began to lose them too. My mother had died the year before. She'd have called Jim my "bit of rough", not that I would ever have let her meet him, of course.'

Daisy smiled again, a wry, self deprecating sort of smile.

'Anyway, I was suddenly, dreadfully lonely. Vulnerable, some might say. Jim made it clear immediately that he found me attractive and, I am afraid, I allowed him into my bed and my life with indecent haste. So, there you have it, Mr Vogel.'

'I see,' said Vogel, voice and face as expressionless ever.

Daisy smiled for the third time. A wider, easier smile this time. It lit up her face.

'Are you shocked, Mr Vogel?' she asked, almost mischievously.

'Certainly not, madam,' replied Vogel, blinking away.

He took his leave and led Dawn Saslow to the door. Walking towards the squad car parked by the curb outside, Vogel was overwhelmed with a sense of sadness.

Saslow had been watching him carefully.

'Everything all right, sir?' she asked.

Vogel grunted. 'Life can be so damned futile, Saslow,' he muttered.

It was about as close to an emotional outburst as Vogel would ever get. To a police colleague, at any rate.

The young DC knew better than to probe for more.

'Yes, sir,' she said.

AL

I suppose nothing lasts for ever. I'd always got away with it, so never felt in any danger of being caught before. I'd been visiting schools – primary schools – on and off, for years. I'd not been to this one before, though. I liked to ring the changes. It was safer and more exciting too.

I looked at my watch. 12.20 p.m. It wouldn't be long now. Very soon, the little dears would be leaving their classrooms for their dinner break. Some would go home. Almost all would be in the playground at some stage and that was right by the road, with just a wire netting fence for protection. You could see through wire netting well enough.

A few days earlier, I had driven by, as slowly as I dared in

my own car, to suss out whether or not this was a good venue
for my purposes. It was. I figured that, if I parked a little way
off and on the other side of the road from the school gates, I
would not be that conspicuous. It was where some of the teachers
left their cars and where all the mothers parked, when they
came to pick up their children at the end of the day. With the
help of a pair of powerful binoculars, I had a pretty damned
good view.

I wasn't in my own car now, of course. It would only take
one eagle-eyed observer to decide that I was acting suspiciously
and jot down my car registration number, then I'd be for it.

Oh no. I was cleverer than that, far cleverer than anybody who
knew me realised.

As a lad I'd run with a wild crowd. So I'd learned early on
how to open a vehicle door without drawing attention to myself
through the noise of breaking glass; I could use a wire and a
hook. Then I'd hot-wire the engine. It only worked with old
vehicles, of course, where the windows didn't quite close or
could be forced a fraction or two. Any sort of alarm system, let
alone the sophisticated modern sort, certainly deterred the likes
of me. It just made things too difficult.

These school-watching visits of mine were very important to
me. I told myself that they stopped me seeking out more active
encounters and, up to a point, that was true.

So I feared the day when I could no longer find vehicles old
and shoddy enough for my burglary skills. Fortunately, there
were still quite a few about if you knew where to look, more
often than not there were vans. Your average man with a van is
unlikely to want to spend a fortune on his transport, even if he
was actually successful enough to do so.

I'd been encouraged to read a newspaper report indicating that
modern, state-of-the-art, keyless vehicles were proving to be not
as secure as had been assumed. Indeed, one British police force,
Essex, so alarmed by the rise in theft of such vehicles, recently
advised keyless owners to install a crook lock, just in case.

Anyway, on this particular day, I procured my transport, as
usual, from a location as close as possible to my target school.
There was always a risk in what I got up to, but I tried to keep
it to the minimum. Therefore, I also did my stealing right before

I intended to do my watching. This limited the time I needed to be on the road in my stolen vehicle and how long I would be in it after it was reported missing by its rightful owner, if at all. I didn't push my luck. Or I tried not to, anyway.

So that's how I came to be sitting outside Moorcroft Primary School in my stolen van of choice: an elderly, white, Ford Transit. It's not only the commercial van driver's favourite, but also the car thief's favourite. The Transit is by far the most frequently stolen vehicle in the UK. There are so many of them about that they are curiously inconspicuous in spite of their size. Most people would assume that there was work being done somewhere close by or a delivery being made. That's what I hoped for anyway.

As always, I parked carefully. The conveniently available front slot of the row lining the far pavement from the school meant that I could make a quick getaway, if necessary. I'd been lucky to find a space right by the white zigzags, which forbade parking any closer to the school gates.

I wound the window down and I could just hear the sound of the bell that signified the end of morning lessons. After a couple of minutes, a group of boys and girls came out and started to walk in the direction of the council estate, which bordered the school to the right.

It was an exceptionally warm April day. Most of the girls were wearing their summer uniform: striped dresses, in the school colours of blue and yellow, and little white socks. This was a traditional sort of school, requiring traditional school attire.

I liked that. I liked it a lot.

I let my left hand drop to my crotch and began to massage myself there through my trousers. I started to swell. I unzipped my fly. I was already hard. I felt the excitement rising in me.

The little girls and boys walked past without even glancing in my direction. I was wearing dark glasses, made to look quite normal by the warm weather and a hoody. It was a size or two too big and not so well-suited to the temperature, but common enough at any time of year. I'd pulled the hood down over my forehead, partially concealing my face. I had become fairly well versed in the whereabouts of CCTV throughout much of the city and my stolen vehicles would lead anyone trying to trace me to a dead end but, with my predilections, you couldn't be too careful.

I hunkered down, pushing myself well back into the seat. My head slotted into the headrest with which the van was most conveniently fitted. Even if they glanced towards me, it was unlikely that any of the children would spot me.

They were gone far too quickly.

I removed my hand from my penis and let it become flaccid again. I did not zip up my fly. The best bit was still to come.

After about half an hour, the children who had stayed at school for their midday meal – the vast majority of them – came running out into the playground. I had a good enough view across the road, but I needed a close-up. I reached for the binoculars I always carried on these occasions and raised them to my eyes.

There was a trampoline in the corner at the nearer end of the playground. The children, supervised by a woman teacher, were taking it in turns to have a go. There was another teacher, a man, on duty at the far end of the playground. You always had to keep an eye on the teachers, but the woman supervising the trampoline was far too busy, making sure her charges didn't kill themselves, to even glance in my direction. The man was watching some boys have a kick about and seemed more interested in giving them advice on their footballing skills, than anything else.

Even if either of the teachers looked towards me, the way in which I was sitting, with my head tightly pressed against the headrest, would make it unlikely that they would even realise anyone was inside the van. Mine would appear to be just another empty vehicle. That's what I hoped, anyway.

There was a girl bouncing about on the trampoline. She would have been seven or eight, I thought. She was pretty, with fluffy, blonde hair. A picture-book child. She did a kind of somersault and ended up pretty much upside down. The skirt of her dress dropped over her inverted upper body, revealing sturdy, little legs and a flash of white knickers.

I lowered my free hand between my legs and began stroking and fondling myself again.

I was vaguely aware of children walking right by the van, but I couldn't stop.

Suddenly, I realised there was a face at the window, on the

passenger side of the van. It belonged to a little girl, also aged seven or eight, I thought. I guessed she must be standing on tiptoe to make herself tall enough to look through the window at me. I found that exciting too.

The child was clearly curious.

I put down the binoculars. With one hand still on my penis, I reached with the other for the handle to the passenger window, the old-fashioned, manual sort, and wound it down. I always used gloves, of course, apart from when I was touching myself. It had to be flesh-on-flesh then. I never took unnecessary risks. Even though I knew my fingerprints were not on any police records, I wasn't stupid. My free hand remained gloved throughout.

'Hello,' I said.

My voice sounded wrong, high-pitched, squeaky, forced. The girl didn't seem to notice.

'Is that a kitten you've got there?' she asked.

I glanced down at my lap. My hand very nearly concealed my otherwise exposed penis. I wondered if she could see tufts of my pubic hair, leading her to think I was stroking some sort of pet animal. A kitten? The very idea of that stimulated me even more.

I looked back at her.

'Would you like to stroke it?' I asked.

She looked doubtful.

I stretched across to turn the handle on the passenger door, then pushed the door ajar. She stepped back to allow me to do so.

'Come on,' I said. 'Jump in. It won't bite.'

She smiled, her eyes fixed on my crotch.

It was madness of course, sheer madness. Some things a man like me knows he can never get away with, but neither can he always stop himself.

Had she realised yet that I was not holding a kitten? I had no idea. My blood was up. I wanted her to put her hands on me and stroke me there more than anything in the world. I needed her to.

'I don't know,' she said.

She sounded doubtful, but still interested. I pushed the door a little more open. She took another step back, still staring at my crotch. I was close to exploding. I could almost feel her touch. I could imagine her lips. I could imagine touching her private parts. Gently. So gently. I was crazy for her.

Another girl's voice cut through the moment.

'C'mon on, Alice.'

Alice looked away from my crotch. I looked away from Alice.

The second girl, of around the same age I thought, was standing about 100 yards away calling for her schoolmate.

Alice still seemed uncertain.

'It's all right, Alice,' I said.

I knew her name now. It was always easier when you knew their names.

'It won't take a moment, Alice,' I continued. 'Jump in. You can have a stroke too. You'd like that, wouldn't you?'

Alice looked back at me and smiled again.

I'd got her. Surely I'd got her. I reached out towards her with my free gloved hand. She only had to take it and I'd have her in the van quick as a flash. She'd be there for me. I'd be able to do what I liked with her. Drive away with her. Make her my own.

I was breathing fast. I was nearly out of control.

Then I heard another voice. An adult voice. Sharp and commanding. It came as a total shock.

'Alice Palmer! What are you doing? Who are you talking to?'

The voice came from across the road, but I could tell that it was getting nearer. I looked up. I had been so preoccupied by Alice, not to mention my throbbing penis, that I hadn't even noticed playtime had ended. The children, including those I had been only half-aware of walking past the van, were all trouping back into the school.

The woman teacher who had been overseeing the trampoline was crossing the road now, striding purposefully towards us.

'Alice Palmer,' she called again. 'Come here *at once. Move away from that van.*'

Alice duly backed off, her face flushed and turned towards the teacher. She looked uncertain. Confused. So she might. She had so nearly been mine.

I slammed the passenger door shut, switched on the engine, thrust the van into first gear and took off with a screech of tires.

SEVEN

It was just after noon, when Vogel and Saslow arrived at the North Bristol Academy. This sprawling complex of red-brick buildings, dating back to the 1960s, was now reincarnated as one of the latest, educational innovations of modern government. An independently run school funded directly by the Ministry of Education.

The buildings, which were in good order, retained the feel of being from another time. They were, it seemed, the only aspect of the North Bristol Academy which was not thoroughly modern. Apart from the smell, of course. The place smelt exactly the way Vogel remembered his own school smelling twenty-five years earlier. A distinct odour of powerful disinfectant wafted his way, as they passed the cloakrooms.

The school secretary took them straight to the headmistress's office.

The head, Christine Chapman, was a handsome woman – in her late thirties, Vogel guessed – who had the manner and appearance of a senior executive high up in the business world, rather than a schoolteacher. Well, Vogel's idea of a school-teacher, anyway. But he reminded himself that is more or less what head teachers had to be nowadays. The wife of one of his team in the Met had been head of a primary school. When Vogel had asked her about her work, at, for him, a rare social gathering, she'd said that the most difficult part of her job was ensuring that she did not become totally distanced, both from her pupils and the art of teaching. Head teachers, like senior police officers, were expected to be managers before anything else nowadays. A concept with which Vogel consistently struggled.

Christine Chapman rose to her feet, as Vogel was shown into her uncluttered, second-floor office, overlooking tennis courts and a playing field beyond. She stepped from behind a big, solid-looking desk made of pale wood, walked across carpeted floor and shook hands with both him and Saslow as they introduced themselves.

Christine Chapman didn't smile. She didn't prevaricate.

'I do hope you are not here to tell me what I think you are,' she said.

Vogel was momentarily surprised. Then he noticed the television mounted on the wall to the left of Chapman's desk. The sound was off, but he saw that it was tuned to Sky News.

The head teacher followed his gaze.

'I saw a report earlier about the body of a girl, as yet unnamed, having been found in Bristol,' she said.

She gestured towards the computer on her desk top.

'That led me to check this morning's register, just in case. We have only one unexplained absentee today. Her name is Melanie Cooke. I was still trying to stop myself putting two and two together, when the office rang through to tell me that two police officers had arrived at our school. I so want you to tell me I am wrong, Detective Inspector.'

'I am afraid I can't do that,' Vogel replied quietly. 'She has yet to be formally identified but the young woman, whose body was found this morning, almost certainly is Melanie Cooke.'

Christine Chapman said nothing. She stared at Vogel for a few seconds then returned to her desk and sat down behind it. She waved an arm towards two easy chairs, silently inviting the police officers to also sit.

They did so.

'I've been a teacher for eighteen years and a head for six,' said Christine Chapman. 'I've never had to deal with anything like this before. You'll have to forgive me, Detective Inspector, I'm stunned. I can only imagine the effect this is going to have on the school, everyone . . .'

Her voice tailed off. She straightened a pen on the desk in front of her so that it was perfectly in line with the edge. Habit, thought Vogel. Everything about the head mistress smacked of order. This was a highly organised, capable, woman on top of her job, he was quite sure. Now she just looked stricken.

'We are very sorry for your loss, Miss Chapman,' said Vogel. 'But we do need to talk to you – as a matter of urgency – and to Melanie's class teacher, any special friends and anyone else who might be able to help us. We need to know what sort of girl she was, what her day-to-day life was like away from home. We have a brutal killer on the loose and the first twenty-four hours in a murder investigation are vital.'

Christine Chapman nodded.

'I teach every class in the school for one period a week,' she said. 'It's easy to get out of touch when you're the head. As far as I know, Melanie was quite an average girl, although prettier than average, that's for sure. She was bright enough, but worked only just hard enough, like so many of them. Popular too. No particular problems that I'm aware of, but I don't know the girls like their class teachers do. I'll call in Melanie's class teacher.'

Melanie's class teacher, Marion Smith, was a grey-haired woman in her fifties, rather more resembling the slightly starchy schoolmistresses Vogel remembered from his own schooldays. Once she had got over her initial shock, been given a glass of water and received a few words of comfort from Christine Chapman, Marion Smith was able to provide a rather more detailed picture of Melanie Cooke, just as the head had predicted.

'She was very good at art, worked hard at the things she liked to do and not so hard at the subjects she had trouble with. She was a fairly easy pupil, never got in trouble. A happy, likeable girl, I'd say.'

'And friends?' enquired Vogel. 'Any particular friends?'

'Oh yes. Sally Pearson. Inseparable, those two.'

'In that case,' said Vogel. 'Could we have a word with Sally straight away?'

The head agreed. A very nervous looking Sally Pearson arrived just minutes later. She was another potentially pretty girl with an abundance of red hair, but unfortunately suffering from a severe dose of teenage acne.

Christine Chapman broke the news to Sally, as she'd requested she be allowed to do.

Sally Pearson barely seemed to react. Her eyelids flickered, her lower lip trembled very slightly, but she said nothing. It was as if she wasn't quite taking in the grim news she'd just been given, thought Vogel. He had been in this kind of situation before.

It was not unusual for people to fail to grasp such a reality until much later. That could sometimes help with a police inquiry, though, because they were inclined to answer questions more factually and without personal bias whilst still in shock and before emotion sets in. But sometimes they just became unable, or unwilling, to respond properly.

'Sally, I can only imagine how difficult this is for you, but we really need your help,' began Vogel gently. 'Do you know where Melanie was planning to go last night?'

Sally shook her head, still remaining silent.

'She told her parents that she was going to have a homework evening with you. Were you expecting her?'

Sally shrugged and spoke for the first time, her voice little more than a whisper.

'She said she might come round.'

'So weren't you anxious when she didn't turn up?'

Sally shrugged again without saying anything more.

'Was she in the habit of not turning up, when you'd arranged to meet?' Vogel persisted.

Sally looked up from the floor and finally returned Vogel's steady gaze.

'Mel only said she *might* come round,' she said, with heavy emphasis on the word 'might'.

Then she looked back down at the floor again.

Vogel continued to question the girl for a few more minutes. It was not a fruitful exchange.

Sally Pearson insisted that she had no idea whether or not Melanie had a boyfriend. She had no idea if she'd ever had contact with a man online. She couldn't remember when she'd last seen Melanie outside school.

Indeed, it seemed she knew nothing, at all, about anything.

'All right, Sally,' Vogel said eventually. 'I'm sure you are very upset. I'll not bother you any more today.'

The interview wasn't getting him anywhere. A murder investigation is like any other police investigation. You have to prioritise your resources and your time.

SAUL

I wanted to meet Sonia too. I really did. After all, it had been my express aim to find someone I might ultimately marry. Someone who could give me the kind of family life I longed for and save me from the life I feared I may be stuck with.

But the picture I'd painted of myself was so far removed from what I really was, I wondered if she would ever accept me. I had created a depiction to which, I feared, I could do no justice. I had a heck of a lot more to explain away than the facial hair I'd doctored into my Marryme.com picture, the colour of the hair on my head and the definition of my chin. A heck of a lot more.

Why had I been such a fool?

I told myself that I could not be the first person to build themselves up a bit in order to impress a potential date online. In fact, it was probably pretty common. Sonia would understand, surely. But I suspected I had gone a lot further than most.

It was eventually agreed that we would meet in Bath, a beautiful town, and easily accessible to us both.

She said she would drive. I said I would come by train. She said she would meet me at the station. She supplied me with her mobile phone number, just in case.

I said I'd had an accident with my phone – drowned it in the bath – and that I hoped my new one would arrive very soon, certainly by the time of our arranged meeting.

Just before I left home, I emailed her to say that my new phone hadn't yet arrived, but I would have her number with me. If there appeared to be any problem with our arrangements, I would find a way of calling her.

I dressed the way I thought she might like me to be dressed. Indeed, the way she might expect me to dress.

I wore a dark jacket over jeans. Surely just right for a school-teacher on his day off.

My perfectly pressed, pale blue shirt was open at the neck. I had spent a long time ironing it and even longer deciding on my footwear. Silly, I know, but at the time I felt that my whole life rested on this meeting.

I put on a pair of nearly-new, Adidas trainers first. They were exceptionally white and they didn't look or feel right at all. Then I tried my best, shiny, black, lace-up shoes. They were old fashioned, but smart. I felt that Sonia would rather like me to be a bit of a young fogey. Well, youngish.

All the same, they didn't seem quite right either.

Eventually, I settled on a pair of elderly and rather battered, but good quality, brown, suede slip-ons. They had a touch of the young fogey about them too, I thought.

As the train trundled into Bath, I wondered desolately why I had spent so long and wasted so much time worrying about my feet.

My face was the problem and even more so was the unlikely background I'd invented. All those silly stories. Why on earth had I told her I'd been in the foreign legion? It was so stupid. Why was I such a fantasist? Why could I not just be myself?

The Saul I had created for Sonia was really so unlike me. It was so ridiculous, because she was one person who might have accepted the real me. I got the impression she would accept almost anything in order to have someone to share her life with.

Now I feared I would not be able to pull off this first meeting and that she would realise just how much I had oversold myself.

Even if I succeeded initially, then what?

I remembered the old Irish joke. A motorist visiting Ireland stops to ask directions from a local. The Irishman looks thoughtful.

'Well now sir,' he says eventually. 'If I were you I wouldn't start from here.'

It's a good joke, I think. But there was nothing funny about my situation. Just like the visitor to Ireland I had no choice; I had to start from where I was. Or rather from where I had put myself.

It wasn't going to be easy.

I put on the pair of spectacles, fitted with plain glass and slightly tinted, that I was carrying in my jacket pocket. They were probably the only thing about me that matched the two photographs Sonia had of me in any way.

As the train began to slow down, I walked out into the corridor and positioned myself by a door. I didn't open the window before the train had stopped, but pressed my face close to the glass and peered along the platform.

Sonia was standing by the buffet, just as she'd said she would. She was unmistakeable, exactly like the photographs she had sent me: fair, a tad on the plump side, not unattractive, but clearly as unsure of herself as her emails had always indicated.

Her whole body language spoke volumes of anxiety. She was staring at the train, her eyes following it, sweeping the windows. She was looking for me. She was eager to see me. She was excited, I thought, as well as being so clearly anxious.

I felt much the same, but I had far more reason than Sonia to be ill at ease.

If only I wasn't so damned shy and insecure, I wouldn't have delved into fantasy land and got myself into this mess.

The train jerked to a halt. I'd arrived. I tried to gulp back my uncertainties. I was here. What could the worst result be? I supposed it was that she would realise I wasn't at all how I had presented myself and she wouldn't want to see me again. I wondered if I should try to continue the charade, on this first meeting anyway, but that would surely only make things worse.

I steeled myself. There was a click as the train's doors were unlocked. I opened the window and prepared to lean out to reach the handle outside and open the door.

We had pulled to a halt, with me standing on the train almost opposite the buffet. Sonia was just yards away, directly facing me.

I leaned forward out of the window and grasped the handle in my fingers.

I couldn't stop staring at her. Suddenly, she caught my eye. She frowned. Puzzled, I suppose. I wasn't sure if she would recognise me at all. I looked so different from my picture. I'd thought about warning her, at least, about the absence of facial hair and the colour of the hair on my head. Both of those were, after all, easy to explain, but it had seemed like opening the floodgates. If I was honest about anything, the rest of it would have to come tumbling out. So I'd said nothing.

And now, there she was before me. She was wearing a cream jacket, grey, tailored trousers and little, black, ankle boots, with straps and shiny buckles. I took it all in in a flash. I wondered if she had taken as long to decide what to wear as I had. I suspected that she had.

I thought she looked lovely. She had a classic timelessness about her. She wasn't like one of these modern women I couldn't cope with. I was sure of it. She really was the one I had been looking for. I began to smile. I couldn't help myself. Surely, this was meant to be. I could sort it, couldn't I? I could make this work. I had an inventive enough brain, that was for sure.

Sonia's frown deepened. Her face tightened. She shook her head slightly. Then she looked away and continued to stare up and down the train.

She hadn't recognised me. She'd appeared to think she had, for a moment, then decided it couldn't be me. That was what I'd been afraid of. All the doubts and fears overwhelmed me again.

'Come on mate, you're blocking the door.'

The cry from behind came as a shock, jerking me back to the reality of the moment. I opened the door and began to step forward, one foot poised above the step. Sonia's eyes swept along the train again. She paused her gaze once more, just for a second, as she saw me and then moved on.

I couldn't do it. I just couldn't do it.

I turned around and squeezed myself past the man behind me, pushing him to one side.

'Sorry, sorry,' I muttered, aware of the heat rising in my neck. I was blushing on top of everything else.

There were other people in the corridor waiting to disembark. Probably only three or four people in all, but it felt like a massive, threatening crowd to me.

'Sorry, sorry, wrong station,' I said.

'Oh for God's sake,' grumbled the man I had pushed out of the way.

I forced a passage through the rest of them.

'Ouch,' cried a young woman upon whose foot I trod heavily. 'Be careful.'

Once back in the carriage, I headed for where I had been sitting before. For a few seconds, I remained standing by my seat, back from the window, but positioned so that I could see out quite clearly. Sonia, I hoped, would be unable to see me. I watched her step forward and begin to walk along the platform yet again, peering in the windows. I turned my head and stepped further back.

This was terrible. I had made a complete fool of myself before I'd even met her. What had I been thinking of? Why couldn't I have been honest with her? Or as honest as I can ever be. What was wrong with the real me? I wasn't that bad, was I? No worse than a lot of others, surely.

Was this train never going to move, I wondered? By then, I just wanted to get away from this ridiculous situation. And from Sonia, I suppose. Yet I had so wanted to be with her, to be with the right person. I'd been sure, too, that Sonia was the right person.

I sank back into my seat, hopefully out of her sight line. There was a lurch as the train finally began to move. I craned my neck for one last glimpse of her. There she was, standing quite still, at the far end of the platform, near the engine, just staring at the train moving slowly forwards.

I was sitting by the window on the platform side. I had an excellent final view of her as the carriage, in which I was travelling, passed by her

She still looked puzzled and what else? Disappointed? Hurt?

I had no idea whether she could see me or not. But I knew she was thinking about me, as I was about her.

I'd let her down so badly, before I'd even met her. What had I been thinking about? I always let people down. I'd been a disappointment all my life. To almost everyone with whom I'd crossed paths, but I'd never meant to let Sonia down. I really hadn't.

I just could not face her. There was to be no new chapter of my life, no soulmate with whom to share everything. I was incapable of sharing anything. I had always been unable to share.

The newspaper I'd been reading or pretending to read really, before the train pulled into Bath, was still on the table where I'd left it. I picked it up and held it up in front of my face, so that nobody could see the tears coursing down my cheeks.

By the time I eventually reached my home railway station, I had at least managed to stop blubbing and pull myself together. I still felt sorry for myself, but I had every right to, didn't I?

I walked home slowly, keeping my head down. I really didn't want to have eye contact with anyone and I certainly didn't want to be recognised by anyone and have to speak to them.

It was after dark by then and I kept away from the street lights.

As soon as I got indoors, I fetched my laptop and switched on. There were two emails from Sonia.

The first said simply: 'Where were you?'

The second was a little longer.

'I thought I saw you when the train, the one you told me you'd be on, pulled into the station,' she wrote. 'Then I thought it probably wasn't you, only someone wearing glasses like yours. I waited for the next train, just in case. Then I realised I was probably making a fool of myself. You had my mobile phone number. You could have called if something had gone wrong. Even if you'd merely changed your mind, you could have called. Now I realise how significant it was that you somehow never had a phone number you could give me.

'I don't know why you have done what you have done, after all that we said to each other, or at least after what I said to you. I opened my heart to you. I thought we already meant something special to each other.

'Were you just playing a game with me? I feel so stupid. What you did today was cruel. Please tell me, what is going on?'

I wrote a reply straight away, making no reference to whether or not I'd been on the train. She could think what she liked about that.

'Dear Sonia, I am sorry if I have hurt you and I am sorry that I could not meet you as arranged today. But I'm afraid the truth is that whatever there was between us is now over, albeit before it really began. Not only could I not meet you today, I cannot ever meet you. I hope you will find someone who is worthy of you. I am not. You may not think it now, but you have had a lucky escape. Saul.'

I was crying again as I pushed the send button. It was a sparse, blunt message. I felt I had no choice. Whatever Sonia might think, I am not a cruel or callous man. Really, I am not. I am a mixed-up wreckage of a man, that's all. That is the reason why I couldn't have a proper relationship with Sonia, nor even meet her. It wasn't anything to do with her. She seemed perfect. It was down to me being me, the me I have had to learn to live with.

I sat looking at my computer screen. There was a ping within just a few minutes of my emailing Sonia. Up popped another message from her.

'How could you do this?' she asked. 'How could you behave like this? You haven't even given me any sort of explanation. Couldn't we at least talk on the phone? You have my number. Call me.'

I switched off the laptop, fetched a bottle of whisky and a pint glass from the kitchen cupboard and took them both with me into the bathroom, where I ran myself a very hot bath.

I climbed in straight away, without adjusting the temperature, even though the water was almost burning and turned my skin an angry red. I didn't care. After a while, the sensation became quite pleasant. I poured the best part of half a pint of whisky into my glass, topped it up with cold water from the bath tap, lay back, and tried to relax. I hoped the whisky, combined with the restorative powers of the bath, would make it possible for me to forget the horrors of the day and move on to dealing with the rest of my life.

Today was over. Sonia was over. I would never call her and I would never email her again.

She knew me only as Saul. I hadn't told her my full name. She had no idea where I lived, although she may have thought she did. She had no phone number or address for me and the email address I'd used throughout our correspondence would never be used again.

I wouldn't even look at it. I would cancel it, that's what I would do. Then her emails would bounce back to her.

That would be kindest, because it would surely make clear to her that there was no hope, that I had disappeared from her life for ever. Like I always do.

EIGHT

Willis took PC Claire Brown with him to interview the second Mrs Terry Cooke, at the unkempt, council house she shared with her husband and their three

young children. As Vogel had hoped, the woman was taken totally
by surprise. She seemed rather alarmed.

'It's just routine, Mrs Cooke,' Willis told her. 'I'm sure you
know by now that Mr Cooke's daughter has been found dead?'

Willis turned the remark into a question, although he was
pretty sure of the answer.

'Yes, of course,' replied Susan Cooke. 'My Terry called me
almost as soon as he knew the worst. Terrible. Terrible. But I
can't help you, I don't know nothing about what happened. She
was murdered, wasn't she? Well, how would I be able to tell you
anything? I barely knew the girl. Her mother didn't like Terry
bringing her here, bloody snob she is. Thinks folk who live in a
council house are beneath her. Well, she's only got her place
because she took all my Terry's money when he left her. He
don't like living in a council house neither. Blames me for how
we live. He certainly wouldn't bring that girl to this place, not
his little princess.'

She paused, waving a hand wearily at the small, front garden,
which was a brown desert growing only the odd stinging nettle,
an old bedstead, a rusting bicycle and a pile of bulging, black,
plastic, rubbish bags. She touched a fading bruise on her left
cheek.

'Anyway, they didn't ever meet here,' she continued with a
forlorn little sigh. 'They used to go out. My Terry and the girl.
He never wants to spend any more time here than he has to. Not
nowadays. That's just how it is. So I don't know . . .'

Willis brought the avalanche of words to a halt with a raised
hand. Susan Cooke was still standing in her own doorway. The
two police officers remained outside.

'Please Mrs Cooke,' he remonstrated. 'Can we come in and talk
about this indoors?'

Susan Cooke didn't look too sure at all. She pushed a strand
of lank, peroxide hair back from her forehead. Willis noticed
how dark the roots were. He hated that sort of thing. This was
a woman who might once have been pretty, but now, he thought,
her pale face merely reflected the damage wreaked by a lifetime
of disappointment.

Willis glanced pointedly up and down the street, as if looking
for curious neighbours or twitching curtains.

'Yes of course, come in,' said Susan Cooke finally, holding the door wide open. She led the two officers past a kitchen, where dirty dishes overflowed the sink, and into a grubby, ill-furnished sitting room. Every available space seemed to be covered with something: newspapers, magazines, beer bottles, dirty cups and glasses, abandoned coats and scarves, assorted children's toys, a broken railway carriage, a teddy bear with one arm, a grimy looking Game Boy and a toy mobile phone.

The woman began to clear a space on the sofa big enough for two. It was several seconds before Brown and Willis were able to sit down.

Willis did so with some distaste and, only with the greatest effort, avoided trying to brush clean the seat of the sofa, with one of the tissues from the small packet he always kept in his pocket.

Willis did not know what a far cry this slovenly home was from the two Vogel had visited on this case so far, that of the first Mrs Cooke and of her second husband's mistress, Daisy Wilkins. He did know this was his idea of hell.

Susan Cooke seemed to read his mind.

'It's the children,' she said, as if that explained everything. 'The 'ouse is too small, you see. Three came along almost straight away. The first before we were married, then the other two. Twins. Never been twins in either of our families, but we 'ad 'em. The council won't give us a bigger one. It's got three bedrooms, they say, and that's enough. But the third one's a box and you can't swing a cat in this room. We'll never be able to afford our own place, not on his wages. With what he gives that ex of 'is too and I can't work, not with they three. He gets that mad about us living like this. I can't cope, that's the trouble. It's me nerves you see.'

She finally stopped talking.

Her glance strayed to the table alongside the chair she was sitting on. Willis followed her gaze. A small bottle of pills stood next to a glass of water. Prozac, or something similar, guessed Willis. Happy pills. A powerful tranquilizer of some sort, for sure. He watched the woman stare longingly at the little bottle, as if fighting a battle within. Finally, it became clear that the battle had been lost.

'You'll have to excuse me, I need to take my medication.'

With a trembling hand she reached for the little bottle of pills, extracted two, took a sip of water and swallowed. Her eyes closed, as if already in anticipation of relief.

'How old are your children?' asked PC Brown gently. She was one of the older women constables and of the old school, having left the force to bring up her own children and then returned. Her quiet manner and the note of sympathy she injected into her voice whenever appropriate, often made her invaluable in a situation like this. Willis had chosen her deliberately from the women officers who had been available.

'The eldest's eight and the twins are seven,' Susan Cooke replied. 'They're all at school now, thank God. It's the only rest I get. We've got no space, that's the problem . . .'

Claire Brown made one of her sympathetic noises.

Susan Cooke waved an arm desolately at the small, cluttered room, which Willis suspected hadn't seen a duster or a vacuum cleaner in months.

Suddenly she sat up straight.

'I'm forgetting my manners,' she said. 'Would you like a cup of tea?'

Willis tried not to let the sheer horror of the prospect show on his face.

'No, thank you, we have to be as quick as we can when we're on an inquiry as serious as this,' he said politely.

PC Brown quickly acquiesced.

'Not for me,' she said. 'But thank you so much for the offer.'

She smiled kindly at Susan Cooke, who managed a small, tired smile back.

Willis had had enough. He decided the time for prevarication was over.

'So Mrs Cooke, we need to ask you some questions about your husband's whereabouts over the last few days . . .' he began.

'You mean last night?' the woman queried sharply, interrupting him.

It seemed Prozac, and the other prescription drugs Willis reckoned she was taking, hadn't completely numbed her senses.

'Not entirely,' he said. 'Let's start with the past week or so. Do you know when your husband last saw his daughter?'

Susan Cooke didn't answer at once. She seemed to be thinking.

'It must have been a couple of weekends back,' she said eventually.

'That's almost three weeks ago,' said Willis. 'Did he usually see Melanie that infrequently?'

'Well, he was supposed to be seeing her last Sunday. He usually saw her every other Sunday, at least. Or used to, anyway. They were going to the pictures, then for a burger. But she cancelled, said she couldn't make it.'

'Do you know why?' interjected PC Brown.

Mrs Cooke shrugged.

'Well, she's that age, isn't she? Tricky. Claimed she was having a bad period. They do that you know, these girls from split homes. Reckon their dads will be too embarrassed to ask any questions. He didn't believe her, though, my Terry. And later on he found out by chance that she'd spent the afternoon with one of her mates.'

'How did your husband feel about that?' asked PC Brown.

Willis decided he would let Claire Brown have her head. He'd noticed before that, along with her sympathetic manner, she had an effectively neutral way of asking questions. She seemed to be doing rather well with Susan Cooke.

'Well he wasn't best pleased, but then nobody would be.' She paused again.

'Look, uh, you're not trying to suggest . . . I mean, I can tell you now. My Terry would never hurt that girl, not his princess.' Susan Cooke spat out the last few words. She touched her bruised face again.

'How did you get that bruise, Mrs Cooke?' Claire Brown asked quietly.

The woman looked startled. 'What? That? Oh, I was putting the twins down the other night. They've got bunk beds. They was playing up. I knocked my face against one of the uprights, while I was trying to get them to settle.'

Brown and Willis exchanged glances. Neither made any direct comment.

'You're quite sure your husband would never hurt Melanie?' asked PC Brown, keeping her voice expressionless.

If Mrs Cooke grasped the particular significance of the question, she showed no immediate sign of it.

'Not in a million years,' she said, with a sniff. 'He worshipped her. Worshipped the ground she walked on. His little princess, as I keep saying, that's what he called her.' She paused then and seemed to be thinking things through. 'He'd never hurt his princess,' she repeated.

'Look Mrs Cooke, we just need to learn everything we can about Melanie, her family, her friends, her behaviour patterns, everything. In your opinion, what sort of girl was she?'

'I told you, I hardly ever saw her. But I know she was spoiled right enough, by her father, that's for sure. He was always spending money he didn't have on her. And by her stepfather by all accounts. Competing for her affections, the pair of 'em, if you ask me.'

'What about her mother?'

Mrs Cooke shrugged.

'Caught between the two men, I reckon. Takes the easy way out. Turns a blind eye to all sorts of stuff, I shouldn't wonder.'

Willis thought it was time for him to take control again.

'So let's move on to last night,' he said. 'Can you tell me where your husband was, Mrs Cooke?'

'I knew you'd get to that soon enough,' the woman muttered. 'Here, in bed with me, of course, like he always is. That's one thing about my Terry. He's not got enough life in him anymore to play around.'

'And earlier in the evening, before you went to bed?'

'He had a long job on yesterday. Left home soon after five and didn't get in til gone seven. We had something to eat, then he slumped in front of the telly. Sometimes he goes to the pub, but he was too knackered. We were in bed by ten o'clock, or thereabouts. So we were together til Sarah called.'

Willis glanced toward the pill bottle.

'What are those?' he asked.

Sarah Cooke coloured slightly. 'Oh, just something the doctor gives me for me nerves.'

'Do you take any other medication?'

The woman nodded.

'Sleeping pills by any chance?'

She nodded again.

'And did you take any sleeping pills last night?'

'Yes, I take them every night.'

'How many?'

'Two. I always take two.'

'What brand?'

She told him.

Willis knew about sleeping pills. His mother had been on them for years after his father went, until she met her new man.

'That's about as strong a brand as you can get, Mrs Cooke,' he said. 'I would imagine they really knock you out, don't they?'

'Well yes, they do. But it's the only way I can get any sleep, you see, with me nerves and the children . . .'

The woman's voice tailed off. Willis thought she might be beginning to grasp the significance of his line of questioning.

'So how can you be sure your husband was with you all night?' he continued. 'If he'd popped out for a couple of hours after you'd fallen asleep, you wouldn't have even known, would you?'

Mrs Cooke looked confused. 'Well, I mean, we sleep in the same bed. Anyway, he wouldn't have. He didn't. Really. I'm sure.'

She didn't sound that sure.

'I think you have to admit it would be possible, Mrs Cooke,' Willis persisted.

'Well, I don't know about that.' The woman still wouldn't commit herself.

'Mrs Cooke, did you wake when your husband's ex-wife called him in the early hours?'

'Yes, of course I did.'

'Do you know what time it was?'

'Not exactly. The middle of the night or that's what it felt like. Maybe three or four.'

'Weren't you pretty woozy, disturbed at that hour, after taking your pills?'

'Well, yes, I probably was, but I knew he had to go out and it had something to do with Melanie.'

'Did you go straight back to sleep?'

'I think so, until the kids woke me just after six. You don't need an alarm in this house!'

'I put it to you again, is it not highly unlikely that anything would have wakened you, before that call from Melanie's mother?' Willis persisted further. 'Your husband could have slipped out for two, or even three, hours without you noticing. You must agree with that, surely?'

Susan Cooke shook her head stubbornly. 'He didn't go anywhere, he was in bed with me all night,' she insisted.

But Willis was smiling when he and PC Brown left a few minutes later.

'Few holes in that alibi, then,' he murmured contentedly.

LEO

After returning home from my night with Tim, I forced myself to stop thinking about him. I am strong. Surely, I am strong. I have had to be, living the life that I do. I concentrated on my work. I am not unsuccessful. I am not an unintelligent man. I think I am quite good at what I do. I think I would be good at anything I chose to put my hand to, actually.

It is just my personal life, my personal predilections, that I can't cope with. I do not lack confidence in any regard, other than that of my sexuality, of course. I tell myself that it is fear of the prejudice of others, which makes me live the way I do: hiding, skulking and keeping my true self hidden from the world around me.

I tell myself that prejudice against homosexuality in the workplace is still rife, particularly in less cosmopolitan parts of the UK. I don't want to have to deal with that; I am unable to deal with that. That and the scorn of family and friends. Some, I know, would pity me and that, of course, would be even worse.

I have constructed an image of myself, as well as being strong, I am tough. I am 'all man'. I have to be. The men I know, in the part of my life that I live from day to day, are the sort who make irreverent, unpolitically correct jokes about almost everything. So when it comes to people's sexuality, I ensure that, if necessary, I am as unpolitically correct as the best of them. Most of the time I just listen, smile, and laugh when appropriate. But, just occasionally, I will tell the crudest jokes of all, the sort that actually make the others wince.

I enjoy that in a curious sort of way. It's my cover. I like the fact that they lap it up, that they do not suspect for a single second that I am anything other than one of them. That is the public me. I'm one of the boys. I make crude jokes about women whenever it seems called for and I invent stories of fictional, sexual encounters. Not often, but often enough. It has become a habit.

I have grown to accept that I cannot get by without regular, if not necessarily frequent, sexual encounters with men, whilst also accepting that I will never come to terms with being open about that, with revealing myself to others for what I am.

So I cannot see Tim again. That would break my golden rule. There have been men before with whom I'd shared more than one sexual encounter, although not many. But if ever there was even the merest suggestion of a relationship developing, I backed away. I disappeared.

And that was the way it would be with Tim. The way it had to be with Tim.

So I don't really know why I kept that half torn, hotel bill, with his phone number scribbled on the bottom. I told myself it was because I might be able to make some sort of expenses claim on it, but that was nonsense, of course. I am not stupid enough to put myself under any unnecessary risk of being found out, in order to save a few pounds.

About two weeks after my night with Tim, I made another trip to London. I remained determined to stay away from Tim and to stay off Grindr, which was so dangerous as well as seductive. I'd failed totally, however, in my greater resolution. I could not suppress my homosexual side. I'd been unable to stop myself looking for alternatives. I surfed the net and found a new, gay club that intrigued me. It had just opened in a basement off Old Compton Street. Discreetly hidden away, it seemed, like Larry's. Also like Larry's, it was the sort of place married men would visit, I thought. The sort of place where anonymity was still respected, required even. Not a place, I didn't think, for the modern set of gays so far 'out' that I sometimes felt they were the biggest threat of all to a man like me.

It was, according to the website I found, a kind of gay, lap dancing joint. A sort of Larry's with benefits, maybe. It called itself Adonis Anonymous and boasted, quite blatantly, that it had been modelled on a pole dancing club in New York called Adonis, where allegedly gorgeous, young men gyrated before an eager clientele.

Adonis NY had 'champagne rooms', which could be hired at a cost and sounded like a euphemism for something more. London's new Adonis Anonymous also offered private 'champagne rooms' and was rather more blatant about the purposes of those. 'For the full experience with your personal Adonis,' it said enticingly on its website.

The temptation was too much for me. I decided I must visit.

The basement room I entered was dimly lit. There was loud music too. It was all rather confusing. It took a while to realise what was going on.

When my eyes began to focus, I could see that there were a series of raised platforms lining the room, each bearing a pole around which scantily-clad, young men danced provocatively.

The punters, whom I knew I would not be able to resist joining for long, prowled up and down, assessing the dancers like judges at a cattle show.

As in straight lap dancing clubs, folded money was passed to the performers. At Adonis Anonymous, it seemed the tradition was that the young men took the notes between their teeth, which was somehow wonderfully provocative. Then, of course, they swiftly removed it to check the amount.

I watched carefully. One young man checked the notes handed him and just carried on dancing. The punter, middle-aged but quite nice looking, reached into the pocket of his trousers and produced another fold of money, which the dancer glanced at before taking it between his teeth. He then beckoned the punter forward and led him through one of several doors in the wall behind the dancing platforms. Then, I noticed that each door bore some kind of crude Bacchanalian image and was labelled 'champagne room'.

The alleged golden rule of straight lap dancing clubs, 'look but don't touch', did not seem to apply at Adonis Anonymous.

I was aware of the sordidness. I acknowledged that the place was distasteful. Or one half of me did. But, as at that sex party, I couldn't stop myself becoming aroused. There was an overt eroticism about Adonis Anonymous. Sex was clearly freely on offer – well not freely, exactly. Probably quite expensively. But that was all right, I had come prepared. I'd brought with me as much money as I could afford.

This, surely, was what I wanted. A place I could come back to as often as I liked, with little or no fear of anyone wishing to take an encounter any further. A business encounter. I had dealt with male escorts before; it was inevitable for a man like me. But there was invariably the problem of where to go, as with all casual pick-ups. I had broken one of my rules with Tim, because I'd been so desperate to be with him. Previously, I had avoided booking into hotels, even on an off-the-street cash-in-advance basis, just in case anyone ever recognised me from my ordinary day to day life. I am, of course, fairly paranoid about that.

I did not enjoy fumblings in alleyways and dark corners. I found it squalid to the point of being repugnant, albeit rarely repugnant enough to stop me. Some might think a euphemistic 'champagne room' in this environment was little better. By the time I had watched the oh-so provocative dancers for several minutes, I didn't care.

I gave in to my overwhelming, inner craving and joined the prowlers. A young man of mixed race gyrated before me. He had the most beautiful, olive skin and the body of a Greek God. In the lust of the moment, he seemed to me to be an Adonis indeed. He was beautiful. A truly beautiful boy. Far better than anything I'd expected to find in this place.

His chest was bare. He wore only a pair of dancer's trousers. Every detail of his well-muscled, young body was on show, above and below the waist. I realised that I could see not just the bulge, but the shape of his cock.

I felt my erection growing. It was almost hurting. I had to do something about it. I glanced around me. I was just one of a throng of like-minded men. No one was looking at me. None of them were interested in anything except their own needs.

I had little idea what the financial protocol might be. In the dim light and at a certain distance, I hadn't been able to be sure of the denomination of the bank notes being passed over. I thought the middle-aged punter I had watched so carefully may have handed over bundles of tenners. I was pretty certain the notes were pink. But, of course, they could have been fifties. Surely not? I decided I would start small and maintain my options. Although the ache in my groin was making that difficult.

I passed the beautiful boy three twenty-pound notes. He leaned forward to take them in his teeth. I pressed them into his hand. I wanted this business over with.

'Uh, c-could we go to a champagne room?' I asked tentatively, stumbling slightly over my words.

The boy glanced at the money with a kind of mild amusement. Then he laughed out loud. All the while he carried on dancing, provocatively thrusting his groin towards me.

I passed over three more twenties. This time the boy merely half smiled. He still carried on dancing.

It was going to be more expensive than I had expected, but then, the quality of the goods appeared to exceed my expectations. I couldn't mess about. I was now in a hurry. The money didn't matter any more.

I passed over five more twenties.

The boy beckoned me forward. He led me into a 'champagne room.' It was small, like a cell, and very hot. The atmosphere was thick, heady, but any lurking hint of the fetid was well enough disguised by a heavy perfume, perhaps some kind of incense. That might have been a relief, if I hadn't been so past caring. The only furniture within was a short, low couch covered by a velvet throw. Well-used, I imagined, but I didn't care about that either. The door closed behind us.

I reached for him. He shook his head and backed off.

'First you have to buy this,' he said, producing a bottle of champagne. It cost me a further one-hundred pounds. I paid up without a murmur. We never even opened the bottle.

I was desperate for relief. I reached for him again. This time he did not back away. I could feel him now, as well as see him. His flesh warm and smooth. His lips full and instantly responsive. He surely was a God, sent to give me peace again.

I didn't think a man like me could hope for anything beyond that, nor even wish for it.

So how was it that as I succumbed to the relentless grip of my desire, all I could think of was Tim.

Nice, ordinary, Tim. Tim who wanted more than sex.

Tim who wanted me.

NINE

Right after leaving the North Bristol Academy, Vogel received a text from Hemmings to say that the formal identification had been completed as expected. The dead girl was Melanie Cooke.

He called Willis to relay the news and to suggest they compare notes over lunch.

'Don't know about you, but I'm starving,' said Vogel.

He'd been woken before 6 a.m. and eaten nothing that day, other than a couple of Daisy Wilkins's biscuits. He was pretty sure the same went for Saslow too. Vogel believed in feeding the brain, even though he frequently forgot to do so. His brain, he feared, was not working at anything like full strength. He doubted that Willis had stopped to eat either. The DS seemed almost as driven as his boss, when he was on a big case. He told Willis to meet him and Saslow at the big, new, vegetarian restaurant down by the floating harbour. Vogel had been a vegetarian for years. He had no wish to be a participant, albeit by default, in the death of any living creature. He wasn't interested in pub lunches and didn't drink alcohol. He just didn't like the taste.

Most of the officers he worked with would have moaned about his choice of venue, preferring a pub or a burger bar. But Vogel knew Willis was only a moderate drinker, who rarely seemed to care what he ate. As for Saslow, he was quite sure she would like nothing better than a fancy salad or a plate of grilled root vegetables. She was always watching her weight, though Vogel had no idea why, he thought she was a perfect shape. He'd never found excessively skinny women attractive.

Willis, looking dapper as ever in a well-cut, navy blue suit, was waiting at a table, when Vogel and Saslow arrived. The DS had already ordered sparkling water, a plate of garlic bread and a dish of mixed olives. It occurred to Vogel that his little team were a tad different to most CID people. Gone were the days when everyone in a male-dominated world of police detection fortified themselves with several pints at lunchtime, as a matter of routine. Though, Vogel mulled, the odd one or two still slipped through the net and quite a few CID men, and women, carried a packet of polo mints close to their warrant card.

'Oh well done, Willis,' muttered Vogel, taking a large bite out of a slice of garlic bread, before he'd even sat down.

Saslow contented herself with nibbling an olive.

Vogel watched Willis cut a piece of bread into neat sections of almost identical size and shape, that was typical of the DS, thought Vogel. Willis was an organised, precise sort of man, who liked to put things into boxes. Vogel understood. He was much the same. He was aware of a number of similarities between himself and the somewhat pedantic sergeant. Not in personal appearance though, Vogel was incapable of looking dapper. His wardrobe consisted primarily of a selection of honourable, corduroy jackets in various states of dilapidation.

'Come on then, Willis,' said Vogel. 'Tell us how you got on with the second Mrs Cooke.'

Willis gave a fair and balanced account of his interview, the flat vowels of his native, Manchester accent still evident in his voice, even after thirteen years in Bristol. He didn't unduly stress the strained relationship between father and daughter or the matter of Susan Cooke's sleeping pills. He did not need to, instead he gave just the correct amount of emphasis to both. He was that kind of copper, thought Vogel, who noted automatically that both the present and previous Mrs Cooke apparently had 'trouble with her nerves.'

Willis did draw attention to the bruise on Mrs Cooke's face.

'Claire Brown and I both reckoned Terry's been knocking her about. Bastard.' Willis spat out the last word.

'Steady,' said Vogel. 'Not the first wife beater you've come across, John, and it won't be the last. Doesn't make the man a killer.'

'Maybe not. Makes him a vicious bully though. I can't stand it, boss. Saw too much of it as a kid.'

Vogel and Saslow glanced at Willis in surprise. It wasn't like him to remark on anything so personal. They both waited for the DS to tell them more, but he didn't. Vogel, of course, was secretly relieved.

'Anyway, on the basis of fact alone, we certainly can't rule

Terry Cooke out,' Willis continued. 'I don't think an alibi from his missus would stand up for long in court, that's for sure.'

Vogel nodded his agreement. 'All the same,' he said. 'Looking at the family on the usual basis of who would be the likeliest suspect, I still lean more towards the stepdad. Although we know he's a lying, cheating toerag, it no more makes him a killer than being a wife beater. Plus, his alibi seems pretty cast-iron to me.'

Vogel then enquired about any results from the officers knocking on doors in the vicinity of the crime scene.

'Not a lot, I'm afraid, boss,' responded Willis, glancing up from dissecting a second piece of garlic bread, 'Stone Lane is tucked away just off the beaten track, which is why the girl was taken there, presumably. Turns out neither of those two big houses up the lane are occupied. They're up for redevelopment, so nothing there. West Street and Old Market Street always have some sort of life going on, but the shops would all have been closed, of course, except the sex shops.

'We've contacted most of the people who live in flats above the various business premises. Only one had anything to say really. The woman in the flat on the corner of Stone Lane, nearest to where the body was found, did hear something suspicious, though it doesn't amount to a lot.

'She was woken by what she described as "a screeching sound", just before ten thirty. She goes to bed early, apparently. She looked out of her window and saw a couple of tomcats squaring up to each other. So she just assumed she'd heard a cat fight, went back to bed and thought no more of it.'

'The time probably fits, doesn't it?' remarked Saslow. 'Was she sure of that, John?'

'Said she checked her bedside clock when she woke up.'

'CCTV?' queried Vogel.

'Still being looked at, boss. We're also trying to track down as many as we can of the bar and restaurant customers. We've put out an appeal, but nothing more so far. I checked on the phone with the lads right after I left the Cooke's place.'

'Right, well, let's hope we get luckier this afternoon,' said Vogel. 'We need to order now, then get out of here.'

Saslow chose a beetroot and goat's cheese salad, much as Vogel had predicted. He went for a cheese and potato bake, with roasted tomatoes and basil on the side. Willis said he'd have what the boss was having. He didn't even look at a menu.

'Will you fill me in a bit more on the stepdad, boss?' Willis asked. 'What did his bit on the side have to say? You said his alibi checks out?'

Vogel nodded. 'Yes, I think so. Of course, Fisher won't be out of the frame until we have the DNA results and they may not be conclusive either, but his, as you call her, "bit on the side" . . .'

Vogel paused, a wry smile flickering on his lips. It was not a description he would ever have used of the woman he'd just met in Bath. But it was typical enough of the attitude of most male coppers he knew.

'. . . Daisy Wilkins, is quite adamant that he spent the entire night with her,' Vogel continued. 'And I don't think she is the sort of woman who would lie to the police.'

Willis's expression gave nothing away. But Vogel was aware of Dawn Saslow regarding him somewhat quizzically. He ignored the DC.

'We need to go through that girl's life and the whole extended family with a damned toothcomb,' Vogel continued. 'Let's check the whereabouts of everybody close to her on the night she died and hope to God we come up with something, or someone who's a real suspect.

'Because, if it's nobody from the family, if we have the unusual one, if it is an outsider, well, you both know what that means, don't you?'

Saslow nodded, her mouth full of beetroot and cheese.

'Yes, boss,' said Willis. 'It means we are looking for a random killer, probably a total nutter. At the very least, a sexual pervert. More than likely somebody who kills for kicks, with no motive, just because they damn well like it.'

'Yes,' agreed Vogel. 'And those bastards are the hardest of all to catch.'

Saslow swallowed hard, clearing her mouth.

'But we are going to get this one, guv, whatever the MO aren't we?' she asked.

Vogel pushed his quickly-emptied plate to one side and wiped the back of his hand across his mouth. 'I hope so Saslow,' said Vogel. 'I really do.'

'I think we should have a damned good look at the girl's father,' said Willis, diverting attention back to the man who was clearly his favourite suspect. 'It's a pretty ropey set up he has with his second wife and she indicated that he always put Melanie on a pedestal. If the girl's been running a bit wild, potentially dating on the internet, hanging out with the wrong crowd or even if he just thought she was, that could have made him pretty mad. Plus, he's sure to have been pissed off about her not bothering to see him half the time.'

'But is he the sort to sexually assault his own daughter?' asked Dawn Saslow.

Willis shrugged. 'He's the sort who knocks his missus about, I'm damned sure of that,' he said.

'Doesn't mean he ever laid a finger on his daughter,' responded Vogel. 'Not in any way at all.'

'OK, but we don't know that, do we?' Willis persisted. 'The girl's clothing was ripped and torn, her breasts were bruised and exposed, as were her private parts, but we don't know yet whether or not there was penetration. Certainly, there was no obvious presence of semen. He could have lost his temper with her and attacked her. Then realised he'd gone too far and deliberately faked signs of sexual abuse to lay a false trail.'

Vogel looked thoughtful. His phone buzzed. He took the call straight away.

'Well, that's fascinating,' he murmured. He looked as if he was being told something of considerable significance. By the time he'd finished the other two officers were both staring at him intently.

'We've just had Melanie Cooke's phone records from her mobile provider,' he said. 'Seems like her father made no less than twenty-one calls to her over the three days before her death. She didn't pick up any of them, nor respond with a text or call back.'

Willis looked as if he wanted to say he'd told them so, but remained silent.

'There must have been something going on then,' said Saslow.

Vogel nodded.

'Shall I bring him in, boss?' asked Willis. 'We need to get him processed fast. There's always a wait for DNA.'

'Hold on a minute,' said Vogel. 'Cooke's supposed to be coming in this afternoon under his own steam. We made an appointment for two thirty at Patchway. He's just formally identified his daughter, which is always an ordeal. Before we get heavy, let's see if he turns up. I think we could get more out of him if we don't alarm him too much.'

'Fair enough,' said Willis. 'But we shouldn't just leave him to the process boys, should we? He should be watched throughout. Do you want me to get over there?'

'That wouldn't be a bad idea, Willis. Go and babysit him through it. Be sure to treat the man like the genuinely bereaved father he purports to be, whilst at the same time try to wheedle all you can out of him. If he doesn't turn up by three o'clock at the latest though, the gloves are off. Go get him.'

'You got it, boss,' said Willis, putting down his knife and fork at once and preparing to stand up.

Willis was a slow and methodical eater, almost half of his meal remained on his plate.

'Finish your food man,' ordered Vogel, shaking his head. 'It's not two o'clock yet.'

Obediently, Willis sat down again.

'You need to look after yourself more,' said Vogel. 'And I forgot to ask. You were fighting a migraine yesterday, are you OK?'

'Oh fine, boss, yeah. Well over it.'

'Thank God,' said Vogel. 'Would hate for you to go sick on me with this lot on our hands.'

'No chance, boss,' said Willis.

'I know,' responded Vogel, grinning.

He turned to Saslow.

'Get back to headquarters, Dawn,' he instructed. 'Liaise with DI Hartley. Then start checking recorded paedophile behaviour in the Bristol area, particularly dating websites aimed at young-sters and anything to do with grooming. Start with the most recent records.'

Saslow looked mildly surprised.

'I thought we were concentrating on the family, boss,' she said.

'We need to keep an open mind,' responded Vogel. 'It's all too easy in an investigation like this to lead yourself up a blind alley.'

'Right boss,' said Saslow, who had finished her salad.

She pushed back her chair and stood up.

'I shall try to avoid that then,' she muttered over her shoulder, as she turned and headed for the door.

'Please God,' said Vogel, even though he didn't believe in any God at all, never had, and privately thought those who did had something wrong with their brains.

AL

As soon as I was out of sight of the school and the advancing teacher, I made myself slow to a proper speed and proceed normally, zipping up my fly as I drove.

I was heading to the far side of the council estate, where I knew there were some playing fields with parking alongside. No CCTV. I'd checked earlier. I was a good planner, I told myself, that was why I'd never been caught. Not yet anyway. Even on this occasion – when I'd got carried away and forgotten about being careful – it had been a tight call but I had still escaped.

When I reached the playing fields, I took off my hoody and reversed it. I always wore a reversible jacket of some kind on these outings. This one was a nondescript grey on one side and red on the other. Grey was for when I wanted to watch inconspicuously and red was for when I turned myself into an innocent passer-by. Red stood out. Had the teacher reported me, the police or anyone else would be looking for a man in grey. That was the idea, anyway.

I stepped out of the van and walked to the nearest bus stop, which was a couple of streets away and frequently served. I knew exactly where it was. I always did my homework. However, standing at the bus stop, trying to look casual and normal, I was still finding it difficult to control my breathing.

What on earth had I been thinking? What would I have done if that child had climbed into the passenger seat beside me? What would I have wanted her to do? What would I have made her do? How could I have imagined that I could get away with it parked opposite a school?

And afterwards, if *miraculously* I had not been spotted, then what?

Would I have just let her jump out and trot off back to school for her afternoon lessons? Was it remotely possible that she would have done my bidding and then left quietly? Or would she have yelled and screamed, when she realised exactly what sort of kitten I was holding in my lap? You could never predict how they might react, after all. Would she have cried for her mummy? Would I have had to silence her?

I pushed my hands into the pockets of my hoody. I wanted them tucked away, so that they couldn't do any harm. No. Not that. I would never do that. I would never hurt one of them. Really, I wouldn't.

Never again.

TEN

Willis made his way to Patchway and settled in to wait for Terry Cooke, as Vogel had instructed. He sat at an unused desk in the front office and, whilst he made some phone calls, kept a constant eye on the public entrance beyond. At around five minutes to three, he was just beginning to fidget when Cooke walked in. Willis hadn't met the man before, but recognised him from a photograph Vogel had shown him. Cooke looked both nervous and upset, just like a man who had just lost his daughter.

As soon as Willis saw Cooke enter, he stepped up to the counter to greet him, introduced himself and then uttered the almost mandatory remark of policemen everywhere under such circumstances.

'I am sorry for your loss, Mr Cooke.'

Cooke nodded in an absent sort of way. 'I'm sorry I'm late,' he said. 'I went back to be with Sarah after . . . after doing the identification.' His voice faltered, just for a moment. 'Then my car wouldn't start. That woman PC who took me to the morgue offered to drive me, but Sarah needed her more. I didn't want to leave Sarah alone. I got a bus, which took for ever. Damned car's had it, but I can't afford a new one, with three young kids and child support for Melanie.'

He paused. His eyes filled with tears.

'Not any more,' he muttered. 'Not any more.'

Willis wasn't impressed. He had, more than once, seen the most elaborate outpourings of grief from allegedly distraught family members, who had turned out to be vile murderers.

He made no comment as he escorted Cooke through the building to the custody suite. Here, Cooke was photographed and fingerprinted. He had samples of his saliva extracted, with an instrument like a cotton bud, and placed on a slide. Willis oversaw the entire operation. He was meticulous, even to the point of taking over the DNA testing and fingerprinting himself. The young officer, who had expected to be conducting the tests, made no protest but looked mildly offended.

Willis didn't care.

He wanted no mistakes. This was a major murder investigation. DI Vogel might be mild-mannered for a senior policeman, but he wasn't a patient man. Not when conducting a murder inquiry, anyway. Willis wanted the case closed as much as his boss did. An early result would make for a much quieter life. Willis took the DNA slide to the custody sergeant to be recorded and sent off to forensics. The results would take several days.

Willis already believed that Terry Cooke could well end up being arrested on suspicion of the murder of his daughter, but these situations were always tricky. It was imperative that if the man were to be charged, brought to trial and ultimately convicted, the case would have to be watertight. Willis intended to do his damnedest to make sure of that. Indeed, he intended to do more than his damnedest. He was determined to succeed and he would start by getting to know Terry Cooke better, just as Vogel had suggested. Nothing he learned this way would be admissible in any court case, but his purpose was primarily to gather ammunition for any future formal interviews.

Willis more or less insisted on driving Cooke home, albeit in the most commiserate of terms.

'C'mon mate, you want to get back to your family,' he said. 'I'll take you in my own car. Nobody will know I'm a copper and even if anyone did, well, under the circumstances you would be expected to be having dealings with the police.'

Cooke looked doubtful.

'I need to go round to Sarah's first,' he said. 'Sort out my car. It's all right. I don't need to bother you. I'll get the bus again.'

Willis persisted.

'Look mate, we both want to get the bastard who killed your daughter, don't we?'

Cooke agreed. He still looked very shaken. Willis thought he might be able to trade on that.

'Well come on, let me be your chauffeur and we can talk about it on the way, man to man. Away from the station. You might know something that would help, without even being aware of it. You'd be surprised how often that happens.'

Meekly, Cooke allowed himself to be led out to Willis's car. The policeman began his questioning as soon as they were both sitting in the vehicle, albeit in as casual a fashion as possible. After all, nothing said in such circumstances could ever be used as evidence, and Willis was aiming for a friendly chat rather than anything resembling an interview. Or to make it appear that way, at least.

'Do you mind telling me again, mate, just so I'm sure I've got it right, when you last saw your daughter?' Willis asked as they pulled out of the station yard.

Cooke looked exasperated.

'Do we have to go over everything repeatedly?' he asked.

'You don't have to do anything you don't want to, mate,' replied Willis. 'This is just an informal chat, but you do want to help, don't you?'

Cooke nodded glumly. His body language was resigned.

'OK, then please help me check a few details. Doesn't mean you're a suspect or anything.'

Not yet, thought the policeman. But pretty soon you might be, if I have my way.

However, Cooke seemed to accept the matey approach for what it wasn't.

'OK, Mel comes to me every other Sunday, you see.' He paused. 'Or she used to.'

'What do you mean by that?' asked Willis, striving to continue to sound casual. This was beginning to back up what Cooke's wife had said, that there had been some sort of rift between father and daughter.

'Oh, you know, she's growing up . . .' Cooke appeared only to realise what he'd said after he'd said it. 'I mean she was growing up,' he amended grimly. 'She had her own friends. She didn't seem to want to hang around with her old dad so much any more.'

'So, when did you actually last see her?'

'Nearly three weeks ago. She missed last Sunday.'

'And do you know why?'

'Yep. She spun me a yarn, but I found out that actually she'd been off with her mates. She preferred to be out and about with them, any chance she had. Well, why wouldn't she? At her age.' Cooke sighed. His shoulders slumped even lower than before. He seemed to be a man resigned to life serving him one cruel blow after another, thought Willis; the most recent being the death of his daughter.

The policeman might have been moved to feel a certain sympathy for Terry Cooke, were it not for the bruises on Susan Cooke's face and her nervous response when asked what had caused them. Cooke came across as a weak and ineffectual sort of man, both mentally and physically, Willis suspected. But he would be a heck of a lot more physically powerful than his wife – and his daughter – and Willis reckoned it was the weak ones who were the worst. After all, he knew that only too well from personal experience.

He would have liked to have challenged Cooke about his wife's bruises and given him a hard time. However, he knew that would only be counterproductive at this stage. They had nothing on Cooke. They needed information. Retribution would come later though, Willis was quite determined about that.

'What about her stepdad?' he asked, his voice still without expression.

'What about him?' countered Cooke, just a tad aggressively.

'Well, was Melanie close to him?'

Cooke shrugged. 'Always told me she didn't like him. That I was the only dad in her life, but they seemed to get on all right.

Sometimes I thought she probably used the same approach with him. Knew how to get round you, did our Mel.'

'It can't be easy having your daughter brought up by another man,' Willis continued.

'No it bloody well isn't,' Cooke responded tetchily. Then he paused. 'What are you getting at, Mr Willis?' he asked.

'Nothing,' said Willis. 'Nothing at all. Just trying to solve a crime, mate. And I'm very grateful for your help, really I am. I know how hard this is for you, but perhaps you wouldn't mind going over your whereabouts on the night Melanie died? Just so I have it straight.'

'All right,' he said. 'Like I told Mr Vogel, I was in bed asleep with my missus, when Sarah called my mobile. I woke up and checked who was phoning in the middle of the night. By the time I realised it was Sarah, she'd ended the call. I phoned back straight away. I knew it had to be something important for her to call me at that hour.'

'What time did Sarah call you?'

'I know exactly. I checked. It was quarter to four.'

'And you'd been in bed for how long?'

'Since about ten. We went to bed early. I was knackered. I'd left for work at five in the morning yesterday.'

'So you guessed at once that something serious had happened?'

Cooke nodded. 'Yes, but I was shocked rigid when she told me that Melanie hadn't come home. She'd never stayed out til that hour before. She is only fourteen for God's sake.' He paused, perhaps realising that he had used the present tense again. He didn't bother to correct himself this time. 'I just got out of bed, into my car and drove right round there.'

Then he paused again.

'But you know, I didn't expect wh-what happened, n-not even then. Perhaps I just didn't let myself think it.' Cooke stumbled over his words and his voice trembled. He wiped one hand over a sweaty forehead. 'She was a teenager, right at that tricky age. She'd always been a good kid, but lately, well, she'd started to play up. I expect her mother told you that?'

Willis didn't respond.

'Maybe not. Rose-coloured spectacles with our Melanie. She let her do exactly what she wanted, half the time.'

Willis smiled to himself. That was more or less what Cooke's wife had said about him. That he put Melanie on a pedestal and could see no wrong in her. That she wrapped him around her little finger.

'Anyway, I was shocked rigid at first, right enough,' Cooke continued. 'But as I was driving over to Sarah's and I started to think a bit more clearly, I told myself Mel was probably just off with friends doing what kids do, the things they never tell their mums and dads about . . .'

'Until four o'clock in the morning?' queried Willis.

'Well, there's always a first time for something like that, with teenagers. That's what I wanted to believe. Then you lot turned up with the news that she was d-dead, and . . . and . . .'

Cooke paused again and looked as if he might break down. He pulled himself together enough to continue speaking.

'I've lost my princess, Mr Willis,' he said. 'And I'll never get over it. Never.'

SAUL

There could never be another Sonia. That was one thing I had to make sure of.

She'd got too close to me. I nearly met her and almost let her see me in a public place. She was a quintessential, old-fashioned Englishwoman, who lived in Cheltenham and thought I was the quintessential, old-fashioned, English schoolteacher. I came so near to letting her into my life and that would never have done.

Yet, deep inside, it was what I wanted. A normal, ordinary life with a normal, ordinary woman at my side.

If only I wasn't what I was and hadn't done all that I had. If only I could roll back the years, reinvent not just my present but also my past.

My experience with Sonia had really upset and surprised me, because I'd half convinced myself that I would be brave enough to meet up with her and take my chance, but I couldn't. Despite this failure, however, I still wanted the same things: the wife and the children . . .

I had to find a different way.

It was a story in *The Sun* – about a 69-year-old, British man married to a 23-year-old, Thai girl – that got me thinking. The man had used a specialised, online dating agency called *Thaibrides-introductions.com*.

This turned out to be a bit more than a dating agency. They provide you with a video featuring around 400 girls. You compile a shortlist of about a dozen and then fly out to Bangkok to make your choice.

The agency sends over about eight men a month and boasts one hundred per cent success, claiming that most men proposed within ten days of meeting and choosing one of the girls on their shortlist. Presumably that was what they meant by success, I thought, not necessarily what might or might not come afterwards.

You were allowed limited browsing without signing on. The women had many different looks, from the clearly flirtatious to the demure, and sold themselves on the site in different ways. The one thing they all seemed to have in common was a desire to find a partner they could settle down with for the rest of their lives. That was what I wanted. It was just unfortunate that there was so much about me which made that difficult. However, I felt cautiously optimistic that, with a woman from a different culture, it might be possible after all. I felt I wouldn't have the same pressure to reveal myself fully. Everything I read and heard indicated that these women, with their dreams of a western-style marriage, would be more accepting, more pliable.

I set up a new email address, *Saul1949@mailme.co.uk,* and began to fill in the profile. I was asked to say something about myself and also to describe the type of woman and relationship I was looking for.

'*Divorced solvent man looking for life partner,*' I wrote. '*I am a 33-year-old sales executive, divorced without children. I have a nice home in a pleasantly suburban UK location. I am looking for a woman to spend my life with. Someone who wants the same things as me – children and a traditional home life.*

*My interests revolve around the home and I have the financial
means to give a partner a good and easy life.'*

I thought I made myself sound pretty plausible and presented
myself in a way that would make what I was offering sound
attractive. Particularly the financial side of things and the stable
family life. I'd done some googling. The common consensus was
that most Thai women were looking for those things.

I wrote that I wanted: *'a family-minded, traditional woman,
who wants to be a traditional wife to a traditional husband. She
does not have to be beautiful, but she must be of childbearing
age and want to have children.'*

I thought that said it all and I started to move on to the rest
of the registration process. It was when I reached the section,
where I was supposed to post a photograph of myself, that I
began to have second thoughts. I realised I had the same old
problem. If I intended to follow this through and travel to
Thailand in search of a bride, I would have to use my passport
and expose my real face. I certainly didn't want that plastered
all over the internet.

I backed off at once, leaving the site without completing the
registration process or entering any more details. I tried to concentrate on my everyday life. I told myself I should stop fantasising. I
tried to kid myself that my life was OK the way it was.

After a few days, idly playing with my computer one evening,
I went into my new email address. To my surprise, even though I
hadn't registered properly, I'd had an email from *Thaibrides-
introductions.com* telling me my profile had been accepted. I
logged in. My spot on their website contained photographs and
profiles of dozens of young, Thai women. There was a section
where you could express interest and send a message.

I did so, choosing a dozen women at random and writing the
same message to all of them.

*'Hiya, I hope you will contact me. As you know I am a 33-year-old
Englishman looking for someone to share my life with. I like
your profile. I hope you like mine and I hope you get in touch
with me soon.'*

I pushed send and waited to see what would happen next.

The next thing to pop up was a payment page. The platinum
option allegedly gave me unlimited online access to hundreds of

Thai women. It cost seventy-five pounds for six months. I paid with a debit card for a bank account that was linked to an accommodation address. I had set it up with a cash deposit some years previously, when these things were much easier and called for little or no identity checking or proof of address. It had come in useful more than once before. Now I hoped it would assist me in transforming my sad and lonely life.

Within seconds I was in and my message would now be passed on to the young women I had already selected.

ELEVEN

The CCTV footage was waiting for Vogel, when he returned to Kenneth Steele House. He and Hemmings pored over it together. An unidentified man and a young girl had been captured the previous evening by a West Street CCTV camera. They could be seen weaving slightly as they walked along the pavement. The time was 10.17 p.m. Stone Lane was just ahead of them, to the left.

The footage lasted only a few seconds. The man appeared to be more or less holding the girl upright. He had an arm around her and her head was against his shoulder. At one point she looked up at him. There was a clear shot of her face. The girl was Melanie Cooke.

The man, however, who was wearing a hooded jacket, kept his head down and his face so deliberately turned away from the angle of the camera, that it seemed likely he knew it was there. There was not a single shot of him which offered any chance of identification. It was difficult even to tell his size or height. The jacket might have been padded, or else just large and shapeless. He was bending over the girl. All his clothes were dark and anonymous, although, of course, every effort would be made to further examine them for any detail which might be of use.

Hemmings and Vogel played the footage several times.

Vogel found it harrowing to watch. Minutes later, Melanie Cooke would be dead.

'This is almost certainly the poor kid with her killer,' he said aloud. 'But it does bugger all to identify the bastard.'

'Well, we'll get the tech boys onto it.'

'Of course,' said Vogel. 'I don't hold out much hope though, do you? It could be her father, her stepfather or a complete stranger, from this.'

The footage was thoroughly disheartening.

Vogel was about to finally give up for the day and leave for home, when Saslow came into his office clutching a wad of computer printouts.

She slapped them on his desk.

'I've been checking out weirdo behaviour, like you told me to, boss. Particularly any incidents of paedophilia that might fit,' she said. 'Seems there've been a number of reports of some pervert parking up outside schools, getting his rocks off more than likely.'

'Is there a reason for believing it's the same man every time? We've got more than one perverted bastard in Bristol, that's for sure.'

'Yes, boss, but it's the same MO. He's always in a nicked motor, for a start. Carefully chosen, of an age not to have a modern security system, usually a Ford Transit or some other kind of common van and, more often than not, it's white, also very common, of course. He always parks carefully, somewhere he can get a good view of the school gates and playgrounds, but not too close and in such a way that if he's spotted, he can make a quick get away. The vehicles are usually recovered later not far from the schools. He's been caught on CCTV several times, though it's never been much help.'

Vogel grunted. For the second time that day, and for the umpteenth time in his police career, he wondered if CCTV was ever much use, except for catching otherwise law-abiding, tax-paying motorists, who happened to be speeding.

'So, not even a halfway decent shot of him?' Vogel enquired.

'No boss. Not so far anyway. There's a lot to go through. I've got the team on it, but he's clearly streetwise and I don't hold out a lot of hope. Bastard hunkers down in his seat and always wears a hoody, with the hood up and pulled down as far as possible over his face. Has sunglasses on too.'

'A hoody eh? Same as the character we have footage of with Melanie Cooke.'

'Yeah, that narrows it down to a few thousand then, boss.'

Vogel responded with a wry smile.

'OK, well, carry on trying to ID the bastard, Saslow, but he could just be a voyeur, of course. Plenty of those about.'

'Yes, but there's more, boss. Teacher at Moorcroft Primary school saw him trying to get an eight-year-old girl into his van.'

'Ah. What happened?'

'The teacher called out. The girl backed off and the weirdo gunned his stolen motor, a white Transit, and beat a quick retreat.'

'When was that?'

'Just under a month ago.' Saslow checked her notebook. 'Tuesday, April 18th, during the school's dinner break. It was reported and looked into at the time, but there was bugger all to go on. No CCTV footage at all that day. The van was found not far away, where there aren't any cameras. He'd probably checked that out in advance and had a camera-free, escape route. Seems probable he always does that, so whenever he's been picked up, the camera has never been near enough or the angle good enough for there to be any chance of identifying him.'

'Right, then leave the camera footage to the specialists, Saslow, and go yourself for a chat tomorrow with that kid and the teacher. Being a Saturday you'll have to go to their homes, but that might be better, for the kid anyway, it's less formal. Take a woman PC with you. All plain clothes. Maybe the kid remembers something that might give us some sort of lead without realising it. I presume she'll have been talked to before, but let's try again.'

'Will do boss. Shall I also get the usual suspects rounded up?'

'Check with Hemmings and DI Hartley. They'll already be onto that I expect, but it might be worth probing more deeply. If we can put all this together, plus anything you might glean from the child, or anyone else up at Moorcroft, we might just get somewhere.'

Saslow left the office. Vogel was thoughtful for a moment. Like all police forces throughout the UK, the Avon and Somerset had a list of known sex offenders on their patch, but Vogel was well aware that there were probably just as many again out there, who'd never been caught. Plus many more who merely watched children whenever they got the chance and surfed the net for child porn, but didn't take things any further.

Yet Vogel never totally accepted that. He always thought that, for almost all of those sort of men, it would only be a matter of time until they did take things further. Until they suddenly couldn't contain themselves any longer. Until they made an approach to a child. It could be years, but the day would come. Then maybe that approach would go wrong. The child might cry for it's mummy, might scream and wriggle and weep. Then they had to be quietened didn't they? *Nobody was supposed to get hurt, that wasn't intentional.*

How often had Vogel heard that apology of an excuse for crimes of shocking violence? How often would he hear it again? Would he, in the next few days, or weeks, or months, hear that about poor Melanie Cooke?

I didn't mean to hurt her, guvnor, honest I didn't. I was just trying to shut her up.

That was bad enough but, worst of all, were the toerags who protested that the children welcomed their intentions and enjoyed their groping and probing.

It only went wrong because she changed her mind, got scared, it wasn't my fault.

Vogel had heard it all. Vogel was a calm, mild-mannered man, but sometimes, listening to the whining of such men, he was aware of coming scarily close to violence himself.

LEO

My visit to Adonis Anonymous worked up to a point. I found it highly erotic and it did stop me thinking about sex for a while. Sex for its own sake, that is. But, unfortunately, it seemed to make me think about Tim all the more.

After two weeks I could stand it no longer. I called him, from my untraceable, pay-as-you-go iPhone.

'Leo,' he said. 'I'm so pleased to hear from you.' He sounded it too.

'I've been thinking about you,' I told him, truthfully.

'Good,' he responded quickly.

Then there was a pause and he sounded a tad ill at ease when he spoke again.

'I, uh, tried to call you, but the number you gave me didn't work so—'

'I know.' I interrupted him. 'I lost my phone, had to get a new one and a new number. It's caused me chaos. One of the reasons it took me so long to call you. And I've been really busy at work. Sorry.'

'That's all right.' He paused again. 'I thought maybe you'd deliberately given me a wrong number . . .' He laughed nervously. I laughed too, perhaps too loudly.

'No way,' I said. 'I really want to see you again.'

'I'm glad. Me too. I just thought . . . Well you know, I thought you didn't feel the same . . .'

'I do feel the same,' I said. That was also true. I wasn't used to so much truth. I seemed to have spent most of my life living one sort of a lie or another.

'Look, shall I book that Premier Inn again? It's OK, isn't it? And it's central.'

'All right.' He didn't sound enthusiastic. 'Are you sure we can't meet at yours?' he asked. 'You're not married or something, are you?'

'No, I'm not married,' I told him honestly.

'But you have a partner? You live with someone? Is it a man or a woman?'

'Nothing like that, I promise.'

'What then?'

'Well, apart from anything else I live miles out of town, I have a flat in a new build in Stevenage,' I said. 'Look, I'll explain when we meet. See you there.'

Both Stevenage and my promise to explain were lies, of course. I had little idea what I would tell him about me and my life, but it would not include much truth.

I'd briefly considered taking Tim somewhere nicer, somewhere special, and splashing out on the Strand Palace or the Waldorf, even. I could afford it, just about. For one night anyway. I was far from rich, but I earned reasonably well, was careful with my money and I had no extravagant tastes.

But the most important thing for me, really, was anonymity. There are few places more anonymous than those big, budget hotels. So the Premier Inn it would be.

I walked in off the street so I could pay cash. That made it more expensive, but I didn't want my credit card details on record. I didn't even have a credit card with me, just a thick wad of notes in the inside pocket of my jacket.

The girl on reception barely looked at me. I carried my rucksack, as I always do, on my trips to Soho. So, as far as she was concerned, I had luggage. If she even noticed, I doubted clients checking in without luggage were that unusual at The Leicester Square Premier Inn. I'd already transformed my appearance at the pub around the corner. I preferred to arrive at the hotel looking the part. In any case, although I was early, it was always possible that Tim might already be there and waiting in the foyer. Although I'd instructed him otherwise.

This time the rucksack contained more than my straight clothes. I'd packed a bottle of champagne in a cooler bag – because Premier Inn rooms don't have fridges – a bottle of decent claret and a picnic dinner of: smoked salmon, pate, French bread, some cheese, fruit and two slices of rich, chocolate cake.

I wanted Tim to realise that I wasn't just after his body, though God knows I lusted after it. I would have liked to take him out to dinner, to wine and dine him in a smart restaurant and to lavish affection on him in a more romantic setting. But, as ever, I was determined to avoid unnecessary risks. Even in London, I felt the need to protect my secret self.

There was CCTV everywhere nowadays, but footage was only checked when there was a reason to do so. In any case, I'd developed a knack for knowing where the cameras were. A knack nurtured at first by working at it and then it became habit. I was good at keeping my back turned away and I usually wore a hat of some sort, or a hoody. Though you had to be careful with both. Sometimes, they actually attracted attention. Hoodies, in the wrong context, could make people suspect you were some sort of thug. By and large they were OK in the street, but if you walked into a shop or a bar with your hood up, it could make people uneasy. They might study you more carefully than otherwise and that went for hotel receptionists too. A baseball cap was usually all right and common enough.

I laid out the food and the wine as best I could on the narrow desk-come-dressing table, which stood by the window. There wasn't much other furniture, just a small built-in wardrobe and one chair. That didn't matter. I suspected we would eat our picnic in bed. I'd brought proper glasses, plates and cutlery, all wrapped in kitchen paper. I arranged everything as attractively as I could.

At the appointed time I texted Tim, as arranged, to give him the room number.

He must have been waiting nearby, probably inside the hotel. The knock on the door came far more quickly than I'd expected. I was just opening the champagne and called out for him to wait a moment. I quickly poured two glasses and carried one of them with me, holding it aloft, as I opened the door.

'Welcome to the Ritz,' I said.

He stepped into the room and I passed him the glass. His face broke into a smile, that big, crooked, lovely smile I feared I was becoming more or less incapable of doing without, whatever the dangers. He took the glass, leaned forward and kissed me lingeringly on the lips. After a bit, I backed away.

'First, dinner,' I said, waving an arm at my picnic.

He looked gratifyingly surprised.

'I uh, hadn't expected,' he stumbled. 'I mean, I didn't bring anything. I, uh, wasn't sure . . .' Of course he hadn't been sure. How on earth could he be sure of anything? I'd done nothing but send out mixed messages ever since we'd met.

'I didn't want you to bring anything,' I said. 'I just wanted . . .' It was my turn to stumble over the words. 'I wanted to make things special . . . well as special as I could in a Premier Inn,' I finished a tad apologetically.

'The Premier Inn is fine,' he said.

I suspected, however, that he was wondering why, if I wanted to give him dinner, I hadn't arranged to do so in one of the restaurants Soho is teeming with.

'I just wanted us to be alone all night,' I offered, again apologetically.

'It's fun, really, it is,' he said, flashing the crooked smile again, even more broadly.

'Enjoy,' I said, topping up his glass.

I'd barely touched mine. I didn't want to drink too much and for anything to take the edge off what was going to happen. I hadn't even brought any poppers. I didn't think either of us needed them and I wanted to see what it would be like without.

I couldn't believe I was with him again and I was going to be able to spend all night with him. Well, most of it anyway. I couldn't believe how much he already meant to me. I supposed I really was falling in love with him. I wasn't entirely sure, though, because I had never been in love before.

Tim drank most of the champagne and at least two large glasses of the claret. I don't think he noticed that I just took sips. By the time we climbed into bed and lay naked alongside each other, he was more than a little tipsy. But he somehow seemed all the more attractive to me. I'd wanted us to have a good time in more ways than the obvious. I'd wanted to show him that I cared about more than the sexual gratification I had when I was with him. I was only sorry that I hadn't felt able to do so in a less secretive way.

He was an eager lover. Ever since the last time we'd been together, I had done little but dream of this, of touching and caressing him, of feeling his hands and his lips all over me and, ultimately, of entering him.

My every expectation was, if anything, exceeded. It was as if my whole being came alive. When we'd finished I was a trembling wreck. He fell asleep almost at once, in my arms. I lay wide awake through the night.

I left just after five, before the city was awake.

I climbed back into my clothes in the half light and loaded the glasses, crockery and cutlery I had brought for the picnic back into my rucksack. Although I moved as quietly as I could, this time I had nothing to worry about. It would have taken a lot more than me dressing and packing to wake my young lover. The alcohol and the sex combined had done their job. Tim was dead to the world, lying flat on his back, snoring. His outrageously beautiful, young body was spread-eagled across the bed. His organ lying limp and damp now. I felt aroused just looking at him, but that was no good. I had to go. I walked softly across the room to the door. There I paused. I couldn't leave him with nothing, not even a goodbye.

I reached into my pocket for a pen and a piece of paper, on it I scribbled a brief note. *Farewell, sweet Tim. You were magnificent.*

Then I left the room, pulling the door quietly shut behind me. I put on my baseball cap and pulled the peak low over my forehead. I walked with my head down and kept out of the way of the CCTV cameras as much as possible, both inside and outside the hotel. I walked down to The Strand and on to Waterloo Bridge. In the middle, where the Thames was deep, even at low tide, I stopped and stood looking down into the murky waters. Then I reached into the pocket of my jacket, took out my pay-as-you-go iPhone and threw it into the river. I felt a tug on my heartstrings and a renewed sense of longing in my groin, as the phone sank without trace.

But I had been forced to take drastic action. I could no longer trust myself. My feelings for Tim were such that I was in danger of taking huge risks just to be with him, just to spend a few hours with him.

I had to end it.

As long as I had the phone, I knew I would not be able to ignore him if he called or texted me. Or rather, when he called or texted me, because I was sure he would. Neither would I be able to stop myself calling him. After all, his was the only number stored in that phone. It would just be too easy. If I no longer had the phone, Tim had no way of contacting me. He knew nothing about me. He thought he did, but he didn't.

And maybe, just maybe, without that phone I would be able to resist even attempting to contact him again. And eventually, day by day it would become easier.

I lasted for two weeks. It felt like two years. No. Two decades.

I could not get Tim out of my head. Whatever I was doing and however hard I tried, his presence was there within me. Nothing, it seemed, could block Tim out.

Eventually, I gave in.

That original hotel bill, with his number scribbled on it, was still in the top drawer of my bedside cabinet. I'd got rid of the phone, which was my main connection with Tim, but had proved quite unable to destroy that scrap of paper. I suppose it had always been just a matter of time. I guess I'd only been kidding myself otherwise. After all, I'd bought myself a new pay-as-you-go phone at the end of the first week. Just in case.

On the day that I attempted to contact him again, I took that piece of paper from its hiding place several times and then replaced it, before eventually dialling Tim's number.

I knew it wouldn't be an easy call. He was going to be angry and hurt. Yet again I'd blown hot and cold. I'd allowed him to think that he was special to me, which he was, whatever he now thought and however much I denied it to myself.

However, I had walked out on him again, whilst he was asleep and without even saying goodbye, then effectively cut our cord of communication.

I was right too. He was angry.

'I don't bloody believe it,' he said. 'You have a nerve, Leo, I'll give you that.'

'Look I'm really sorry, I can explain—'

'What?' He interrupted me. 'With some piece of fiction about another lost or stolen phone, I suppose? I don't want to hear it. I don't want to hear from you again, not ever. Go play your stupid games on some other poor sucker.'

And, with that, Tim hung up.

It took me several days to find the courage to call him again, but it was inevitable that I would, eventually.

He didn't seem quite so angry this time, at least he listened when I told him I'd never come to terms with my sexuality. That I'd always kept everything about it a secret from my family and friends, that I had previously been content with occasional, casual, sexual encounters to satisfy my needs and that I'd never before found a man I wanted more from.

'It was hard for me to take the next step,' I said.

'And you really think you are ready to take the next step now, do you?' he asked. He seemed a little mollified, at least.

'Yes,' I said. I was lying of course. Or was I? There was *some* truth in it.

'All right,' he countered swiftly. 'Let me into your life. You say you live alone. Let me visit you at your home.'

'I will,' I said. I was definitely lying about that. 'But can we do the Premier Inn one last time?'

He remained silent.

'I think of it as our special place,' I persisted desperately. 'I feel so relaxed and happy there with you. It would help me a lot.'

'You need help to be with me?' he queried. His voice had edge.

I feared I might lose him for ever. I couldn't lose him. I had to say something he would want to hear, quickly. Anything at all that would make him see me again.

'Look, you know that's not what I meant,' I said. 'Go along with me on this, Tim. I will explain more when we meet and, if you like . . . if you're free, I'll make sure I have a day off the next day and you can come back to my place in the morning.'

I heard him sigh. 'You expect me to believe that, after what you've done?' he asked.

'I'm hoping you will believe it,' I said. 'Hoping with all my heart. We have something together, you and me. Something special.'

There was another pause.

'All right,' he said. 'We'll do it your way, but you'd better be telling the truth, because I won't let you mess me around again, do you hear?'

I said that I heard.

'And I want us to meet somewhere else first, have a drink, go out to dinner, like a proper couple. OK?'

A proper couple? I loved the idea, just as I so feared I was beginning to love Tim. But it could never be, of course. Not for us. Not for me. I was different.

All the same, I said that was OK.

I'd got to the stage where I would agree to anything so that I could see my Tim again, to lie with him, stay in the same bed as him and make love with him.

One more time.

That was probably all it could be now, but it was better than nothing.

TWELVE

It was almost midnight before Vogel got home. His wife was used to it. As usual, she had waited up for him. Well, half waited up. When he entered the living room, he saw that Mary was sound asleep on the sofa. She was wrapped in her favourite, fluffy dressing gown. It was turquoise coloured and just a shade darker than the bedsocks keeping her toes warm. Mary liked coordinated colours.

The room wasn't yet cold. Vogel reached out a hand towards the wood burner. The fuel had gone out, there was no longer any glow at all, but there was still a little heat coming from the stove.

He leaned over his wife and touched one shoulder, shaking her gently. She woke straight away, the anxiety in her eyes fading as she focused on him. She was always apprehensive when he was on a big case, particularly if he was late home, even though he almost always was.

They had moved to Bristol from London the previous year, not long after Vogel had been badly injured in an incident in Soho. Mary told herself that The Avon and Somerset Constabulary was surely a less dangerous force for a copper to serve in than the Met. She still worried, though.

That was not why they had moved, of course. Vogel would never allow personal safety to influence him professionally. But Mary wouldn't forget, for as long as she lived, the night she was told that her husband had been rushed to hospital following a clash with a violent criminal. Back then, they had been living in a flat in a mansion block in Pimlico. A far cry from a suburban bungalow on the outskirts of Bristol and – if it hadn't been for their daughter, Rosamund, and her special needs – they would still be there. Mary was quite sure of that.

Vogel was a Londoner through and through. To be a detective in the Met had been his only, real, professional ambition. To most people, Bristol was a vibrant, modern, cosmopolitan city but, to

Vogel, it was merely an outpost of the capital and virtually green-wellies territory. But then, so was everywhere.

However, thankfully, to Mary's relief, he was proving able to immerse himself in his work in Bristol, just as much as he had in London. That was what Vogel did. Mary knew that her husband loved her; she considered herself very happily married, but it was only Rosamund for whom Vogel would ever have been prepared to move out of his beloved metropolis. Mary suspected he would even give up the job altogether for Rosamund, if it ever became necessary. He would do anything for Rosamund, anything at all to make her life better.

Rosamund had been born with cerebral palsy. She was a happy and intelligent girl, trapped within a body that consistently failed her, except when she was in water. Swimming was Rosamund's greatest joy. The water gave her freedom. In water, her body was no longer an encumbrance and this small, apparently very ordinary, suburban bungalow was the reason Vogel had been prepared to move out of London. The previous owner had installed a seventeen-foot-long pool, equipped with a jet swimming system, in the garage. It presented an opportunity to make swimming an experience Rosamund could enjoy whenever she wanted, instead of on occasional and often quite difficult visits to municipal swimming pools.

Mary had accidentally discovered the property advertised in a copy of *Somerset Life* magazine, which she'd picked up in her dentist's waiting room. And David Vogel, who had not imagined in his wildest dreams that he would ever be able to afford any sort of home swimming pool for his daughter, quickly put in an offer. He told his wife it was clearly fate that she had found the bungalow and Rosamund must come first.

'How's it going, David?' Mary asked.

Vogel had left home before six that morning and made his way straight to the Melanie Cooke crime scene. He hadn't called Mary since. He rarely did when embroiled in a major case, but neither would she expect him to. All she knew, so far, was that a girl's body had been found in a Bristol backstreet.

When Vogel came home though, it was different. Mary was the DI's sounding board, his release. She knew that he trusted her implicitly and that she was the only person in the world with whom he shared his innermost thoughts. Mary took her feet off the sofa and made room for her husband. He sat down next to her, allowing weariness to show for the first time that day, as he slumped backwards and gratefully kicked off his shoes.

'It's hard,' he said. 'The dead kid's about the same age as our Rosamund. That was all I could think of, at first.'

Mary didn't intend to let him dwell on that.

'And since then?' she asked. 'Why don't you tell me the rest of it? Shall I make a pot of tea first? Have you eaten?'

'Not since lunchtime,' Vogel admitted, which was better than it often was.

Mary retreated to the kitchen, where she made tea and a pile of cheese salad sandwiches, liberally laced with mayonnaise, the way she knew Vogel liked them. Meanwhile, he'd brought the log burner back to life, throwing a couple of firelighters at it and a handful of sticks, before stoking it up with bigger logs. Mary poured the tea and then sat down beside him. Vogel drank most of the first cup and hungrily bolted down one of the sandwiches, before he told his wife everything.

She was the only one who heard about his gut feelings, his worry about the lack of evidence so far and his fears of a random killing. Everyone David Vogel worked with thought he was totally self-contained and so he was, in public. But at home, Mary was his rock and on that first night after the discovery of Melanie Cooke's body, Vogel needed her as much as he ever did. Mary rarely commented until her husband had finished, allowing him to talk everything through. He always told her how much it cleared his mind to do so.

When she did eventually speak her remarks were often significant and, not unusually, focused on an aspect of a case Vogel had not yet considered.

'You said you interviewed the friend, what was she called? Sally? At her school?'

'Yes.'

'Where exactly?'

'In the head mistress' office.'

'So was the head there?'

'Yes, and Dawn Saslow.'

'David, a best friend at school would never tell tales in front of the head mistress.'

'Come on, Mary, it's a murder investigation. I'm trying to find the bastard who killed the girl's friend, I'm sure she understood that. It's got nothing to do with telling tales.'

'I really don't think that's how it would have seemed to Sally,' Mary persisted gently. 'Girls of that age are conditioned not to tell their teachers, their parents or anyone in authority, anything. Also, she would have been in shock too. I expect she just shut down, saying nothing and giving nothing away. She probably did it quite automatically, without thinking it through.'

Vogel looked thoughtful.

'You think she could be holding something back?'

'I think it's very possible, particularly if Melanie was doing something all the girls know they shouldn't – like, as you suspect, planning a date with someone she met on the net.'

Vogel smiled.

'OK,' he said. 'I expect you're right, as usual. I'll make sure we talk to her again. Away from school and without the head teacher.'

'And who will you get to do that?' Mary asked casually.

'I'll probably try to get round to her house myself, with Saslow, some time tomorrow,' said Vogel. 'She knows us now, after all.'

'Might you think about sending Saslow on her own, or with another woman officer?' Mary enquired in her most neutral voice.

Vogel was not fooled.

'So now you don't think I should even interview the girl, is that it? Honestly, Mary. I am a trained, senior police officer of many years' experience, you know.'

'Exactly,' said Mary.

'And what does that mean?'

'David, you are a sensitive and caring person, you don't even look like a copper, but you still are one. You're a middle-aged man in a position of enormous authority. You say yourself you prefer your computer to dealing with the public. You hate outward displays of emotion and you're well over six feet.'

'So now I'm too tall?'

Mary raised one eyebrow.

'Of course not. But if you put all that together, even you have to admit that you might appear more than a little intimidating to a fourteen-year-old girl.'

Vogel grunted. Mary was right of course. She almost always was.

But this time, this day, he did not get the feeling of release that usually came after talking with her. He knew exactly why. He was hiding something from his wife. Something very important. Something, unconnected with his work, which he had so far found himself unable to reveal.

AL

I tried to do what I always did. As soon as it was over, I did my best not to think about it again. I endeavoured to blot it out. I told myself it was already in the past.

I should never have tried to coax that child into my vehicle. It had definitely been in my head that I would drive away with her. Take her somewhere where I could do anything I wished with her.

But is that what I would have done? I no longer knew myself well enough to be sure either way. If I had been rash enough to do that, it could only have led to one end. I couldn't have just let her go when I had finished with her. Or could I have?

I really didn't know.

What I did know was that I'd entered into highly dangerous territory. Looking was one thing. Touching was another. And I knew, more than most men, just how different the two were.

I also knew that, in the future, I should content myself with what the internet had to offer.

However, images and videos on the web never quite hit the spot with me. I liked my children in the flesh: laughing, playing and gyrating right in front of me. Sometimes I could smell them, or I thought I could anyway. Celluloid images did not have the same effect.

I told myself they would have to do. I had a life separate from this monstrous side of me. Oh yes, I recognised that side was monstrous, but that made no difference to me. It was part of me, a part I could not deny.

However, I wanted to protect my other everyday life. My job. My friends. Well, I didn't really have friends, of course. I could never let people close. But there were those, mostly at work, who probably considered themselves my friends. There was family too, although I no longer had much to do with them.

I really would have to stick with the internet in order to satisfy my voyeuristic instincts. I would have to avoid chat rooms too, or any websites which encouraged people to correspond with children and then to meet them.

I couldn't cope with that. I knew I couldn't. I'd weaken. I would just have to be strong and stay away from those sort of sites. I had no choice.

But I wasn't strong, was I? That was the whole point. I was a weak man. The internet was a smorgasbord to someone like me. I wasn't going to be able to stop myself reaching out for more, not for long.

And that was what happened, I reached out to grasp what I longed for. I meant no harm. I never meant harm, but once a man like me has started on a certain course of action he cannot stop.

Now I had to deal with the consequences.

I am clever though, cleverer than almost anyone I know. Clever without necessarily seeming to be. I still believe that I can cover my tracks. I still believe that life can continue for me, in the way that it always has.

THIRTEEN

Mary knew, of course. She had probably known from the beginning. She was staring at him, in silence. Sometimes he thought the expression she 'could read him like a book' had been invented for his wife.

'David, something's wrong isn't it?' she asked.

'A young girl has died, the same age as our Rosamund, I've told you all about it . . .' Vogel began.

He let his voice tail off. He could see that Mary was not taken in.

'I know how involved you get in your work, David,' she said. 'But I also know what's going on inside you, even though you give so little away. This is different. You haven't been right for days. Won't you tell me what it is? I can't help you if you don't.'

Vogel said nothing.

After a few seconds, he reached into the pocket of his old corduroy jacket and withdrew the letter which he'd kept with him constantly since its arrival nine days previously.

Puzzled, Mary took the letter from him. She glanced at the envelope. It was addressed to Vogel, care of the Avon and Somerset Constabulary. She looked up at him again. His face bore little expression, as usual. If he were affected by anything, his first instinct was to fight against that emotion. Mary removed the letter and began to read.

When she'd finished she took her husband's hand.

'My God, David,' she said. 'Is it true?'

'I have no idea,' Vogel replied.

'Well, you could ask your father.'

'Yes,' Vogel replied.

'When did you get this?'

Vogel told her.

'And you kept it from me, for nine days?' Mary queried gently.

Vogel nodded.

'David, I know that you've spoken to your father at least twice in that time. Didn't you mention the letter?'

Vogel shook his head. Vogel's father, Eytan, now lived in Israel with Vogel's younger brother, Adam. David Vogel was a secular Jew. He believed in no god, actively practiced no religion and privately questioned the intelligence of anyone who did. His father was a devout Jew, who had never quite come to terms with his elder son's rejection of the faith. Adam, on the other hand, was always so committed to the faith that he ultimately became a rabbi and moved to The Promised Land. After the atrocities against the Jewish race during the second world war, the Israeli Knesset passed the Law of Return in 1950. This allows all Jewish people, as their birthright, to resettle in Israel and become Israeli citizens. It had seemed quite natural that, when Vogel's mother died a few years previously, the widowed Eytan had followed his rabbi son and gone to live in Tel Aviv.

Mary persisted, her tone even more gentle.

'David, why haven't you asked Eytan about it?'

Vogel blinked rapidly behind his spectacles.

'Because I'm not at all sure I want to hear his answer,' he said.

'Oh David, it must be so difficult for you,' responded Mary quietly. She glanced at the clock on the wall. 'Look it's nearly two a.m. Let's go to bed. You must get some sleep, perhaps things will seem clearer in the morning.'

Vogel smiled wryly.

Mary knew he was unconvinced of that. She followed him out of the sitting room. As usual, when he was late home, he quietly opened the door of Rosamund's bedroom and stood, for a minute or two, watching his sleeping daughter. He would now have very little time for sleep himself. Mary was well aware that he'd leave the house before six.

She also knew how disturbed her husband had been by the extraordinary revelation that he had just shared with her.

SAUL

The replies started coming in within days.

The first two girls didn't sound right at all. I thought one, reading between the lines, was just after western money. I had seen a lot of warnings online about that happening. The other seemed like the sort of good-time girl, who were ten a penny in any pub or club in the UK. I hated that type. Six didn't reply. Another two didn't appeal to me, for reasons I couldn't explain.

I entered into correspondence with the remaining two who had responded. Manee and Apinya. I didn't know if those were their real names but, nonetheless, I looked up the meaning of both. All oriental names have meanings: Manee meant *precious stone* and Apinya meant *magical power.*

I guess I leaned towards Manee from the start. I realised it was silly to be influenced by names, particularly when they may not even be real, but I felt it might be too dangerous for me to become involved with a woman whose name meant *magical power.* Who knows, she might see right through me.

Manee began to sound more and more like Sonia, I thought. But a Sonia who was prepared to travel halfway across the world to be with a man she'd never met. A woman who told me she'd been brought up in an orphanage, her only relative being a sister she hardly ever saw. A woman who was so desperate to start a new life, to have any sort of life at all, that I thought she might even put up with me. Just as I was, as I had to be.

'*I am not like western girl,*' she wrote. '*I want to look after man. I want to have his children and look after them too. That all. I do not want partying. Manee hate partying. Want home with her man.*'

She seemed very trusting too, which was absolutely necessary to me. She agreed at once to exchange email addresses, something the site warned against. I told her that was only because they wanted more money from us. She did, however, ask why I hadn't posted a picture of myself on the site. I replied that I was a very private person, which was surprisingly near the truth. As we were now in direct contact via email, I sent her the same heavily Photoshopped picture I had posted on *Marryme.com.*

Things moved quickly then. I understand they often do.

I had circumnavigated Thaibrides-introductions.com protocol. I explained to Manee that I was too busy to travel to Thailand. We needed to move to the next step.

Manee agreed to fly to England to be with me. If we liked each other, we would be married. I became carried away by it all, just as I had with Sonia, but I told myself that this time would be different. Thai girls were different and Manee would have to rely on me totally, in a land that was foreign to her. This time there was hope, surely. This time maybe I could make it work. I could fulfil my dreams.

I sent Manee the money for her fare. I did wonder if I was being naïve, perhaps she would just take my money and I would never hear from her again. I wouldn't be able to do anything about it. But, within days, she emailed me to say she had booked her flight for the following week. Unlike Sonia, who'd wanted to speak to me on the phone before even agreeing to meet me – let alone flying across the world to me – Manee had not asked to speak to me at all. I wasn't sure if I was glad or sorry about that. It did mean I was really thrown into the deep end.

I had a lot of planning to do and the short period of time, before she was due to arrive, flew by. As soon as the reality began to sink in, the realisation of what I'd done and what was about to happen overwhelmed me. I couldn't bring Manee to my home, that was for sure.

I already had the basis of a false identity, which I'd started to build some years ago, just in case! I'd used the old Frederick Forsyth, Day of the Jackal trick to obtain a passport and taken it from there. I was aware of that idiot who faked his own death in a canoeing accident and had successfully done the same thing. It seemed crazy that the scam had still worked, more than forty years after Forsyth taught us all how do it. But, knowing that it had worked so much more recently for canoe man, I'd decided to give it a go. It worked for me too and hadn't proved too difficult either.

I'd homed in on a male, who'd died as a child, but would have been about my age had he lived. and visited the national records office to gain the necessary papers, starting with a birth certificate. It was easy enough to follow through the required steps to acquire a passport, set up a bank account and so on. That gave me the debit card, which I used to pay for my online dating activities and anything else which necessitated plastic rather than cash. I'd opted for internet banking, of course, so all correspondence with my bank was online. Even acquiring a driving licence hadn't been difficult, I'd just had to apply for a provisional and take a test. I was a good driver and sailed through it.

I scanned the internet for affordable, rental properties in Bristol. Most of what was on offer was out of my budget and I was looking for a private rental; a property being advertised directly by the landlord. I wasn't sure that my false identity would stand up to the scrutiny of a bona fide estate agent.

Eventually, I found a furnished, two-bedroomed flat, albeit in an area where I would not normally choose to live, which seemed suitable and was being advertised by a private individual. Apart from anything else, someone who wanted to avoid estate agent's fees was more likely to bend the rules.

I arranged to meet the landlord at the property the same evening, it wasn't much. The kitchen was dirty, the furniture had seen better days and the whole place needed redecorating. But, after a cursory glance around, I decided to take it. I didn't have the time to be choosey. I just had to hope that Manee accepted the story I was planning to tell her.

As soon as the landlord began to talk about needing bank references, I offered him six months rent, at his asking price, in advance. Cash, if he liked.

I saw his eyes light up.

'I'm in a hurry you see,' I said, by way of explanation.

He didn't seem to really need one by then.

I went to the bank, drew out the cash, and I was in. Then I hired a car, using my driving licence and the debit card from my phoney bank account. I didn't want to risk using my own car, any more than I wanted to use my own home.

I did some shopping, bought flowers and made the apartment as nice as I could. I scrubbed the kitchen and even found the time to slap a new coat of paint on the walls in the sitting room, in order to brighten the place up. I wasn't an insensitive man. Then I was ready, or as ready as I would ever be, to drive to Heathrow to pick up Manee.

One half of me was excited. The other half already regretting what I'd done. I parked in short-term parking and walked swiftly into Terminal Three. Manee was flying Thai Air.

She arrived on a Saturday evening. I'd made myself look as much as possible like the picture I'd sent her. I'd given my hair a dark rinse and grown some facial hair, albeit little more than a hint of stubble after a day without shaving, which I planned to remove before returning to work on Monday morning. I was also wearing the tinted glasses.

I spotted her as soon as she walked into the arrivals hall. She was very small and pretty, prettier even than her picture had suggested.

Just as I'd told her I would, I'd printed out her name in big letters and stuck it on a piece of cardboard, like the chauffeurs do. Manee. Manee Jainukul. She'd said she was sure I would recognise her and she me, from our photographs. But I knew I didn't look at all like my photograph, even with the amendments I'd attempted to make to my appearance.

I watched as she first spotted the name board I was carrying, then looked up at my face. At once, I saw the doubt in her. My stomach lurched. I forced my features into the most welcoming and reassuring smile I could manage.

Suddenly the doubt seemed to lift and she smiled back, brightly, excitedly. We walked towards each other. I put my hand on her trolley, proprietorial already.

'Manee?' I queried, though the question was unnecessary.

'Saul?' her voice was high-pitched, childlike, full of hope.

I felt like a rat. I suppose I was behaving like a rat and not for the first time, but I was already in too deep to do anything about that. I'd feared we might not even get beyond the airport, however things looked promising, so far. Manee was still studying my face though, scrutinising me.

I thought I'd better deal with that straight away.

'Sorry about the picture,' I said. 'I know it's not a good likeness. It isn't very up to date, you see.' I turned my smile of welcome and reassurance into a disarming boyish grin. Well, the best shot I could make at it anyway. 'Vanity, I'm afraid.' I continued.

It seemed ages before she spoke.

'But you very handsome,' she said eventually, 'Very much more handsome than picture.'

I liked that. I liked that a lot. This was the sort of woman I'd been looking for all my life. I leaned forward and kissed her on the cheek, in a chaste sort of way. It seemed I did the right thing. She beamed at me.

I steered her out of the arrivals building and led her to the hire car in the car park. It was only a small Ford but, being a rental, it was nearly new and very clean. She looked at it approvingly or I thought she did, anyway.

On the way back to Bristol, we made polite and somewhat stilted conversation. I thought she was probably nervous. I was certainly nervous. Not least because I had another little problem to surmount before we reached our destination.

Stupidly perhaps, I'd emailed her a photograph of my real house when I'd invited her to the UK. I'd been trying to impress her, you see, to do my best to ensure that she would fly halfway across the world to be with me. It wasn't anything special, but it was quite a nice house and was in keeping with the picture I had painted of myself and the profile I had created. But I couldn't take her to my house, it would reveal far too much about me and I was afraid that things would go wrong. After all, they always had before, then I'd be trapped.

'My house,' I said. 'I sent you a picture. Do you like it?'

She nodded enthusiastically. Her whole face lit up.

'For me, very beautiful house,' she said.

'Yes, well it's going to be even more beautiful for you,' I told her. 'I'm having some work done on it. A new bathroom and kitchen.'

'Me very excited, Saul,' she said.

'Yes, but it's meant quite a lot of structural work and disruption. I'm afraid the house isn't liveable in at the moment,' I lied. 'There isn't even any running water. So I've rented a little flat. It won't be for long, few weeks at most.'

I watched her face fall.

'I so want to be in your fine house, Saul,' she said.

'Me too,' I responded. 'We will be there together soon. It won't be long, I promise and the flat is quite nice.'

She looked doubtful, very doubtful. I changed tack slightly.

'It has two bedrooms,' I said. 'One each, if you like, until we are married, which will also be soon, I hope. And, I want you to know that I won't be, uh, expecting anything until then. First, we can just get to know each other. No obligation to do anything else. Nothing like that.'

For a second or two she looked confused, then her face split into the big smile again. It seemed I had said the right thing.

'You honourable man, Saul,' she said. 'Very fine, honourable man.'

I touched her hand lightly, affectionately.

Her assessment of my character, of course, could not have been further from the truth.

FOURTEEN

In the morning, Vogel made himself put all thoughts about the bombshell letter to the very back of his mind. He needed all his energy and brain power to be concentrated on the investigation into the death of Melanie Cooke.

He left the house just before six, as Mary had predicted, and caught the little train to Temple Meads Station. It was fifteen minutes or so walk from Kenneth Steele House, which he always said he didn't mind, because it was the only exercise he got.

In keeping with Mary's advice, he intended to call Dawn Saslow as early as he reasonably could, after the previous extended day. He didn't expect his team to keep quite the working hours that he did – although very nearly.

It was extraordinary how often Mary had the knack of stating the damned obvious.

He'd been in too much of a hurry. It wasn't a mistake he'd usually make, but all police officers were aware of the importance of the golden first 24 hours in a murder inquiry. He'd wanted to get the school visit over as fast as possible and move on, but Sally Pearson was 14, the age of keeping secrets. And, although he prided himself on his interviewing skills, Vogel, in common with most middle-aged men, was totally bewildered by both the mental and physical complexities of a young, teenage girl.

Vogel called Saslow just after seven.

'I'm going to get Claire Brown to talk to that teacher and child from Moorcroft,' he began. 'It's a long shot that either of them have any further information and, if they do, Brown's just the sort to winkle it out. I've got something for you that could be more important. Have another go at Melanie Cooke's friend, Sally Pearson, will you? I've a feeling she knows more than she's letting on. As it's Saturday she'll be at home, presumably. I'm hoping it might help to be talking to her in her home environment, away from teaching staff, and without a bloody, great plod like me putting his size elevens in it. Get round there will you. Take Polly Jenkins. Tell Margot Hartley where I've sent you.'

Saslow smiled. Anyone less plod-like than Vogel was hard to imagine. She supposed he had a point though and she understood his choice of an accompanying officer well enough. Polly was a sassy, young, black constable, five foot nothing and super skinny. She dressed streetwise and although actually twenty-four, only three years younger than Saslow, at a glance probably looked more like a teenager. She also had a brain like a bacon slicer and had been drafted into the major crimes unit at Kenneth Steele House six months earlier as a crime coordinator.

Saslow called her straight away. She knew Polly would be delighted to be asked to be actively involved in a murder inquiry. It would not be the first time she had been called on because of the way she looked, more than anything else, but nobody ever remarked on that.

All she said was: 'Oh cool.'

'I'll pick you up in an hour,' said Saslow. 'Brief you on the way.'

Saslow dressed in tight, black jeans and a tan, leather jacket. It was the nearest she had to streetwise clothes.

Jenkins, with her braided hair, faded, denim jacket, short, black skirt and well-worn, silver trainers, looked rather more the part, as both Vogel and Saslow had known she would.

They arrived at Sally Pearson's house just after 8.30. It was a semi-detached property in one of Bristol's better suburbs. Saslow had been careful not to make it any earlier, even though Vogel might have wished for that. Two police officers calling much before 8.30 would smack rather too much of a dawn raid she thought. It was still earlier than she would have liked to make the call.

The girl's mother answered the front door. She seemed anxious, but not altogether surprised, to be confronted by two police officers, even at that time in the morning.

'Sally's not up yet,' she said, ushering the two women into the sitting room and gesturing for them to sit. 'I'll fetch her down. Though what she can tell you I don't know. She's ever so upset. We all are.'

Saslow and Jenkins made sympathetic noises. Saslow lowered herself onto the big, squashy sofa against the far wall. Jenkins sat in one of four upright chairs set around a small dining table by the window. It was ten minutes or so before mother and daughter reappeared. Sally was still wearing her pyjamas with a dressing gown over them, which was pink with a rabbit motif. Dressed like that, she looked like the child she really still was and she was clearly near to tears.

'Please don't worry about anything, Sally,' Saslow began. 'We just want an informal chat, to see if there's anything you know that might help us catch whoever did this to Melanie. Sometimes people know things they don't realise the importance of.'

Sally nodded unenthusiastically.

'Look, why don't you sit down here next to me.'

Saslow gestured towards the other half of the sofa she was sitting on.

Sally Pearson rather pointedly perched herself on the edge of an armchair as far away from Saslow as possible.

Nonetheless, Saslow persevered.

'Why don't you tell us again about the few days leading up to Melanie's death? We think she may have arranged to meet someone that night, possibly a man. Do you know anything about that?'

Sally glanced towards her mother.

'If you know anything, my girl, you tell this officer now,' instructed Mrs Pearson. 'I never understood what you were doing going around with Melanie Cooke anyway.' Mrs Pearson glanced towards Saslow. 'Not our sort of people,' she said. 'If you see what I mean.'

Then she looked at Polly Jenkins, as if seeing the black PC for the first time and blushed slightly.

Saslow was afraid that she saw what Mrs Pearson meant all right. Particularly as the woman very nearly sniffed as she made her last remark. It seemed hard to believe that she disapproved of Melanie Cooke and her mother because of their colour, but the glance towards Polly Jenkins had said a lot. In addition, there could be a misplaced sense of class superiority. Saslow knew that Mr Pearson was an insurance salesman and that Mrs Pearson worked part time as a doctor's receptionist.

They clearly saw themselves as aspiring middle class. The family home was spacious and well appointed and Mrs Pearson would consider it far superior to the Cooke's little, terraced house, even though that was so well kept. No doubt she also saw her family set up as superior to that of Melanie Cooke, who came from – what Mrs Pearson would likely describe as – 'a broken home' and had a common, jobbing, brickie stepdad and a lorry driver for a father. The woman's intervention was not helpful.

Sally's lower lip began to tremble. She really did seem to be on the verge of breaking down.

It was then that Jenkins – who hadn't reacted at all to Mrs Pearson's not so subtle expression of racism, even though there was no chance that the sharp, young PC could have missed it – intervened for the first time.

'Don't suppose there's any chance of a cup of tea, is there, Mrs Pearson?' she asked cheerily. 'I missed breakfast this morning.'

Mrs Pearson looked uncertain . Saslow was doubtful too. Police officers were not really supposed to interview under 16-year-olds without the presence of an appropriate adult. But this wasn't an interview, she reminded herself, just an informal chat, as she had told Sally.

Jenkins smiled her most girlish and matey smile.

'All right,' said Mrs Pearson, who clearly did not know quite what to make of the disingenuous PC and left the room for the kitchen.

Jenkins turned to Sally immediately.

'You want us to get this bad arse off the streets, don't you, Sally?' she asked.

Sally nodded. 'Course I do,' she said.

Jenkins pulled her chair closer to Sally's.

'So please, darlin', tell us what you know. You were besties with Melanie. I'll bet there wasn't much she got up to you didn't know about. I remember when I was your age I told my bestie everything and me mum nothin'!' Jenkins grinned disarmingly. At that moment, Saslow thought, Jenkins would almost have passed for a fourteen-year-old herself.

Like Saslow, Polly Jenkins was a local girl who spoke with

more that a hint of Bristolian in her voice. Sometimes a regional accent could be reassuring, thought Saslow, comforting even.

Sally sniffed away her tears. She even managed a small smile. It looked as if Jenkins might be working her magic.

But Sally said nothing.

'She snitched on me in the end though,' continued Jenkins.

Something seemed to stir in Sally.

'That's terrible,' she said.

Jenkins shrugged.

'I didn't have a home like yours, Sally,' the PC continued. 'Me mum didn't care who I was seeing, girl or boy, as long as I wasn't bothering her, and she had a boyfriend who wouldn't leave me alone.' Jenkins paused. 'You know what I mean?' she asked Sally.

Sally nodded, colouring slightly.

'My bestie was the only person in the world I told. I swore her to secrecy, but in the end she told her mum. I remember how frightened I was when the social services came round. And me mum still didn't want to know. She either wouldn't believe it or didn't care. I never knew which. I was twelve. I was taken into care and eventually put with a foster family, who did care. I don't know what would have happened to me if my bestie hadn't snitched.'

Sally stared silently at Jenkins for what seemed like a very long time.

'I can't tell,' she said eventually. 'I can't. Mum'll kill me.'

'No she won't,' said Jenkins. 'But your best friend has been killed. Murdered, Sally.'

'So I can't help her, can I?' protested Sally, with more than a hint of stubbornness.

'Oh yes, you can,' said Jenkins. 'You can help us catch the bastard who did her in. You owe that to Mel.'

Sally still looked doubtful.

'You're not that scared of your mother, are you?' Jenkins persisted, rather to Saslow's concern.

The promised tears came suddenly. Sally's shoulders began to heave.

'Well, are you?' Jenkins repeated. She clearly wasn't going to back off.

Sally shook her head, just as Mrs Pearson re-entered the room carrying two mugs of tea.

'Now you've upset her,' she said accusingly. 'I hope it's worth it, that's all.'

'I think your daughter has something to tell us, Mrs Pearson,' Saslow interjected. 'And I have a feeling it might prove to be quite important, isn't that so, Sally?'

Sally nodded. She shot a nervous glance at her mother, but all the same began to speak.

'Mel and me, well, we went online a lot, on her laptop because her mum and dad don't know how to check it like mine do.'

Jenkins made encouraging noises.

'We used to go on dating sites.'

'I don't believe it,' interrupted Mrs Pearson thunderously. 'After all we've said, all you've been told . . .'

Saslow gestured to the woman to be quiet.

'It was a game really,' Sally continued, almost as if her mother hadn't spoken. 'Neither of us ever intended to carry anything through. It was just a bit of fun.'

'What were the sites?' asked Saslow.

'Oh we tried out any we could get for free. There was one called *LetsMeet.com* . . .' Sally's voice trailed away.

'So did you actually meet anyone. Either of you?' Saslow asked.

Sally shook her head. 'I didn't. I would have been too scared. Mum is always going on about the dangers of that sort of thing. Mel is, I mean . . . uh, she was . . . hardly ever afraid of anything. There was this man she'd been chatting to online for a bit. I didn't know for certain, but I think she was going to meet him on Thursday night. She asked me to cover for her. She said it was a secret, but she'd tell me afterwards. She liked being mysterious, even with me.'

'Do you know anything about this man?'

'Not really,' said Sally. 'Except Mel said he sounded Scottish, and he'd told her he was nineteen and a student. But we both knew that older men lie about their age online, to get younger girls. I said she'd better be careful. That she shouldn't meet him, not on her own anyway.' Sally turned towards her mother, who had fallen mercifully silent. 'I did, honestly. Anyway, she said I was a wuss and she was going to have some fun regardless and that I'd better cover for her, or she'd tell you what we'd been doing, mum.'

Mrs Pearson still didn't speak, to Saslow's relief.

Sally's shoulders started to heave again. 'It's my fault, isn't it? It's my fault she's dead. I should have snitched on her, like your best friend did.' She glanced towards Jenkins. 'I shouldn't have cared about getting into trouble. If I'd snitched on her, she'd still be alive.'

'You can't know that, Sally,' said Polly Jenkins. 'You thought you were doing the best for your friend and you certainly are now. Did you know his name, this man you thought she might be planning to meet?'

'Only a first name. He called himself Al. Just that. Al.'

As they left the Pearson house, Saslow asked Jenkins if her story about being rescued from an abusive childhood by her snitching best friend had been a true one.

'Of course,' replied Polly Jenkins, smiling an enigmatic smile.

Saslow wasn't sure whether she believed her or not. The approach had certainly been effective.

She called Vogel to give him the news about Melanie Cooke's online adventure. An adventure which now seemed likely to have led to her death. The all-out hunt for a paedophile called Al had begun.

LEO

We arranged to meet at the pub just off Leicester Square. The one with the conveniently situated gents' toilets, right by the entrance, which I used as a place to change clothes. I felt safe there. Safer, perhaps bizarrely, than at The Freedom Bar, which Tim had suggested as a meeting place. There, I'd felt that both Tim and I had stuck out because of our awkwardness among the cool set. Or my awkwardness at any rate. I suggested one of those big, anonymous, Chinese restaurants, which was almost next door, for our dinner. Both the pub and the restaurant were close to The Premier Inn, therefore involving as little public appearance as possible.

As usual, I tried to keep the risk of being recognised by anyone from my day to day life, however unlikely that might be, to the minimum. I made sure I arrived at the pub early and, from just inside the doorway, had a good look around to make sure that there was no one around who might know me. I'd changed earlier, and already been to the restaurant and reserved a table that was close to the door and in a secluded corner booth.

Fortunately, Tim was tickled by the corner booth, which he seemed to find romantic. He did not appear to notice that I positioned myself as far away from him as possible. He talked and talked, and I talked too, rather a lot for me. I told him as much as I dared about myself.

'If you disappear on me this time, if I suddenly can't get hold of you, don't even think about coming back to me again with tales of lost and stolen phones,' he said sternly.

I could see that his eyes were twinkling, but I knew he meant it.

I'd given him my new mobile number and we'd been in touch again several times before this meeting. I hadn't felt the need to confess that this was yet another pay-as-you-go phone.

'No chance,' I said.

Again, he didn't seem to notice my determination not to get too close to him when we were outside, walking together to the hotel. I kept as much as possible of the pavement between us.

Having decided to give me another chance, he threw himself into the occasion with his customary enthusiasm. We were in each others arms as soon as the door to our room had closed behind us. If anything, our lovemaking was even better than before. There was a tenderness between us that I had never previously experienced, either with a man – or with a woman, which I had tried out in my all too frequent attempts to achieve conventionality – and yet there was excitement too.

So it was with a heavy heart that, in the early hours, when I was quite sure he was deeply asleep, I untangled myself from his arms, dressed stealthily in the bathroom and crept from the room as silently as possible.

Yet again he did not wake and that was a relief. I could not stay until morning as I had promised, of course, because then I would be expected to fulfil my other promise; my promise to take Tim home with me. That would never do.

I caught the first train of the day, just after 5 a.m. and spent the journey thinking over the wonderful time I had with Tim and the future. If indeed we could have any sort of future together. I so hoped that we could, although I knew it could never be the kind of future he hoped for.

This time I certainly did not intend to break off communication with him. The pay-as-you-go phone would stay. It was Tim's phone now. I would allow Tim to be a part of my life, as long as he accepted that there had to be limitations.

Of course, I wasn't at all sure that I could get Tim to go along with that. He was going to be pretty angry, when he discovered I had disappeared in the early hours yet again, that was for sure. It was quite possible that he would fulfil his threat to have nothing more to do with me. But I knew how much he cared for me, as indeed I did for him, in my own way. Every time we spent together enhanced those feelings.

I told myself that I was in much the same situation as a married man, who kept promising his mistress that he would leave his wife, but there was always something stopping him. The children. Ill health. Even just money. Those 'other women' often accepted that for many years.

I hoped for something like that with Tim. That he would accept stolen nights at The Premier Inn and similar locations, perhaps even the occasional holiday, somewhere discreet. Even that would be risky, but it might be worth it. Although I suspected it was unlikely that it would be enough for Tim. He had already more or less told me it wouldn't be.

I just hoped I could convince him otherwise.

I had been home about an hour when the doorbell rang.

I did not encourage casual callers or indeed callers of any kind, but I shopped online occasionally. I tried to remember if I had any deliveries outstanding. I was pretty sure I didn't.

Whilst I was thinking about that, the doorbell rang for a second time.

There were sometimes people collecting for charity in our neighbourhood and there was a local election pending. It could be a canvasser. It could also be a Jehovah's Witness, but it was a little early in the day for them, surely.

I took my usual course of action, without any good reason to do otherwise. I ignored the bell.

It rang for a third time. I didn't think political canvassers or even Jehovah's Witnesses were ever that persistent. Reluctantly, I took myself into the sitting room. From the bay window, if I craned my neck, I could see anyone standing by the front door. Obviously, I recognised my caller at once. A cold shiver ran down my spine.

It was Tim. My Tim. My secret lover. He was standing outside my home, about to invade my sanctuary. Clearly he hadn't been asleep when I'd left him earlier. He must have followed me.

I was so afraid. Afraid of what he would do. Afraid of what I would do.

I backed away from the window, moving softly, retreating well into the room. Perhaps he would just go away, if I didn't answer the bell. I knew I was kidding myself though.

The door bell rang yet again. It carried on ringing for a long time. Half a minute maybe. Strident. Threatening. Then it stopped and I heard his voice. He began to shout at me through the letter box and he was angry again, very angry.

As I had known he would be, when I'd left him in our hotel room.

But I hadn't expected him to follow me and vent his anger at me through my own letter box.

'I know you're in there, Leo,' he yelled. 'I watched you going in. I've been standing here outside, looking at where you live, deciding what to do. Now, I'm doing it. I'm confronting you, Leo. I'm calling your bluff. I am giving you one last chance to tell me what's going on. I know you are there and I'm not leaving until you let me in.'

FIFTEEN

The civilian specialists on the internet team hacked their way into Melanie's *LetsMeet.com* account. They found records of several chat sessions between Mel and a correspondent who called himself Al. There was no overt sexual content and, if Melanie had been meeting Al on the night she was murdered, she did not arrange to do so through *LetsMeet.com*. Al had posted a picture on the site purporting to be him. It was of a teenaged boy, in shorts, on a beach. The boy was little more than a pin figure in the distance and when the tech team tried to zoom in on his face, it pixelated. Vogel wondered why on earth that picture alone hadn't warned Melanie Cooke off. It wasn't even a proper, recognisable photograph.

The email address to which Al's account was linked was an anonymous one: Alboy@mymail.com. It proved untraceable and had already been closed down. The computer he used also seemed untraceable. All location tracking software had been deactivated. But, during one exchange, this Al had asked for Mel's mobile phone number, which she had promptly supplied.

Further checks were made into Melanie's phone records. There were no texts or voicemail messages from Al, but there was a call registered on the day before Melanie's murder. It was from an unidentified caller and had lasted six minutes. The phone used was an untraceable, pay-as-you-go mobile.

Vogel suspected that the unidentified phone call had been from Al. He wondered if Al had used the call to arrange a meeting with Melanie, but there was no way of knowing for sure. Text messages remain on the records of mobile phone providers, as do voicemail messages. Conversations made on mobile phones are not recorded, unless a specific phone is targeted by the police or some kind of surveillance agency. Therefore, the content of any phone conversation Melanie may have had with her Al would remain unknown.

Claire Brown's interviews with Alice Palmer, the little girl approached at Moorcroft School, and the teacher, who may have saved her from abduction, provided little further information, as Vogel had predicted. Alice did, however, reveal more details to Claire than had been in the original police report. The report hadn't mentioned the kitten Alice said was on the van driver's lap, nor how he had tried to coax her into the van to stroke it.

Vogel found that quite chilling. There was no way of proving it so far, but he felt strongly that Melanie Cooke's Al and the weirdo in the van were one and the same man. Little Alice Palmer had had a very narrow escape indeed.

In addition to poring over computer and phone records, Vogel and his team continued with the same dogged police work. Knocking on doors, checking sex offenders' lists, interviewing and re-interviewing family, school friends, teachers, neighbours, local shopkeepers and anybody who might be able to help.

Nobody could. Al was totally elusive.

AL

'd told myself there wouldn't be any harm in getting to know a few young girls on the net. Surely I could have some personal contact, without actually putting myself or anyone else into danger.

There were plenty of appropriate websites or inappropriate, a lot of people would say. The names said it all really: *CrushOnMe*, *Chat2Me*, and *FlirtyTeen*, which actually advertised itself as being for kids of 15. My favourite, because it required so little personal detail and was so accessible in every way, was *LetsMeet.com*.

None, except on the dark web of course, presented themselves as deliberately targeting – and offering – contact with children. But it became abundantly clear that many of the teen sites were more than happy to promote kids who were almost certainly not even into their teens yet.

I began to contact girls regularly. I don't think that made me a groomer, not really, because I never had any intention of taking things any further than a bit of internet titillation. Honestly, I didn't.

It was so easy. These girls, sometimes quite little girls, were so trusting and so eager. You only had to watch the news to know what could happen to them. No doubt there were parents and teachers warning them off, telling them not to talk to strangers and certainly never to talk to strangers on the world wide web. Everyone knew where that could lead, but they still did it.

I said I was younger than I was, of course, much younger. I said I was a nineteen-year-old student. You could add about a decade and a half to that and, long ago, I'd given up studying anything except the best way to fulfil my needs.

On most of the teen sites, you had to say you were a teenager. Although it was pretty damned obvious, to me anyway, that many of the male participants had waved goodbye to their teens many years previously.

I invariably posted the photo of myself taken when I was a student, or very nearly, it was just after I left school. It was genuine enough, but a bit blurred and far from close-up. In fact, I was only a tad more than a spec in the distance, but you could see this was a young person, a kid. Me, aged 18 actually, dressed in shorts and a T-shirt, on a beach, running towards the camera. I supposed that was what had so conveniently distorted the image. I would never be recognised from that photograph, not even by somebody who had known me back then. That was why I liked it. My mother had been the photographer. She was dead now, long dead.

One or two of the girls I contacted questioned the photo and asked me to post a better one. So I ignored them.

The majority just seemed to accept it.

You should have seen the pictures some of them sent to me, a total stranger. One girl sent me a selfie of herself in the bath. You couldn't actually see much of her body, just one arm and a little leg, but all the same. I asked her to show some more, but she didn't come back to me. But almost all of them sent provocative pictures. Or they were provocative to me, anyway. I mean what could be sexier than a picture of a girl who looks about twelve, heavily made up and pouting for the camera, even if she's fully dressed?

They knew how to pose, these kids. It was extraordinary.

If I'd thought clearly about it, it was a foregone conclusion that I ultimately would not be able to control myself. That I would want to touch as well as look.

I couldn't help it. It wasn't my fault. Really, it wasn't.

SIXTEEN

The results of DNA analysis of samples taken from Melanie Cooke's father and stepfather finally came through, four days after her murder. There was a direct match between the hair follicles found in Melanie's fingernails and that of her father, Terry Cooke.

Saslow had been the first of the team to pick up the email from forensics. She printed it and brought it to Vogel, who was in the canteen with Willis. In an unusually ebullient display, Willis shouted '*yes*' and smashed a clenched fist on the table.

'There we are then, boss,' he continued. 'I told you I had a feeling about that man, didn't I?'

Vogel nodded.

'And it seems you were right,' he said. 'I must admit though, I wasn't expecting this, particularly after the Al revelation. Sally Pearson actually told Saslow and Jenkins that Melanie had arranged to meet Al on the night she was murdered.'

'Sally could have got it wrong,' said Willis. 'Indeed, it looks like she did. Maybe Melanie chickened out of meeting this Al or perhaps it was all bravado and she was always planning to meet her dad.'

Saslow looked puzzled. 'Why would she lie about that to her mum and stepdad?' she asked. 'And why would a father, who allegedly adores his daughter, kill her?'

Willis shrugged. 'Why do they ever?' he responded. 'Yet more often than not it's a father or a stepfather, or sometimes an uncle, even a mum, rare but not unheard of, who is guilty when a girl of this age is murdered. We all know that.'

Saslow nodded. She wasn't so very long out of police college. She still remembered much of what she had been taught verbatim, including statistics and crime figures.

'"More than seventy per cent of murders in this country are committed by family members or people extremely close to the victim, like a sexual partner, and, therefore, less than thirty per cent are committed by someone the victim does not know,"' she recited. 'It's just that the fact that Melanie had told her friend that she was meeting a man she'd met on the net, that very night, is such a coincidence.'

'I agree with you,' said Vogel. 'But, what if her dad found out what she was planning to do? Perhaps he saw her dressed the way she was, maybe he bumped into her by chance, in the street, even. She wouldn't have dressed like a young tart if she'd actually arranged to meet her father, surely? We know he didn't like the way she was behaving and what she was getting up to. If he'd found out she was going to meet this Al, or indeed any man at all, looking the way she looked that night, he'd have been furious with her, wouldn't he? Maybe he just lost his temper with her, and, like you said before, Willis, made it look as if there had been a sexual assault in order to cover his tracks.'

'I suppose so, boss,' said Saslow doubtfully. 'Meeting her by chance though? That's even more coincidental. It just doesn't seem quite right. Any of it. And Sally Pearson telling us she'd arranged to meet this Al seemed such a good lead.'

Vogel wasn't comfortable with any of this either and he told Saslow so.

'I agree with you, Dawn,' he said. 'But it seems we must both be wrong. You can't argue with a direct DNA match. Hair follicles found in a victim's fingernails indicates a clear attempt at self-defence. Terry Cooke has to be our man. Come on. Let's bring the bastard in.'

SAUL

For about a week, things went very smoothly. I'd stocked the kitchen cupboards with everything a woman could want. I'd bought Manee perfume and a gold chain necklace. She seemed almost happy.

I was fairly happy too. I had so far been able to avoid all physical contact, something I was very nervous about, of course. I continued to say that I respected her, that I wanted us to be married before we had sex. Unfortunately, however, Manee quickly seemed to grow frustrated with that; quite quickly, actually.

'You not normal man, Saul,' she proclaimed. Of course, she had no idea how accurate that assertion was.

'Am I ugly?' she asked. 'You no want Manee?'

I assured her that she was not ugly and that I wanted her very much, which was true. I was just afraid. Afraid of the same old.

But when she began to kiss me, I kissed her back and it felt good, very good. Maybe this time it would be different, I told myself. I allowed her to lead me into her bedroom. Then it all started to go wrong, as usual. The foreplay was successful. I knew what was expected me, but there was, as usual, no way I could achieve full intercourse. My organ remained flaccid, even though I was so aroused I thought I might go crazy.

When I had been a young man, experimenting with girls, I had been able to manage half an erection. Indeed, bizarrely, I had got one of my girlfriends pregnant, almost as soon as we'd started trying to have sex. They say that impotent men are often exceptionally fertile. It had certainly seemed to be true in my case. As the years passed, things went from bad to worse for me. The fear took over. Every time, I was sure that I was going to fail and so I did. Totally.

And this time, it seemed, albeit with a young bride from another country and culture, was to be no different after all. I'd heard that Thai women had certain ways with them, ways that could work miracles for men like me. But Manee was more submissive than anything else and, to begin with, she was very sweet about my problem.

'We try again in morning,' she said. 'Men always horny in morning.'

Well, it was quite likely that I would be horny in the morning but, no doubt, I wouldn't be able to do anything about it. I did sometimes wake with an erection. Like most men, as Manee said. It was when I tried to do something with it that the trouble started. My erection would deflate almost instantly, as would the last vestiges of the totally forced sense of self-belief that I was so desperately trying to cling to.

There was one thing that had occasionally helped me in the past.

I reached for her young bum.

'Turn over,' I croaked.

I was sure I felt a stir in my useless organ at the thought of it, just a twitch.

'Oh no,' she said. 'Manee good Catholic girl. No bums.'

'Come on, please,' I coaxed hoarsely.

'No,' she said firmly, wriggling away from me in the bed. I was beginning to learn that Manee was both stubborn and opinionated, much like most of the English women I'd encountered over the years. It seemed I had failed dismally in my quest for the compliant, Thai girl every other man seemed to have.

'No bums,' she said again. 'It is in Bible.'

'Where in the Bible?' I asked.

'Don't know,' she replied. 'There somewhere.'

And that was that.

I lay back on the pillow full of frustration. I guess I had kind of assumed she would be Buddhist, like so many Thais, or nothing at all. In any case, what had her being a Catholic got to do with refusing to indulge in anal sex? What about all those perverted old priests over the years and what they'd done? Not just to consenting adults either. All too often, children were the victims of their unnatural lusts.

Eventually I fell into a fitful sleep. When I woke in the morning

Manee was already up making tea. I had a weak erection, just as she had predicted. I wondered if I should try to persuade her to have another go, but she didn't seem interested. I didn't blame her.

She made no mention of the night before, instead asking when we were going to go out, to a restaurant or a bar, to meet my friends. I suppose I shouldn't have been surprised. She was a young girl. How had I imagined I could keep her hidden away?

'You said you wanted a quiet life, for us to build a home together,' I reminded her.

'This not our home,' she said in a puzzled voice. 'You tell me this not our home.'

I had indeed told her that. She was supposed to be the naïve one. Actually, I was beginning to suspect it was me. How could I have expected to get away with any of this?

'Soon,' I said 'Soon we will move into our real home and soon we will go out, meet people. I am sorry I have been so busy.'

I'd been blaming pressure of work for not being able to spend more time with her, and claimed to be too exhausted to do anything by the time I returned to the flat at night.

'I have been nowhere,' she said. 'You lock door when you go out. Flat on fourth floor. Manee prisoner.'

'No baby. It's not like that. You're not a prisoner. Not at all. It's just that this flat is in a rough area. I don't want you wandering about on your own here and I told you, this is just a temporary rental. I only have one set of keys, for the front door downstairs too.'

'In England they no have locksmith?' Manee queried, her pretty, little face set into a quite unattractive pout.

I forced a smile. Trust me to find a tricky one. I'd thought Thai girls were supposed to never question their men. Wasn't that why so many Western men wanted them for wives?

'Yes, of course,' I said. 'As soon as I have time, I will get another set cut. I promise.'

'Today,' said Manee.

It wasn't a query. It was an order. This really wasn't how it was supposed to be.

Things just went from bad to worse after that.

I kept making excuses about the keys. She started to get angry. There was no landline telephone in the flat, I'd made sure of that. She had a mobile, but I wasn't too worried about it. I was beginning to get to know Manee. She was impulsive. She had come to England, to me, on an impulse. She was also proud and feisty. She would be reluctant to contact her sister, or anyone else back home, to tell them she had made a mistake. She wouldn't want to admit that and, as far as I was aware, she knew nobody in the UK whom she might phone or text.

However, I felt that Manee's patience was running out.

I had to try to keep her sweet. I took her to a big anonymous out of town supermarket and let her choose the food. She wasn't very impressed. I told her that as soon as I had the time I would take her shopping properly and buy her lovely things. Her look said that she didn't believe a word I was saying any more, but she stayed silent. I made a huge fuss of her. I even told her I loved her. She seemed to like to hear that, but she didn't say it back.

Late one night, I took her to a nearby Thai restaurant. I told her I wanted to make her feel at home, but it was pretty downmarket.

'This is rubbish restaurant,' she said. 'Rubbish restaurant and rubbish food.'

On balance, she was right. I had chosen the restaurant because it was so unlikely that I would meet anyone there who knew me. I was well aware that it wasn't the sort of place Manee or any other young woman would expect to be taken to after flying halfway across the world.

We were reaching a crisis, Manee and me, I thought to myself as we walked home from the Thai restaurant. She wasn't going to put up with this much longer. She wasn't the sort. In any case, I wasn't sure that any sort of girl would be very happy in the situation I had created.

I had to do something about it. I just wasn't sure what, but something had to be done. And soon.

SEVENTEEN

Vogel took Willis and Saslow with him to arrest Terry Cooke, backed up by four uniforms in squad cars.

They went to the Fisher home first, Willis and the family liaison officer, who was already in residence, both being able to advise that there was where Terry Cooke was spending most of his time.

'Much to the annoyance of his second missus, I wouldn't mind betting,' volunteered Willis. 'Or maybe she'll be relieved; no more mystery bruises for a bit.'

Several members of the press were still hanging round outside 16 Carraby Street. The murder of a schoolgirl was always a big story.

Vogel positioned two of the uniforms on the pavement outside. Their brief was to keep the vultures at bay.

Vogel himself led the other two uniforms, Willis and Saslow to the house.

Sarah Fisher came to the door, the FLO, who had been discreetly informed of the impending arrest, just behind her. Sarah's eyes opened wide in surprise at the extent of the police presence which confronted her.

'Has something else happened?' she asked. 'Have you arrested someone?'

'Is Melanie's father with you, Mrs Fisher?' asked Vogel.

'Uh yes, he's been ever so good, well he idolised that girl, you see . . .' Sarah Fisher paused. She looked as if she had begun to put two and two together and didn't like at all the sum achieved.

Vogel had no time to waste. Once he had ascertained that Terry Cooke was inside, he didn't intend to wait to be asked into the house.

'Move out of the way, Mrs Fisher, please,' he commanded, at the same time pushing his way past the woman, closely followed by the rest of his team.

Vogel guessed that Cooke would be in the sitting room. He was right. Melanie's father was sprawled across the sofa in front of the TV. He had a bottle of beer in one hand and a pile of sandwiches were on a plate on a small side table.

Well, he'd certainly got his feet under his ex's table, thought Vogel, remembering Willis's description of the chaotic squalor of the man's own home.

Cooke looked pretty relaxed and content, under the circumstances, until he swung round to face the door and found himself confronted by four police officers.

Alarm spread across his sallow features.

'What's going on?' he asked and then, echoing his wife, 'have you got any more news?'

Vogel strode swiftly forward until he was standing directly in front of the man.

'Terence James Cooke, I am arresting you on suspicion of the murder of your daughter Melanie Anne Cooke,' he began. 'You do not have to say anything, but it may harm your defence if you do not mention . . .'

The standard caution was interrupted by Cooke jumping to his feet with unexpected athleticism, uttering a strange, animalistic wail and lurching towards the door, in what appeared to be an ill-thought-out attempt at making a run for it.

Vogel had chosen his team of arresting officers with care. One of the uniforms, PC Steve Braddock, was a rugby player.

Braddock filled the doorway with his extremely large frame and effortlessly wrapped one muscular arm around Cooke, making it impossible for the other man to move.

'Cuff him,' Vogel ordered Willis, who did so with alacrity, whilst Braddock continued to hold on to Cooke, even though he no longer really needed to. The man made no attempt to struggle and looked totally beaten down.

Vogel thought his ineffectual attempt to run had probably been only a reflex action, but the DI was taking no chances. He completed the caution then told Willis and Braddock to load Cooke into one of the squad cars.

Only then did a stunned looking Cooke speak again.

'Wait, wait, I don't believe this is happening,' he said.

Braddock was already in the process of leading Cooke towards the door. Willis was right behind him, just in case. Braddock paused and looked enquiringly towards Vogel.

Vogel gave a little nod, which indicated that Braddock should hold on for a moment and let Cooke speak.

'I'd never hurt my Melanie,' Cooke continued. 'I'd never hurt her. Why do you think I did it? Why?'

Vogel did not reply, instead he addressed Braddock and Willis.

'Take him away,' he said.

Sarah Cooke began to cry. She joined in her ex-husband's chorused protests of innocence.

'He wouldn't hurt our Mel,' she said. 'He's not done it. I know he's not done it.'

'Mrs Fisher, your family liaison officer will stay with you and answer any questions that she is able to . . .'

It was Sarah Fisher's turn to suddenly lunge forward. She threw herself at Vogel, wrapping her arms around him.

'Please Mr Vogel, please, this can't be right,' she cried.

Vogel disentangled himself, not without difficulty.

'Mrs Fisher, I can assure you we do not make arrests in such serious cases as this without having very good reason to do so. That's all I can say at the moment. Now, please let us get on with our job.'

The FLO took Mrs Fisher by the hand and led her to a chair.

'Come on,' she said. 'Try to keep calm. I'm here to help in any way I can.'

Sarah Fisher obediently slumped into the chair. She, too, looked totally beaten.

LEO

I gave in and opened the door.

I didn't have time to change the way I looked. Again.

I was no longer a gay man. I'd cleaned the gel out of my hair, of course, removed my fake tattoo and given my man tan a bit of a rub in the bathroom at the Premier Inn. I'd dressed in my straight clothes. I couldn't risk being spotted on the journey, or anywhere near my home, looking the way I did when I was in London consorting with Tim.

My 'pulling jeans' and my trendy Year Zero T-shirt were for Soho only.

As soon as I'd arrived home, I had changed swiftly into my usual indoor wear, a baggy sweatshirt over a pair of old cords. Clothes that had never even been to London. I neither looked nor felt like gay Leo.

Tim was purposeful.

'So you don't live in a new-build in Stevenage after all,' he pronounced rather obviously.

I could think of no reply, so I said nothing.

'This is ridiculous Leo,' said Tim. 'We can't continue like this. What's going on?'

'You followed me, then,' I said, dodging the question by making a remark as obvious as his had been.

'Terrible thing deceit, isn't it Leo?' said Tim. The question was clearly rhetorical.

'Look, I'm sorry, this is a really bad time. I know we have to talk, but not now . . .'

'Let me in, Leo,' said Tim.

'Uh, not now. I'm sorry.' I searched desperately for an excuse, not that any were likely to deter him. 'I uh, have to go to work. I've been called in at short notice.'

'Really.'

'Uh, it's a bit of an emergency.'

'You're an accountant, or so you told me, not a bloody fireman.'

'I'm sorry,' I said again.

Tim looked me up and down.

'Are those the clothes you wear to work? I thought an accountant would be suited and booted.'

I shrugged. What was there to say.

'Let me in, Leo,' Tim said again.

I shook my head.

Tim raised his voice.

'Let me in Leo, or I am going to shout and yell as loud as I can, loud enough so that everyone living in your stupid, neat and tidy, middle class road will hear me.'

I just stared at him. I couldn't have him inside my house. That was my place. My sanctuary. I really couldn't let him in.

Tim threw back his head and opened his mouth wide, preparing, rather theatrically it seemed, to fulfil his promise and shout as loud as he could.

I had no choice. I stepped out of the doorway and beckoned him in. I led him into the sitting room. It was an anonymous room. I didn't want anything personal around me. I never had. The furniture was a mixture of IKEA and DFS. The walls were Dulux magnolia and decorated only with two incongruous Alpine snowscapes on either side of the blocked-off fireplace, probably adding to the cold atmosphere. I kept everything very clean and tidy. I certainly wouldn't want the mess of an active fireplace. A fifty-inch TV dominated one wall. I liked to escape into other worlds. After all, I was less than happy in my own.

Tim sat down on the sofa without being invited, leaned back and stretched his long legs, as if he were making himself comfortable. It was all an act, of course.

'No wife then, or live-in lover?' he queried.

I knew he didn't really need to ask, because it was fairly obvious from the austerity of my home that nobody shared it with me.

I decided to go on a kind of attack. It was silly, but I guess I was playing for time.

'I can't believe you would follow me,' I said.

'I can't believe a lot of things, Leo,' responded Tim. 'I don't know if I even believe your name.'

I saw his eyes focus on a small pile of mail on the desk by the window.

I walked across the room, as casually as I could manage, and stood in front of the desk. I started to speak again, trying to reassure him, at the same time reaching behind me to move a magazine on top of the mail.

'Leo,' I said. 'I'm your Leo.'

'Really.' He paused. 'You seem different.'

'It's the clothes and how I am at home, but I'm your Leo and I love you. Nothing will ever change that.'

I was prepared to do or say anything to get him to calm down and, ultimately, to leave quietly.

'I don't understand,' he responded. 'I really don't understand.

If you love me, you sure as hell have a funny way of showing it.'

He didn't sound angry any more, just bewildered and weary.

'Look,' he said. 'Look Leo, you clearly don't have a wife. Nor do you share your life with anyone else, I shouldn't think. You're single, right?'

I nodded.

'You're single. OK. That's something I suppose, but this is 2017. Why all the subterfuge? What are you afraid of?'

'I thought you understood,' I said hopefully. 'After all, aren't we in the same boat? You haven't told your parents you're gay. You've been unable to do that. It's the same.

'It is not the same, for God's sake.' Tim sounded angry again. 'I'm eighteen years old,' he said. 'I'm in my first year at college and I still live at home because I can't really afford to do anything else. I've told you. All that is changing soon, very soon. I will have my own place and I will live my own life. I didn't even know for sure I was gay till I met you and it will not be easy explaining it to my parents. They are kinda old-fashioned but, as soon as I can get myself sorted, I will tell them.'

'You knew you were gay,' I said. 'Don't kid yourself. Look, I'm not a straightforward man . . .'

'You can say that again,' interrupted Tim forcefully.

I continued as if I hadn't even heard him.

'OK, I know its almost fashionable to be gay nowadays, in certain circles, anyway, but I'm unable to be like other people. I've built up this façade over the years. I can't come out. I couldn't face it at work . . .'

'Who do you work for, Leo? The fucking Pope?'

I rather wished I'd thought of that first. Well, not quite the Pope, but if I'd told him I worked for the Roman Catholic church that might have made him rather less puzzled and curious about me. After all, everybody knows the attitude of the Catholic church to homosexuality. Though I thought it was clearly hypocritical.

It was too late for that excuse now, but I could still use his train of thought, even if he hadn't meant it seriously.

'Not the Pope,' I said, risking a small smile. 'But I am a Catholic and I do guilt big time.'

'What's to be guilty about?' Tim was staring at me, his innocent eyes wide open as if he were trying to see inside my head. I so hoped he couldn't. I could see his tears forming. 'I don't understand any of this,' he said. 'I shouldn't have bloody followed you, you bastard. I should have let you walk away, but I love you, that's the bloody problem. I love you and I know you're only trouble.'

I reached out and touched his cheek.

He jerked away from me.

'I love you too, Tim,' I said again.

It was the truth. In as much as anything about me was ever the truth.

I moved closer to him, put my arm around him.

'Will you let me kiss you?' I heard myself say.

I saw that the tears were falling down his cheeks now. He turned to me. I showered him with kisses. It wasn't long before he began to respond. It wasn't long before we were in bed. My bed. In my house. I knew it was madness.

After we had made love, he began to question me again. The same questions. Why was I like I was? Why had I been so dishonest with him? Could I ever change? Could he and I ever have a proper relationship?

I answered everything the best I could, whilst actually telling him nothing. I said I would try to change. I really would. It would be difficult for me after all these years, but I would try. I wanted us to have what he called a 'proper relationship' and I would try to make that happen.

Eventually, he fell asleep. While I just lay there watching him, wondering what an earth I was going to do next. How I was going to get him out of my bed without upsetting him? How I was going to carry on with my life? Wondering whether it would ever be possible for me to do so, with Tim as a part of that life. I wanted Tim. I really wanted Tim, but in my heart I knew I could no longer have him. He demanded too much.

Around 11 a.m. I felt and heard my phone buzz. I'd put it on silent and tucked it under my pillow, where it would be safe from clever fingers and prying eyes.

It was a call I had to take.

I studied Tim carefully. He'd been sound asleep in the same position for over an hour, his tousled hair spread over the pillow, his mouth slightly open. He didn't move. His eyelids didn't flicker.

I tiptoed out of the bedroom, still naked, and took the call in the spare room. When I returned Tim remained in the same position. I sincerely hoped he wasn't just pretending to be asleep. Again.

I sat on the edge of the bed for a minute or two, just watching him, before gently shaking him awake.

He smiled at me sleepily, stretching his long limbs.

'What time is it?' he asked.

'Gone eleven,' I replied, hoping he would assume it was even later than it was. I really had to get rid of him. I needed to leave the house. I had things to do that would not wait. I wasn't sure quite how to go about this without causing another scene. Tim came to my rescue.

'Oh my God,' he said. 'I didn't mean to fall asleep. Is it really that time? I have to go. I've got an exam this afternoon.'

There followed a frantic few minutes of panic: Tim rushing in and out of the bathroom; trying to dress in a hurry; pulling on his jeans, the wrong way round at first; looking for his jacket and a shoe that had disappeared under the bed; me helping him look and going downstairs to make a coffee he didn't drink. Whilst I was downstairs, I stowed away the pile of mail that had attracted his attention in a locked drawer. Eventually, in a surprisingly short period of time under the circumstances, he was on the doorstep preparing to leave.

'Are we going to make this work now, Leo?' he asked.

'I do hope so,' I replied truthfully.

He stepped towards me, looking as if he were going to kiss me goodbye. Automatically I stepped backwards, away from the doorstep, further into the hallway. My hallway. My house. My doorstep. My neighbours. What if anybody saw? It was bad enough that he was there at all, but he could be anybody, I told myself. A relative. An electrician. A plumber. Without tools? I knew I was probably being ridiculous. Why would my neighbours even notice whether he was carrying a bag or anything else? He could have been a workman giving me an estimate on a job, a bit young, perhaps, but surely there was no reason for anyone to assume he was my lover, was there?

I was beginning to feel quite shaky. The last few hours had been madness.

Tim didn't push it.

'You really are a wimp, Leo,' he said, but he was smiling, he wasn't angry any more. Our lovemaking had been as good and as special as it always was. You couldn't stay angry after that and I suspected Tim might be beginning to believe things could work out for us, eventually.

He turned and began to walk away.

Then he paused looking back over his shoulder and swung around towards me again.

'By the way, for how long do you want me to continue to call you Leo?' he asked. I felt a chill engulf my entire body. 'Whilst you were on the phone, I had a look around. You'd left your wallet in the pocket of your jacket, hanging behind the bedroom door.'

How could I have been so stupid? How could I have let this happen?

Tim smiled again, a knowing smile.

'It's all right,' he said. 'I'd guessed Leo wasn't your real name. I told you that, but I know what you do for a living now, too. Can't see that it matters though, plenty of gays in your job.'

'Yes,' I said. 'Yes. Of course. I've just been stupid. I am Leo, though. Your Leo.' He looked a tad confused. 'Everything will be all right, Tim,' I continued. 'I promise. We'll talk it all through properly the next time we meet.'

He took a step towards me, again.

'You've no idea how happy it makes me to hear you say that,' he said.

Was he never going to go?

'Tim, your exam,' I reminded him frantically.

His expression changed.

'Oh, Christ, yes, I have to run,' he said and he did, literally. I watched him run off down the road.

I'd started to shake. I was having a major trembling fit. It was something that happened occasionally and I so hated it. I slammed the door shut and retreated inside. I could feel myself losing control, physically and mentally.

I smashed my right fist into the wall, again and again. I wanted to hurt myself. I hated myself, but then, that was my problem.

I'd always hated myself and I hated what I feared must come next. Something had to be done about Tim. I couldn't get the boy out of my head, but I had to. I had to get him out of my head and out of my life. He'd been to my home. He had pried into my very existence. He knew my other name. He knew what I did for a living. He knew how I lived my life. No man had ever got this close to me before. I hadn't allowed any man to get this close.

For several days, I did what I usually do in every aspect of my life when things get difficult. I stalled. I answered each text and phone call from Tim. I had to. I couldn't risk him turning up unannounced again. For me, that was an unacceptable intrusion. I didn't like intrusion. It felt like I was being stalked. I had to end it somehow. I began to forget that I had fallen in love with him. In the real world, I could not love anyone. I never had been able to. I never would be able to and certainly not another man.

Tim started to become insistent about fixing a date for our next meeting. If I didn't want him to come to me again, then I must make a trip to London. Soon. He said he had to see me. He felt we'd crossed a bridge, made a leap, all sorts of nonsense. The biggest nonsense of all, which he landed on me during one of our many, increasingly angst-ridden telephone conversations, was that he wanted me to meet his parents.

'Your parents?' I gulped. 'Your parents don't even know you're gay.'

'Not yet,' he responded excitedly. 'But the time has come. I know who and what I am, now, and I'm not going to live a lie. No way.'

I'd known that, hadn't I? From the beginning. But I'd still carried on seeing him.

'Neither am I going to let you live like that, not any more,' Tim went on. 'I'm going to tell them this weekend. We always sit down together for a big Sunday lunch. Time to talk. I'm going to tell them then.'

He sounded so sure of himself. I felt weak. My carefully constructed life was about to implode. I was quite sure of it.

I arranged to meet him at the Premier Inn on the Saturday

evening. The night before his planned family revelation. I had no choice.

We would go back to the Freedom Bar and hit those cocktails, I promised. Eat there or at any restaurant he chose. I wanted things to be different too, I said. I wanted us to be a normal couple, just as he did, and we would start on Saturday evening.

I was lying of course, but I had to convince him that I was prepared to change and ensure that he wouldn't be suspicious of me.

EIGHTEEN

Terry Cooke continued to declare his innocence throughout a series of interviews. But then, as Hemmings said, didn't they always?

It was only on the telly that murderers conveniently confessed all to investigating officers.

As Vogel had said, you didn't get much more conclusive evidence than DNA.

And Cooke, whilst quite reasonably protesting that of course his DNA could be found on his own daughter and that meant nothing, could not explain how follicles of the hair from his head had been found in Melanie's fingernails. He also had motive, of sorts, and more than likely, considering his wife's reliance on prescription drugs, the opportunity to perform the murder.

Less than seven hours after his arrest, Cooke was duly charged with his daughter's murder.

The case was put in the hands of the Crown Prosecution Service and Vogel just hoped they made a good fist of it this time. The team all went to the pub to celebrate, like they always did. Vogel, although he didn't drink, almost always went along. Not on this occasion.

He just couldn't face it. There were two reasons.

The first was that it still didn't feel right to him. In spite of the overwhelming forensic evidence, he couldn't quite believe that Terence Cooke was responsible for his daughter's murder.

The second was that letter! After showing it to Mary, he'd decided he really mustn't continue to carry it around with him, not in the middle of a murder investigation anyway. If he wasn't going to do anything about it, then he should leave it alone. He'd tucked it in the desk drawer in the sitting room, where he and Mary kept all their important papers. Out of sight, out of mind. But it hadn't quite worked like that. Even though he'd been so busy, he hadn't been able to get the letter entirely out of his mind. It had somehow lurked there throughout.

As soon as he got home, he sat down at the little desk and, whilst Mary fetched him food and drink as usual, retrieved the letter and read it once more.

Dear Detective Inspector Vogel, it began, curiously formal in view of what was to follow, Vogel thought.

There is no easy way to say this, so I am just going to come straight out with it.

I have reason to believe that you are my half-brother.

Vogel paused there. When he'd first opened the letter that second sentence had come as such a shock, that his first inclination had been to screw the piece of notepaper into a ball and throw it away. After all, it couldn't be true, could it?

But he'd been unable to carry that through. He'd carried on reading, as he was now doing for the umpteenth time.

A few weeks ago, I found papers amongst my mother's belongings which made it clear that she had a child, a son, when she was just sixteen and that the boy had been adopted. My mother – our mother – was seriously ill in hospital at the time I found this out; she had suffered from a severe stroke, from which she is slowly recovering, so it was a while before I could question her about this.

She broke down. She had kept you a secret for so long that it was very hard for her to talk about you, but eventually she told me everything. How she had been given no choice but to give you up. She was a schoolgirl at the time, who fell pregnant after an ill-advised, one-night stand with a fellow pupil. She'd been able to keep track of your progress over the years; the adoption had been arranged through a family friend, who had connections with a Jewish charity which placed unwanted children (not that she didn't want you, please understand that) with Jewish families, rather than through the more anonymous and legally-protected, local authority channels.

That is why I know your name and have been able to write to you at your place of work.

My mother married a few years later and I was born. I am thirty-four. You also have a younger half-brother, William, aged thirty, but he knows nothing of any of this yet.

My mother does know that I am writing to you, and wishes, particularly after having been so very ill, that she had dared to contact you many years ago.

I hope you will forgive this intrusion into your life, David Vogel, and I want you to know that it is meant with only the best of intentions and comes from the heart. From both our hearts, my mother's and mine.

We both hope that you will want to meet us, that is the real intention of this letter, of course, but we will under-stand if you don't. My mother's heart has already been broken – forty-three years ago, when she was forced to give you away.

With all best wishes,

Ellen Hunt

When he'd finished reading, Vogel removed from the envelope the photograph which had accompanied the letter. A photograph, fairly recent he thought, of a woman approaching sixty (his mother), a younger woman (his sister) and a younger man (his brother). His birth family. Did he resemble any of them? He wasn't sure. They were all very dark, as he was, dark-haired and dark-eyed, that is, but quite fair-skinned.

One of the three people in that picture had no idea he existed, until a few weeks ago. One still did not know. But the biggest secret of all had been kept from Vogel, by the two people he'd been brought up by and whom he had regarded as his natural parents.

He'd never been told that he was adopted.

Mary came back into the room, while he was still studying the picture. She was carrying a tray and placed it on the dining table, at the far end of the sitting room. She saw at once what her husband was doing, came over and laid a hand gently on his arm.

'David, why don't you call Eytan? You really should talk to him, you know.'

Vogel nodded in apparent agreement, but made no move to use a phone.

'It might not even be true,' Mary persisted.

'It's true all right,' said Vogel. 'You've read the letter. It wasn't written by a nutter. There is no malice in it, just the opposite. It's the work of an intelligent, articulate woman, someone who had assumed that I at least already knew I was adopted. After all, adoptive parents are supposed to tell their children the truth as they know it, aren't they?'

Mary nodded, 'Call Eytan,' she said yet again.

Vogel glanced at his watch.

'It's too late,' he said. 'Don't forget Israel is two hours ahead of us, perhaps I'll call tomorrow.'

'David, that means it isn't yet nine o'clock in Tel Aviv. Surely not too late to call your father . . .?'

Mary let the last words tail away.

Vogel smiled wryly.

'Yes,' he said. 'And that's the whole point, isn't it? I'm calling a man who, almost certainly, isn't my father at all.'

All the same, he picked up the phone and began to dial.

AL

There was something about Melanie Cooke which particularly attracted me from the moment I first spotted her entry on *LetsMeet.com*.

It wasn't just the way she looked, although she was stunning. The photo she chose to post showed her wearing a skimpy top, those shorts they call hot pants that I so like, torn tights and very high heels. I was turned on by that, certainly, but it was what I could see in her eyes that really got me.

She was knowing, as if she had done and seen it all before.

She didn't look like the kind of kid who would run, when confronted by a man instead of a boy. Indeed, just the opposite. I told myself she was looking for someone like me, just as much as I was looking for someone like her.

We began to correspond.

She told me early on that she lived in Bristol. She might have had a knowing look in her eye, but she was totally disingenuous. I told her I lived in Bristol too. She opened up even more after that. It was if my having said I lived in the same city provided some sort of reassurance. Silly girl.

She wrote to me in detail about her family life, about the problems she had coping with her too-strict stepfather and her too-clingy father and how she hated her younger sister, whom she felt had taken her place with her mother. I couldn't imagine sharing the kind of stuff she shared with me with my closest friend – that is, if I had any close friends, which I didn't.

I was very careful in my replies. I said nothing suggestive at any time. Neither did I ask her to send me any photographs of a more explicit nature. I had a pretty good awareness of the trending interests of young teens. For obvious reasons, I kept up to speed. I was able to talk to her about her interests, as if I too were a teenager. I asked about the kind of music she liked, the apps and games she had installed on her laptop and phone, and I was able use the right sort of language. Or I hoped so, anyway. I could go way beyond cool, wicked, and savage. I kept up to date through the web, because teen slang changes so rapidly. I sympathised with her about her fam (family) and enquired about her squad (group of friends).

I really worked at it. Melanie Cooke was different to the others.

I knew I would just have to make a move on her sooner or later. But I didn't want anything incriminating about me on *LetsMeet.com*, however unlikely it was that anyone would be able to trace me from my entry. After a couple of weeks or so of apparently innocent exchanges, I asked for her phone number.

She gave it to me straight away.

I called her on the untraceable, pay-as-you-go phone I'd bought specifically for the purpose. I kept our first chat light. I tried to pitch my voice higher than usual, and if she noticed that mine was the voice of a man much older than nineteen, she passed no comment. Instead, she asked if I was Scottish. I was surprised. I thought my accent was light,. But it seemed she had a Scottish grandmother, so she had picked up on the nuances.

'That's another thing we have in common,' I gushed, without giving anything more away.

I didn't text her at all. Texts remain on the records of mobile phone providers, as do messages left on 121, but there are no records of the content of spoken calls. We had several more phone calls, only very slightly flirtatious on my part, before I invited her to meet me. She took surprisingly little coaxing, agreeing quite swiftly to meet.

I told her to dress the way she had for her *LetsMeet* picture and that I liked her style. I kept everything light. I was becoming desperate to meet her. I didn't want to say anything that might frighten her off, but Melanie Cooke was putty in my hands. She was asking for it all right and I couldn't resist.

I was ready to cross the line. I had no choice.

NINETEEN

The conversation which followed shocked Vogel to the core. 'Is there something you've forgotten to mention over the years, dad?' he asked casually.

'Sorry son, what are you talking about?' Eytan responded.

'I'm talking about he fact that I am not your son at all.'

'Sorry? You've lost me.'

'No, Dad. Please don't dissemble. I was adopted, wasn't I? And neither you, nor mum, chose to tell me.' Vogel spoke in an even enough tone, but inside he was in turmoil.

'Ah,' murmured Eytan Vogel. It was little more than a breath.

'Come on, dad,' persisted Vogel. 'Show me some respect. Tell me the truth.'

'Uh yes, uh, we never wanted you to find out this way.' The shock was clear in Eytan's voice. David Vogel didn't care.

'Your mother always said it could happen,' Eytan continued. 'That you might learn the truth from someone or something else. She wanted to tell you from the beginning. It was my fault we didn't. You know what Jewish fathers are like with their firstborn, I wanted you to be *my son*. You were my son. You are still my son, every bit as much as Adam. We never expected that your mother would get pregnant after we adopted you. We'd been trying for years, perhaps it was because there was no pressure any more. That's what they say happens sometimes, don't they . . .?'

Vogel let Eytan Vogel's words wash over him, in the distance. He'd known. He'd already known, but having it confirmed on the phone, from three and a half thousand miles away, by the only father he had ever known was an extraordinary moment in his life.

Automatically, he began to reflect on what he'd already learned from this, so far, brief conversation. Adam was the natural son Eytan Vogel had longed for, so what did that make him, David? Not the much desired firstborn, that was for sure.

Another thought occurred to him.

He had stopped listening to his father and interrupted him anyway.

'Dad, am I a Jew?'

'Of course you're a Jew, David. We brought you up a Jew. You were circumcised. You had your Bar Mitzvah, didn't you? What more could we do?'

'So my birth parents were not Jewish?'

'Uh no. But that doesn't matter David. You're a Jew all right.'

'Right. Goodnight, dad.'

Vogel ended the call before his father, or the man he had always thought was his father, could say any more.

Mary stood anxiously by Vogel's side. She looked at him enquiringly.

'I'm not even a Jew,' he whispered. As a little boy he'd sat listening to Eytan's stories of their family history, the good and the bad, the relatives who had died in the Holocaust all over Europe, those who had escaped and forged new lives – as Eytan, one of Germany's kinder transport refugees, had done. Vogel had mourned and rejoiced at these tales of his Jewish heritage, but the heritage was a lie. The Jewish relatives were a lie, even his own father was a lie.

'Is that what Eytan said?' Mary queried.

'No, he said I'd been circumcised and had my Bar Mitzvah, that I was a Jew all right.' Vogel spat the last words out.

'Well that's true, isn't it?'

Vogel shook his head slowly, still taking it all in.

'Mary, I have no religious beliefs. Jews are a race, first and foremost, that is my ideology, you know that. Being Jewish was my birth right and it's always been very important to me. I have always been proud of being a secular Jew. Somebody who has thought through the dogma of The Torah and rejected it, yet would live and die by the ideology of his race. By definition you can't have secular Anglicans or Baptists or Muslims or even Buddhists. I could never practice any religion and I do not believe in any kind of God. I thought I was a Jew by blood, that I'd been born a Jew. I never had any reason to doubt that, but I wasn't born a Jew and I don't have the faith. So what kind of a damned Jew does that make me?'

The phone call to his father and the subsequent revelations weighed heavily on Vogel. After a largely sleepless night, he was in a thoroughly bad mood when he left for work early the next morning.

He tried to put the extraordinary and highly disturbing turn of events in his personal life to one side and concentrate on the day ahead. But he had his final report on the Melanie Cooke case to compile and he was not happy about that either.

In spite of the apparently unquestionable forensic evidence, Vogel remained unconvinced that a satisfactory conclusion had been reached. His mood darkened with every paragraph that he wrote. At home, and now at work, he found himself becoming overwhelmed with a feeling of helplessness, a vague awareness of events spiralling out of his own control.

And that was not usual for Vogel.

He was finally nearing the end of the report, around noon, when Hemmings strode into his office with news of a case that had just been referred to the major crime unit from CID at Trinity Road.

'I need you to finish up the Cooke case and take this one over as soon as possible,' said Hemmings. 'Young Thai woman found dead in a flat in St Pauls. Smothered in her bed. At first they thought it was a domestic with an oriental twist.'

Hemmings smiled at what he apparently thought was some kind of a joke. Vogel obligingly stretched his features into something vaguely resembling a smile back.

'You know anything about it, Vogel?'

'I knew it had happened, and I saw something on the news, boss,' he said. 'Been too busy with the Mel Cooke case to take much notice. Anyway, the inference was that it was a domestic which would be cleared up pretty quickly.'

Hemmings grunted.

'Actually, it seems there's more than a bit of a mystery about it and Trinity Road have been doing some digging, with interesting results. The landlord found the body, three days ago now, after a neighbour reported a smell on the landing. He couldn't raise his tenant, a man who'd said he wanted the place for his new wife while his own house was being done up, so he used his own keys to get in. Forensics reckon the woman's been dead going on two months.'

'Right,' said Vogel, trying desperately to refocus his train of thought. 'So, everything surely points to the man who rented the flat, doesn't it? Husband? Boyfriend?'

'Indeed. Only he doesn't seem to exist.'

'What?'

'Well, he paid cash in advance for six months, so, as you can imagine, the landlord didn't do a lot of checking. The man was seen in a rental car and Trinity Road have already managed to track that down. He used the same name to rent the car that he gave the landlord, Richard Perry, which checked with an apparently valid driving licence. He paid by credit card in the same name. He returned the car about a month later, at night, parked outside the rental place and stuck the keys through the letter box. He left no paper trail worth mentioning. All internet banking, set up with falsified ID, an accommodation address, everything is pretty much uncheckable. The Trinity Road boys are pretty sure he's built a totally false identity.'

'How?' Vogel suspected he knew the answer and Hemmings confirmed it.

'Obviously Trinity Road have tried everything to trace this Richard Perry and the only person they can find so far, who's details check out, died as a boy. It's the old Day of the Jackal trick again. Hard to be believe it still works, though you have to be a pretty smart cookie to get away with it these days, which it's pretty certain this character is. He's clever and the attack was premeditated, it would seem. Anyway, he now seems to have disappeared off the face of the earth.'

'I doubt that, boss. He'll be out there somewhere. What about the Thai woman? Do we know much about her yet?'

'Well, her name was Manee Jainukul, she came here thinking she was going to marry a man she met through an internet dating site. Not a lot of family, they've only just found a sister back in Thailand.'

'You said she'd been dead two months. Did nobody in Thailand raise the alarm when they didn't hear from her?'

'Ah, I said he was a clever bastard, didn't I? He must have taken her phone after he killed her. The sister continued to receive texts and emails from her. She even got one after the body was discovered.

'There's something else too. According to the sister he didn't call himself Richard Perry, Manee knew him as Saul. She didn't even know his last name until she got here. Crazy eh? You travel half way round the world to marry a man and you don't even know his full name.'

Vogel muttered his agreement.

'Did she tell her sister his last name, or alleged last name?'

'Apparently the sister said she thought she did, but couldn't remember it. She had just been told Manee was dead though, so she would have been in shock and she doesn't speak any English. Trinity Road have only been able to go through the Thai police, but I know they've been asked to talk to her again.'

With some reluctance, Vogel completed his report on the Melanie Cooke murder and began to study the files on the murder of Manee Jainukul.

SAUL

'd never wanted to hurt Manee. I'd never intended to kill her. Honestly I hadn't. I'd so wanted her to be my wife, really I had, and to give me the family life I'd always hoped for. It had never been my intention to hurt her. She'd been my last hope after all, that's how I'd thought of her.

But she hadn't been what I'd expected, not at all the way Thai girls were supposed to be. Or not the way I thought they were supposed to be, anyway. It wasn't my fault that she had been so difficult, questioning everything that I did and criticising me all the time. She hadn't been any different to the English girls I'd known.

Indeed, towards the end, she'd begun to remind me of my ex-wife. When I tried to have sex with her, all I could see was that pale judgemental English face I had grown to hate many years ago.

My dream Thai bride eventually began to openly mock me, when I failed in my desperate attempts to enter her – no longer so compliant – little body. Just as my ex had done. Or that's how it seemed to me.

That had been the beginning of the end, I suppose.

Even then, I don't think I ever planned to kill her. More than anything, I just wanted her to shut up. The night it happened, after I'd failed yet again to perform, she actually laughed at me. I told her to stop, but she didn't. She had a high-pitched trilling sort of laugh. A very annoying laugh.

I shouted at her. It made no difference.

I grabbed a pillow and held it to her face. She stopped laughing then. I slackened my grip on the pillow. She pushed it from her face with her skinny, little arms and started to scream, which was even worse. I flung the pillow back over her face and lent on it with all my strength, pressing it into her, filling her nose and mouth with it, so that she struggled to breathe.

She beat on my back ineffectually with her little fists, but after a bit she stopped doing that. I felt her go limp beneath me. I lifted the pillow from her face. Her eyes were wide open and she lay quite still. She was definitely dead.

I had become desperate to find a way out of the hole I'd dug for myself but I hadn't planned to murder the girl. Honestly, I hadn't. I could hardly believe it had been so easy. That she had died so quickly.

I was in an even bigger hole now, of course. Or was I? I wasn't sure. Maybe I would get away with it, I'd always got away with everything before. It all went quiet for a bit. They didn't find her body for a long time; I'd banked on that and on the trail going cold. Even then, it was a while before the press cottoned on to it not being just another domestic.

The Thai bride found dead in a Bristol flat and the way in which she had died, did eventually hit the papers and the TV news, as it had to. But they didn't even know who I was, not really. The police announced that they were looking for a man who had used the name of Richard Perry, but had been known to the dead woman as Saul. They put out a call for anyone who might know him or might have had dealings with him to come forward. This man might be able to help them in their inquiries, they said, and everyone knew what that meant.

It seemed likely that they would have already gone into the dating website I'd used, but found that I hadn't posted a picture of myself. I supposed that ultimately they would unearth the picture I'd emailed directly to Manee, the same doctored picture I had used before with Sonia. But that could take some time, as I had deleted all emails sent between Manee and me and cleared the records as best I could. In any case, I was pretty sure that it didn't look enough like the real me for anyone to recognise me from it.

Sonia would recognise that picture of course, but not the real me.

The landlord I'd rented the flat from and the chap I dealt with for the rental car, would already have been asked for a description of me, I assumed. However, most people, in my experience, are not very observant.

All the same, as I went about my day to day business, I began to wonder if people were looking at me curiously. Perhaps trying to work out where they had seen me before. It was almost certainly my imagination. Someone would have reported me already, wouldn't they? I would have been investigated.

I wasn't though. I couldn't understand how those around me could be so blind. They were stupid. They had to be stupid, compared with me anyway. I was going to get away with it again. They had nothing on me, not the real me. They couldn't touch me.

TWENTY

V ogel took the call just before lunch, the following day, his first day running the investigation into the death of the young Thai woman in St Pauls. He knew he wasn't operating on full power, as half his mind was still with the Melanie Cooke case.

'How are you, you old bugger?' asked Nobby Clarke.

Vogel's spirits rose at once. He both liked and respected his former boss from the Met and one of his greatest regrets at leaving London was that he would no longer be on Clarke's team. He thought the Detective Superintendent was one of the best police officers he had ever worked with.

'All the better for hearing from you, boss,' he responded truthfully.

'I'm not your boss, Vogel,' said Clarke, speaking with exaggerated patience.

Vogel smiled into the phone. It was well known between the two of them that he had never been able to call Clarke anything other than boss and never would be able to. Even though he knew well enough that the DS preferred informality.

The problem was that, in spite of the unlikely nickname, DS Clarke was a woman. A damned good-looking woman at that, Vogel thought. Tall, blonde and elegant. He didn't even know what her real Christian name was and neither did anyone else. Clarke, for whatever reason, and in common with a famous television detective, had always kept it a closely-guarded secret.

And, in spite of her frequent invitations to do so when they'd first worked together, Vogel certainly could not bring himself to call her Nobby.

'Right Vogel,' Clarke continued, after only the briefest of pauses. 'Something's just landed on my desk, which I thought you might be interested in.'

Vogel knew she would not have called for chat, they didn't have that sort of relationship, and that she would cut to the chase straight away. The DS was not one for small talk. Unless she got on the Scotch of course, then she could be quite garrulous.

'There's a connection with a case in your patch,' Clarke continued. 'Are you involved in the Melanie Cooke murder at all?'

Vogel felt his pulse quicken.

'I'm deputy SIO,' he said. Then he corrected himself. 'Or I was, it's done and dusted now, boss. DNA match with the father. He's been charged. We announced it yesterday.'

'I know,' replied Clarke. 'But I'm afraid I may be about to rock your boat, Vogel.'

'I'm hanging on to the sides,' said the DI.

'We've been looking into the suspicious death of a male teenager found in a Soho hotel a month ago,' Clarke continued. 'He died of strangulation, that much was abundantly clear from the start. We don't know yet, though, whether his death was murder or an accident. Have you heard of asphyxiaphilia?'

'I don't just do crosswords, I compile them, boss,' replied Vogel.

'Yeah.' Clarke knew that well enough. She sounded totally unimpressed. 'Not a term that fits naturally into the crossword section of our own dear Daily Telegraph, Vogel.'

'I also read the news pages, boss. Fits in there. It's a deliberate partial strangulation, using a cord – or often a belt – tightened around the neck. It reduces the amount of oxygen to the brain during sexual stimulation, heightening the pleasure of orgasm. Dangerous old game. Michael Hutchence, the INXS singer, was found hanged in a hotel room in Australia amid rumours of auto-erotic asphyxiation. That's the same practice solo, during masturbation. The coroner delivered a suicide verdict but the auto-eroticism theory was backed by Hutchence's wife Paula Yates, who said he would never have deliberately killed himself.'

'How come you manage to sound like an anorak even when you're talking about sex games?' asked Clarke.

'Sorry, boss.'

Clarke grunted acknowledgement.

'Anyway, you are absolutely right, of course,' she continued. 'The assumption here was that this was a sex game gone wrong. Asphyxiophilia is particularly prevalent among certain sectors of the gay community. Our lad had clearly been indulging in some pretty extreme sex with another man. Forensic found signs of quite violent anal sex. The sexual partner was nowhere to be seen, when the body was discovered by a maid in the morning. Like I said, we are not sure yet whether the death was murder or an accident. But my own hunch is murder, the boy's hands were tied in front of him with some sort of dressing-gown cord and there was a belt around his neck. He was in a kneeling position when he was found, but lying on his side. The belt had been pulled so tightly through the buckle, that his neck protruded all around it. I reckon it must have been held in place by somebody pretty strong until he died. I also reckon the whole thing was too violent to have been a sex game that went too far; there'd been no attempt to loosen the belt around the boy's neck or untie the bonds around his wrists. Mind you, if it was a deliberate killing, we are dealing with some cool murderer here. DNA all over the place. Fingerprints too. He used a condom, but he left it in the bin in the bathroom. Arrogant bastard. We have his sperm, for God's sake.'

'Intriguing,' said Vogel, but he couldn't let his brain dwell on it. He really couldn't. He had another case of his own now. He was already having trouble enough moving on from Melanie Cooke, then he remembered Clarke's opening gambit.

'I don't see what it could have to do with the Cooke murder, though, boss?'

'I'm getting to that, Vogel. You're ex-Met. I'm sure you know about our DNA backlog. Everything has to be prioritised. A gay boy found dead in a hotel room is pretty low priority round here. My personal hunch that it could have been murder didn't count for much under the circumstances. This place is still full of homophobes and mysogynists. We didn't get the DNA back til this morning. My lot wacked it into the national data base and hey presto, there was a direct match with the DNA found on Melanie Cooke.'

Vogel couldn't believe his ears.

'What? That doesn't make sense. The murder of a schoolgirl and the death of a gay man during a sex game just don't match at all. It can't be the same perpetrator. How could it be?'

'People can be bisexual you know, Vogel.'

Vogel thought for a moment.

'When did you say you found that dead boy?'

'Nearly a month ago.'

'Well, I suppose that, technically, Terry Cooke could be your killer,' said Vogel reluctantly. 'Melanie died a week ago now and we didn't arrest her father until four days later, after we got our DNA results back, just a tad quicker than yours.'

'Stranger things have happened, Vogel. Remind me how old the girl was, will you?'

'Fourteen.'

'Well our boy is only eighteen. Not quite paedophilia territory, but perhaps your man just likes 'em as young as he can get 'em and of either sex.'

'Perhaps, but we have no evidence of that. We investigated big time whether or not Cooke had been abusing his daughter on a regular basis, but we found nothing to suggest that. Although the girl's clothes were ripped and there were bruises around her breasts and her vagina, there was no sign at all that sexual intercourse had taken place. Indeed, she was a virgin, apparently. The favourite theory is that Cooke killed her out of frustration at her behaviour, because she was running wild and didn't want to know her dad any more. Then he tried to make it look like a sexual assault, but he couldn't bring himself to actually have sex with her.'

'She wouldn't have bruised if she was already dead, Vogel.'

'Well, maybe at the same time he was throttling her. I don't know, boss. To tell the truth I've never liked this one, but DNA can't lie or so we are told. Only, now you've brought this to the table . . .'

'That'll teach you to boast about compiling crossword puzzles, Vogel.'

Vogel didn't bother to respond to that.

'You are sure about the DNA results, aren't you boss?' he asked. 'Not one of forensics' famous cock-ups is it?'

'Pretty sure, Vogel. In any case, it's all being double-checked as we speak.'

'I just find it hard to believe, boss.'

'Indeed. I suppose you have yet to consider that there could be a famous forensics cock-up at your end?'

'The thought was beginning to occur to me.'

'You'd certainly better do some double-checking too, Vogel.'

'Yep. I guess so.'

'Right, then we should reconvene.'

Vogel didn't respond. He couldn't quite take in what he had been told. He was missing something important, he felt sure of it. And, if he was right, Nobby Clarke was missing something too.

It was the DS who finally broke the silence.

'Are you still there, Vogel?'

'Sorry boss, I was trying to think,' he said. 'By the way, I presume you have an ID on the victim?'

'Yes. His wallet was on the bedside table. Cash, credit cards, students' union card, bus pass and so on all still in it. His phone was there too. We were able to ID him straight away: Timothy Southey. First year student at LSE. He lived with his parents in Clapham. They were told as soon as the body was found. Not by me, thank God. One advantage of a highfalutin, damned desk job. No more death calls. Apparently they didn't even know the lad was gay and still won't accept it.'

'Which hotel was he found in?'

'The Leicester Square Premier Inn.'

'Who booked the room?'

'Our likely killer, he walked in off the street and paid cash.'

'Right. He'd still have been asked for a name at least though.'

'Yes, but he wouldn't give his real name, would he? Registered as Leo Ovid. Doesn't even sound like a proper name. There's not a single Ovid listed in the London phone book.'

'Curious. People giving false names usually use something common, don't they? I know John Smith is a cliché too far, but nothing to draw attention, isn't that the criteria if you're checking into a hotel and you're up to no good?'

'I wouldn't know Vogel,' remarked Clarke in a deliberately neutral tone. 'Not bloody Leo Ovid, though, surely.'

'You've got the boy's phone. Was this Leo listed on it?'

'Indeed. Along with more than one contact number. One of them was just a wrong number and the others were all defunct pay-as-you-go phones.'

'So, no way of tracing him?'

'No, not from that anyway.'

'No doubt you've checked the records. Read his texts? Listened to voicemail? Hasn't that lead to anything?'

'Nope, not really. No voicemail messages and most of the text messages were from Timothy to Leo expressing undying love and trying to arrange a date. The ones from this Leo were all vaguely defensive and there'd been a couple cancelling earlier meetings. The only thing clear to us, was that Leo seemed to be leading our young victim a merry dance, but that's no surprise given what happened. Maybe murder was what he'd intended all the time, who knows. I'll email you a transcript. You can have a look for yourself.'

Vogel thanked her and ended the call. He suddenly had a great deal of work to do.

LEO

I suppose it seems crazy to say that killing him hurt me as much as it did him. But that's the truth, I was quite sure of that. Tim is dead. He is at peace. I now have to live with what I have done and I will never find peace. Never.

I left the hotel in the early hours, hovering by the lift until I was pretty sure the attention of the night staff had been distracted. I had my baseball hat on and was keeping my head down. It was highly unlikely that I would be recognised by anyone or be identifiable on any CCTV footage, but I didn't wish to be spotted leaving in the middle of the night. I thought it might look suspicious and draw attention to myself, even in a Premier Inn in Soho.

It might have been safer, of course, to have waited until eight or nine in the morning, when my leaving would have been camouflaged by other guests checking out. But I couldn't spend the rest of the night in a hotel room with a dead body, could I? And his dead body too. My beloved Tim.

I still do not know quite how I managed to tighten that belt around his neck. It was not a problem for me physically. I am a strong, fit man, but I loved Tim. Truly, I did. In as much as I have ever managed to love anyone, of course.

His death was an ordeal for me too. I had to watch the light fade from his eyes, the colour from his cheeks, as I pulled the belt tighter and tighter through its buckle. He struggled too. He was almost as strong as me, but not quite. I had persuaded him to allow me to tie his hands. All part of the game, I'd assured him.

But, as he began to realise that what was happening to him was no kind of game, he thrashed around with his legs, nearly kicking me in the face more than once. I just managed to avoid contact. At the very least, I would have been badly bruised and that might have been hard to explain away in my day-to-day life.

He made terrible gurgling sounds as he died. I shall never forget those sounds, but I did not allow myself to be deterred from my deadly and unavoidable purpose. I'd switched the TV to radio and tuned into a music station on high volume. To drown the sounds of our love-making, I'd told Tim. He'd smiled and accepted it. He'd trusted me totally, my young lover. In the physical sense, at any rate.

God knows, I hadn't wanted to kill him, but I cannot kid myself that it was an accident, nor even that it wasn't premeditated. I'd planned every bit of it. I'd had to. Tim had got too close to me. He knew about me. He knew who I was. If only he'd been prepared to step back, to stay away from my other side, but Tim was incapable of that. He'd wanted what he called a 'normal relationship'. I didn't have the faintest idea what a 'normal relationship' was. Not with a man or a woman. Not with anyone.

But I knew that, in Tim's case, it represented a huge threat to everything that I was. Everything I had become. I had to remove that threat. I had no choice.

TWENTY-ONE

Vogel went to see Hemmings straight away to bring him up to speed with the news from the Met. The shocked DCI agreed that the Melanie Cooke investigation must be reopened and that Vogel should drop the St Pauls murder case to divert all his energies back to it.

'This could leave us with more egg on our faces than you and I are likely to eat in a lifetime,' muttered Hemmings.

Vogel could only agree.

Supported by Saslow, he spent the rest of that day and most of the following morning re-interviewing Terry Cooke. He was still being held in a police cell at Patchway, awaiting transfer to prison where he would be held in custody until trial. Unless the charge against him was dropped of course, thought Vogel.

When questioned closely about his movements at the time of Timothy Southey's death and whether or not he had ever met the young man and so on, Cooke grew more and more bewildered.

Eventually, Vogel told him about the DNA match with samples taken from Southey's body.

'I don't believe this,' said Cooke. 'It's some sort of fit-up, stuff like this doesn't happen to blokes like me. I've told you, I've never been to any Premier Inn anywhere, let alone one in Soho. I've never even heard of Timothy Southey. I'm not an effin' shirtlifter, for fuck's sake. Anyway, it's bloody simple now, you've got to do another DNA test on me right away. The stupid bastards have got my sample mixed up. That's all it can be.'

Cooke's brief stepped in for the first time then.

'Clearly you should arrange that at once, Mr Vogel,' she said. 'And you should know that I shall also be advising my client to undergo a private and independent DNA test.'

Under the circumstances, Vogel didn't blame her and Cooke's request for a second DNA test hadn't actually been necessary. It had always been Vogel's next move.

Vogel was well aware that mistakes of this magnitude were,

as they used to say in the Met, rare as a silent cabby. But everything about Cooke and the way he dealt with each questioning session was leading the DI to strongly suspect that one had been made in this instance.

DNA was generally regarded as a magic bullet by police forces throughout the world and with good reason, but laboratory error was not totally unknown. If that was what had happened in this case, then Vogel had never had personal experience of anything so major.

He suspended the interview. He and Saslow, accompanied by a uniformed officer, took Cooke around to the custody suite and supervised the second DNA test, taken by the custody sergeant himself. Then they headed back to Kenneth Steele House.

The transcripts of Tim's text exchanges with his probable murderer and the records of phone calls to and from unidentified pay-as-you-go phones, still lay on Vogel's desk. The DI prepared to go through them again, and every report, and every bit of evidence compiled on the Melanie Cooke murder too.

Logic told him that the Terry Cooke DNA match had to be a massive blunder by forensics. The results of the latest DNA test would be at least a couple of days, even though a request had been made at the highest level for fast-tracking. But, until Vogel knew for sure that Cooke's DNA had been a mix-up, he intended to check and double-check every possible detail of Melanie and Timothy's murder cases.

AL

I had waited anxiously, at our appointed meeting place. It was a bar which was always busy, not just at weekends, and where I knew there was no CCTV. I made sure I was there early and bagged a table by the door. I spotted Melanie as soon as she walked in. She looked all around, her eyes searching faces. They swept over my face and onwards. She did not recognise me and I had not expected her to, not from that photograph.

I stood up and took a few steps towards her. Her back was turned to me by then.

'Melanie,' I said quietly.

She swung around to face me, her smile of greeting quickly fading.

'You're not . . .' she began. 'You can't be . . .'

I nodded.

'*You* are Al?'

I nodded again, smiling.

'But . . .' She let the word fade away.

She didn't really need to say anything else.

'I'm Al and I am so pleased to meet you at last,' I said, reaching out to shake hands with her. She ignored my hand.

'You don't look much like your picture,' she responded sharply.

That was an understatement.

'I know, I'm sorry,' I said, trying to sound friendly and reassuring and nothing more. 'Not close up enough and a bit whiskery, I fear.'

'So are you,' she said.

Razor blades for breakfast, I thought. I tried to rise to the challenge.

'I was afraid you wouldn't meet me, if I sent you an up-to-date photo.'

She didn't reply. She looked uncertain and suddenly very young, in spite of the provocative way she was dressed. That reignited my interest, of course. I saw her glance towards the door. I couldn't let her go, not now I was so close.

'Don't leave,' I said. 'Just have one drink.'

'Uh, I shouldn't have come.'

'Yes, you should. Look, I really like you. I'm not so bad am I? Still fit?'

She pursed her lips and half smiled.

'Just the one,' I coaxed. 'What do you like to drink?'

'I'm underage.'

I damned well knew that, didn't I? That was the whole point.

'So have you never had an alcoholic drink, then?' I asked in a teasing voice. 'Not even an alcopop?'

She bristled.

'Of course I have,' she said. 'And wine, well, just once or twice.'

'So is it an alcopop then?' I persisted.

'All right.'

'Any particular flavour?'

She shrugged.

'How about blackcurrant? I'm told that's very nice.'

She nodded.

I led her to the table by the door, where I'd been sitting before and where I'd left my pint of lager. It was as far way from the bar as possible. I didn't want the staff questioning her age. From a distance, dressed the way she was, she could pass for late teens. I hoped so anyway. I went to the bar to order, keeping one eye on her as best I could, just in case she decided to leave. Not that I had any idea how I was going to stop her, if she simply stood up and went. I could hardly wrestle with her in a busy bar. I would just have to hope for the best.

I ordered the alcopop and a double vodka shot. As soon as the barman's back was turned and making sure that Melanie couldn't see what I was doing, I tipped the vodka into the glass of alcopop.

I hurried back to our table. She hadn't left, that was the first hurdle over with.

She sipped gingerly at her drink. I took a big swallow from my previously untouched glass of beer.

'Go on,' I said. 'Take a proper swig. It won't bite you.'

She did so. This was encouraging, I thought.

I was good at talking to kids. Men like me always are. The trick is to be ever so interested in them and totally sympathetic. She'd already told me quite a lot about her life and, like so many teenagers, she wasn't happy with it.

'I can understand how hard it must be for you, living with your stepdad, you know,' I said. 'I had a stepdad. I hated him.'

She smiled.

'Jim's all right really,' she said. 'But he's so strict. He's stricter than my own dad. It's like he's trying to control me all the time and I just think, yeah, right, who are you, anyway, ordering me about like that?'

'Of course,' I said. 'That's exactly how I felt.'

She finished her drink quickly. That pleased me.

'Just one more?' I asked.

'I shouldn't,' she said.

But she did. And had another. Each time I added a double vodka shot to her alcopop. Once I'd got her going, she couldn't stop talking. It was like our online exchanges, only more. She gave me the run down on her entire family, her school, her school friends, everything.

The colour rose in her cheeks. Her eyes brightened. She was halfway through her third drink and a detailed account of a disastrous family holiday the previous summer, when she said she had to go to the loo. I hoped she wasn't going to be sick, but I didn't think she would be. Not yet. I didn't care what happened to her later, after I'd finished with her.

I watched her carefully, as she walked across the room. She already seemed unsteady on her feet. If she wasn't she soon would be. I was going to make sure of that. I nipped to the bar while she was away and ordered another shot, which I swiftly poured into her glass. What a cocktail she now had.

I listened, apparently intently, to more of her silly, childish ramblings, whilst she finished her, now heavily doctored, alcopop.

Then I suggested we leave.

'Perhaps you'd like to eat something?' I asked. 'I know a really good restaurant down the road.'

She giggled.

'Whatever,' she said.

Her eyes were becoming glazed. I had to help her to stand. I needed to get her away from this public place, before her condition became noticeable and unwanted attention was drawn to us.

I wrapped one arm around her and steered her outside. She was giggling quite uncontrollably now and when the fresh air hit her she leaned more heavily against me. I adjusted the position of my hand. I could feel the shape and warmth of a firm, young breast beneath my fingers. I had her. Surely, I had her. The question was, what to do with her?

I suppose I hadn't really thought I would get this far. I don't know if I had even intended to get this far. I had no idea where I was going to take her. I hadn't made a plan. I couldn't take her to a hotel, a kid with an older man, and certainly not in that state. Clearly, I wasn't going to take her to my home. I had vaguely considered driving my car to our assignation, but I was afraid of CCTV. In any case, I knew I would need a drink to steady my nerves. I had never done anything like this before. Well, not quite like it.

So it was really down to a kind of beginner's luck that I found myself in this position. I hadn't expected the silly girl to get quite this drunk this quickly. I suppose I might have done, if I'd thought about it. After all, she wasn't likely to be a hardened drinker at fourteen, even in this day and age and I'd been pretty liberal with those vodka shots. But I'd imagined her becoming mellow and compliant, not out of her head.

I was wearing a hoody, albeit a rather trendy one, I thought. I now pulled the hood up, and kept my head down as I helped her along the street. Actually, I had to half carry her. I knew what I ought to do next. I ought to just prop her in a doorway or something and do a runner. Anything other than that was so dangerous. But my fingers had found their way inside her flimsy little top. I began to squeeze a small hard nipple. She didn't protest. I'm not sure if she even noticed.

That other side of me, the side I so often fail to control, began to take over.

I could feel my erection rising and the gnawing, urgent desire take a hold of me.

Her head lolled against my shoulder, her eyes were rolling, the pupils were very big, but she smiled up at me. Or at least I think it was a smile. I leant towards her and kissed her on the lips, thrusting my tongue inside her mouth.

She didn't actually respond, but neither did she protest.

Nobody took any notice. This was Bristol's hinterland, a part of the city where it was perfectly usual to see couples walking about, entangled with each other and often one, or both of them, unsteady on their feet. I knew there was a network of shadowy alleyways and cul-de-sacs behind the bars, pubs, restaurants, and providers of sexual titivation, which lined Old Market Street and West Street.

I led her into Stone Lane.

I'd once followed a couple up this cobbled cul-de-sac late at night and watched them have full sex against a wall. A knee trembler, I think they call it. I like to watch. I have already said how much I like to watch. That had been an older man and a girl who'd been little more than a kid, not a lot older than the way I like them. Rough around the edges, though, and probably drugged up. I thought she'd almost certainly been on the game.

They hadn't seen me. I know how to conceal myself.

I pushed Melanie against the same wall, pulled up her skirt, tore at her knickers and her puerile, already torn tights, opened my fly, lifted her, wrapping her legs around me and prepared to enter her. I had to be quick. Unfortunately, if I am not quick I am inclined to lose the ability. I still have the inclination, but I can only maintain an erection with a woman for seconds, when it comes to actually trying to do something with it. When I am just watching my erections seem to last for ever, achingly so, because I so rarely reach a climax.

It was at that moment that she sprang to life and began to fight me off. Perhaps she wasn't so drunk after all. Her hands and arms were flailing. She went for my head. I was afraid she might catch me with her fingernails, leaving me with scratch marks on my face or neck, which would be difficult to explain away. I reached to grab her arms. Before I could do so, she started pulling at my hair. I jerked my head away and finally managed to fasten my fingers around her wrists. I smashed her arms back against the wall above her head. She began to scream. I fastened my mouth over hers, which only partially shut her up. She began kicking out with her legs, which seemed to cause her pelvis to move around against me. I found that exciting. But I had to silence her, so I punched her in the face.

She went a bit limp again. Her arms fell to her side. I was able to release her arms then and use my hands to hold her legs around me. The fight had further aroused me. My erection had grown even harder. I tried to manoeuvre myself into her and, of course, as soon as I did so, my penis began to shrink. I had hoped that this time, with a young girl and under these circumstances, I might have been able to keep going, but no. I stepped back, disentangling myself.

Then, just as I was about to zip myself up and do a runner, she started to speak. She only seemed to be able to remain upright with the help of the wall and her voice was slurred, but she knew what she was saying all right.

'You can't even manage it,' she said. 'Are you a poof?'

Her eyes had dropped to my shrunken penis. She was mocking me. I couldn't believe it. She was only fourteen. I remember thinking, yes, fourteen going on forty, and surely she realised the danger she was in, but she didn't even seem to be afraid. Perhaps she was past that or just too drunk and confused to respond normally. She smiled at me, a smile as mocking as her words. She raised one hand and crooked her little finger.

Then she giggled.

It was the last straw.

I threw myself at her, wrapped my fingers around her neck and squeezed.

PART TWO

TWENTY-TWO

Vogel was at his desk continuing to puzzle over the baffling turn of events, when the results of the second DNA test on Terry Cooke dropped.

They were, as Vogel had more or less expected, totally different to the first results. The foreign DNA, extracted from the hair follicles found in Melanie Cooke's fingernails, did not match the new sample taken from her father's at all. It did, however, match DNA taken from the crime scene of murdered Timothy Southey in London, as the Met's forensic people had already reported.

No further match had been found with this DNA on any national data base so far, although forensics would continue to search. Meanwhile, there was no doubt at all that somewhere, somehow, there had been a catastrophic error. Terry Cooke was almost certainly innocent and an extraordinary double murderer was still at large.

Vogel knew that the first thing he must do was to inform his superior officer. He decided he would knock on Hemming's office door unannounced. There was no easy way of doing this. Vogel was expecting a fairly unpleasant confrontation and he was not to be disappointed.

Hemmings was not a man who often swore or raised his voice. He was a thoughtful, measured policeman. He had no time for the ranting and raving looked upon as par for the course amongst many senior officers of his generation.

On this occasion, however, Hemmings hit the roof and his language was blue.

'For fuck's sake, Vogel.' He roared. 'How could this have happened? It's a total cock-up. This force is going to look like a bunch of incompetent idiots. I have absolutely no choice but to order the immediate release of Terry Cooke and get all charges against him dismissed. Not only that, I'm going to have to reveal to the general public that there is some kind of weird monster out there somewhere.'

'Don't shout at me, boss,' remarked Vogel mildly. 'I don't run forensics.'

'I'd like to fucking get hold of whoever does – *or fucking pretends to*,' stormed Hemmings.

After a brief pause, he continued in a more reasonable tone of voice.

'There can't have been a cock-up at this end, Vogel, can there?'

'I don't see how, boss,' replied the DI. 'Terry Cooke's DNA was taken at Patchway custody suite in the usual way. Properly packaged and dispatched, I even sent Willis along to oversee it and make sure everything went smoothly.

'Forensics must have got Terry Cooke's sample mixed up. I can't think of anything other explanation. I know there is supposed to be every precaution in place and it would be highly unusual, but it wouldn't be the first time it's happened. They'll deny it, of course.'

'They can deny all they fucking like, but heads are going to roll over this, Vogel, and I sure as hell do not intend one of them to be mine.'

'No sir,' murmured Vogel formally. 'Will that be all, sir?'

'For the moment. Just sort this bloody mess out as soon as, Vogel, do you hear?'

'Yes sir,' said Vogel, who was already halfway out of the door.

Back in his own office, he called in Willis and Saslow to give them the bad news.

'I can't believe it boss,' said Willis. 'How could a mistake like that have happened?'

'There'll be an inquiry of course,' said Vogel. 'Meanwhile, we can only start from where we are and it pretty much means starting again, but this time with even more cards stacked against us. We'll be liaising with the Met, but they've got bugger all themselves, so far.'

'Are we going back to regarding Al the paedo as our number one suspect then, boss?' asked Saslow.

'He could be our only suspect, certainly our only lead, however weak,' Vogel replied morosely.

It was nearly ten at night. The DI was exhausted and bewildered. He had little of his usual energy. He was having to push himself, but he couldn't even face the walk and the train journey home. He asked if there was a squad car free to take him to Sea Mills, something he almost never did. Vogel didn't think tax payers should be paying to get police officers home. Particularly not police officers who were stupid enough never to have learned to drive. He believed squad cars had rather more important purposes, but on this occasion, he gave in to his total weariness of mind and body and asked for a ride home.

His mood, driven both by his personal and professional dilemmas, was blacker than ever by the time he arrived. It felt as if his entire life was in a mess. The Melanie Cooke case was in total disarray and the revelation that he had been adopted continued to torment him. Then something else happened, the very rarity of which made it all the more horrible. He had a row with Mary. A nasty silly row, which was entirely his fault.

She began to ask about his day, ready to listen and to support him like she always did. He bit her head off.

'Can't you see I've had enough,' he snapped. 'I'm living and breathing this damned case and now there's been a major cock-up, which I'm likely to get the blame for. Do you think I want to bring it back here with me?'

'Well, you usually say how much it helps you to talk things through with me,' Mary began reasonably.

'Well not this time. You should be able to bloody well tell.'

'Really?'

Mary was a good woman, totally supportive of her husband and an exceptionally reasonable and understanding wife. She was not a saint.

Vogel caught the note of icy warning in her voice, but didn't care.

'Yes, bloody *really*,' he stormed. 'I'm dog-tired. I just want to sleep, for a week if I could.'

'David, stop taking this out on me, do you hear?' Mary shouted back. 'Now. Right now. You're going too far.'

'Taking what out on you, for God's sake?' Vogel muttered.

'You know very well what. The Melanie Cooke case may be a nightmare, but you can always cope with your work. Always. What you can't cope with is learning that you were adopted and that you weren't even born a Jew. And you aren't going to cope with it until you come to terms with it.'

'Indeed? As easy as that, is it? And what do you suggest I do about it?'

'I never said it was easy. What you do is your business, but sweeping the whole thing under the carpet isn't going to work. Perhaps you should at least get in touch with your sister and your birth mother. Maybe arrange to meet them. You never know. It might help.'

'Might it? Well, if you're so bloody wise why don't you bloody well do it. I'm too busy for any of this. I'm in the middle of a murder inquiry which has gone totally pear-shaped.'

'Fine. I might just do that. If that's what you really want, I'll call them tomorrow!'

'You know what Mary, I don't care what you do about my bloody birth mother and my bloody half-sister. I'm too tired to care. I just want to go to sleep and I'm sleeping right here.'

He pointed at the sofa.

Mary said nothing more. She simply headed for their bedroom in silence.

Vogel curled up on the sofa as he had threatened, wrapping himself in his coat.

It was not the first row Mary and David Vogel had had in their marriage, but it was the first ever to end with them sleeping apart.

TWENTY-THREE

The next morning, Vogel remained more than a little preoccupied with the events of the previous evening. This was most unusual for him when he was working and on such a major case, especially one so disturbing in so many ways. He had just decided that he would call Mary and try to put things right, when his desk phone rang. His mind was still largely on Mary as he answered it.

'Vogel,' he said absent-mindedly.

Within seconds, his whole body language changed. He sat bolt upright in his chair, clearly listening intently.

'My God,' he said. 'That's extraordinary.'

Then he added: 'Right. Yes. It gets curiouser and curiouser, indeed.'

He spoke for a few minutes more, before replacing the phone in its holder, then he called Willis and Saslow into his office.

'I've just had a call from Bob Farley at Trinity Road,' he began. 'He's now leading the team over there on the Thai girl murder case. They've just had the DNA results back. Another direct match. Actually two direct matches – with both the DNA taken from Tim Southey and from Melanie Cooke.'

'Jesus,' said Willis.

'Are they sure they've got it right, boss?' asked Saslow.

All three knew that was a rhetorical question. A mistake within forensics on the scale they had witnessed was not going to happen twice, let alone three times.

'So, boss, we are looking for just one perpetrator for all three murders,' said Saslow.

'It would seem so.'

'But they're so different. I mean, you'd come up with a totally different profile for each, wouldn't you?'

'Yes.' Vogel concurred. 'Firstly, we have someone whose target was a gay man. But, from what we know, Tim Southey's killer is a homosexual himself, as there was plenty of evidence of sexual activity. We don't know for sure how Southey met him, but the lad did have gay dating apps on his phone. Secondly, we have a killer who murdered a young Thai woman. One whom he had contacted through the net, allegedly with a view to a long-term relationship. The woman apparently thought she was coming here to marry him. Meanwhile, our third killer is a paedophile weirdo, who also met his victim through an online dating site. So, besides the DNA matches, the use of dating websites is the only thing we have so far that might remotely link the three killers. If it really is one man, then that's extraordinary. It's quite unheard of.'

'Presumably there are no other DNA matches on record?' queried Saslow.

'No,' Vogel agreed. 'No matches and our perpetrator clearly knows there won't be. He has not exactly been careful about avoiding giving us samples. Although, if the paedo is the same man who's been staking out primary schools he always kept his stolen vehicles free of prints for some reason. Habit maybe. Or just good paedophile practice.' Vogel stretched his lips into a humourless smile.

'He's an arrogant bastard, all the same,' muttered Saslow.

'Or just confident,' offered Willis.

'Let's hope to God he's overconfident, Willis,' responded Vogel. 'We need him to trip himself up, because right now we are going nowhere with this investigation.'

'That's what usually happens in the end, isn't it, boss?' commented Saslow.

Vogel grunted.

'I'm afraid there's nothing "usual" about this case, Dawn,' he said. 'There's something else that's odd, too. The bastard's choice of names. Trinity Road just heard from Thailand again. When Manee Jainukul's sister was interviewed a second time, she remembered this Saul's last name. Homer. Saul Homer. And we also have Leo Ovid. Both of possible classical derivation.'

Willis and Saslow looked blank.

'You two need to read more. Ovid, the Roman poet? And Homer, the Greek author?' Vogel sighed. 'Look them up. And let's feed all this new information into what we have compiled already.'

After a brief silence, Vogel continued. 'Willis, get the whole team checking and double-checking everything. You can brief them. You know as much as I do. I need to think all this through.'

Willis nodded his understanding.

After the two officers had departed, Vogel tried to do what he did best: study and assimilate. But he couldn't put his personal dilemma out of his mind; the awful and completely needless row with Mary lurked on the fringe of his thoughts, blurring his focus. He shook his head and looked at the names again: Leo. Al. Saul. Surely there had to be significance in the choice of the unlikely names of Homer and Ovid, he thought, both with that classical association? But the significance evaded him. Until things were set right with Mary, Vogel knew he wouldn't feel right in himself.

Vogel called Mary then, told her briefly what was happening and apologised for the night before.

'I can't believe I behaved so badly,' he said. 'I'm so very sorry, sweetheart.'

'I'm sorry too,' Mary responded at once.

'You didn't do anything,' he said. 'I just took everything out on you, just like you said.'

'It's all right,' she said. 'It really is, David.'

He had known it would be, of course. Nonetheless, he breathed a sigh of relief.

'Oh, and by the way,' Mary continued, 'Eytan called this morning, soon after you left.'

Vogel thanked her for telling him. They both knew he was far from ready to return the call. He was also far too busy. Vogel was about to say goodbye, when Mary suddenly said,

'I was just thinking about the names you mentioned: Leo Ovid and Saul Homer and how you thought that they must be connected in some way. You don't suppose that your killer likes word games just as much as you do, David?'

That turned on a switch in Vogel's mind, which – now his argument with Mary was behind them – was suddenly clearer than ever. Vogel said a hasty thanks and a swift goodbye to Mary. He couldn't wait to follow up her idea.

Like many compilers of crosswords, Vogel was a classicist and more than moderately familiar with ancient literature. He knew that Homer, the legendary writer of *The Iliad* and *The Odyssey*, was often considered to be the father of Greek mythology. Then there was Ovid, an important mythographer of the Virgil and Horace era. He felt so certain that those names hadn't been picked at random. The two surnames held a direct link to ancient mythology and perhaps that was the biggest clue. Homer and Ovid were writers, they were creators of characters. Maybe what Vogel needed to look for was a mythological character with some, yet to be revealed, relevance to all that had happened.

He began scribbling the names on a piece of paper, jumbling them up, transposing letters. He kept thinking about what Mary had said: might the killer also like word games? As a crossword compiler, he was an expert juggler of letters and words. He played with all five names at first – an awful lot of letters, even for him. Then he separated the last names from the first names. He got nowhere with Homer and Ovid, so he started to concentrate on Al, Leo and Saul. He felt quite sure there was an anagram there somewhere.

He delved into his memory, dredging the very depths of his knowledge of ancient literature. Eventually something jumped out at him.

He turned to his computer and went into google. The results took just a moment or two.

Vogel leaned back in his chair and closed his eyes. Oh my God, he thought. Could this be possible? Leo, Al and Saul. The whole thing was unbelievable.

After just a few seconds he forced himself back into action. He printed out a couple of pages and reached for his phone to call Hemmings, then thought better of it. This needed to be done face-to-face. On the way through the incident room, he asked Willis and Saslow to join him.

They followed at once and he could feel their eyes on his back, as he strode purposefully along the corridor to Hemmings's office. Vogel was excited and, at the same time, in a state of some shock. He could feel beads of sweat forming on his forehead and his trembling hands were clutching the freshly printed pages.

Hemmings was on the phone when Vogel poked his head around his office door and asked if he could see him for a minute. Immediately, the DCI ended his call and beckoned Vogel and his two lieutenants in. Hemmings had realised immediately that something momentous was afoot.

Vogel knew he was blinking behind his spectacles as rapidly as he ever had in his life. He couldn't help it. He feared that what he was about to say was going to sound crazy, so much so that he wasn't sure he could deliver it with the required conviction.

'We are looking for just one man, for three very different murders,' he began. 'The DNA results have made that virtually irrefutable. The thing is, what I think I have discovered is, that our perpetrator actually thinks he is three different people. Indeed, he lives his life as three different people.'

'You're losing me, Vogel,' responded Hemmings. 'What possible evidence do you have for that?'

'Not evidence exactly, sir, but either I'm right or we have a pretty unbelievable coincidence. I've been playing with the names the bastard's been using, jumbling up the letters and that sort of thing. At one point I removed the duplication. The names Leo, Al and Saul, contain two As and three Ls. So by removing two Ls and one A, I was left with the letters LEOASU.'

'And so?' enquired Hemmings.

'Well I tried looking for anagrams, any combination of all, or some, of those letters that might make a word, or rather a name. One combination forms the word Aeolus. It even uses all the letters. AEOLUS. And it hit me straight away. I was focusing on some kind of connection with ancient mythology – because of the last names our killer had used, Homer and Ovid – and I remembered, or half-remembered anyway, who Aeolus was. I mean, it's pretty unbelievable, but . . .'

'Vogel, get on with it,' instructed Hemmings.

'Yes sir.'

Vogel looked down at the Wikipedia printout in his hand.

'"*Aeolus, a name shared by three mythical characters, was the ruler of the winds in Greek mythology. These three personages are often difficult to tell apart and even the ancient mythographers appear to have been perplexed about which Aeolus was which.*"'

Vogel lowered the printout and looked directly at Hemmings. 'It was Aeolus who gave Ulysses a tightly closed bag containing captured winds, so that he could sail easily home on a gentle, easterly breeze. But his men thought the bag was filled with riches, they opened it and unleashed a hurricane. And Homer relates that story in The Odyssey, his masterpiece.'

Vogel paused, waiting for the response of his fellow officers. Saslow was the first to speak.

'Well, our man has certainly unleashed a hurricane and he may not have finished,' she said. 'It's crazy all right, boss, but I reckon you might be on to something.'

'S-so you actually think the bastard believes he is three different people, boss?' Willis enquired haltingly.

'I think we are probably dealing with someone who is suffering from multiple personality disorder or dissociative identity disorder, as it is more usually known nowadays. His transition from one self to another is not always voluntary and when he is in one identity, he may have no memory of the others, or not all of them anyway,' said Vogel. 'That's my basic understanding of this condition, but this would be a particularly extreme case.'

Hemmings looked stunned.

'Well one thing's for certain,' he said. 'We can't afford any more mistakes on any of this. To start with, we need an expert medical opinion, Vogel.'

'Yes boss. I was about to suggest that. There's a trick cyclist in London, who Nobby Clarke called on in the aftermath of the Sunday Club murders. She's a chum of Nobby's, big in the world of criminal psychiatry. Our killer there had a personality disorder too, but nothing like this, though.'

'All right. Well, get on with it then, Vogel. Try for a meet today, if you can. DCS Clarke will be the one to fix that for you, then, won't she? And let's keep this between ourselves, shall we, until we know a bit more.'

'OK, boss.'

'Meanwhile, we carry on looking for Al, Leo Ovid and Saul Homer as if they are three different people. I don't see what else we can do.'

'OK, boss,' said Vogel again.

He led Willis and Saslow towards the door.

'So, if you're right, which would be his real self, then boss?' asked Saslow as they stepped into the corridor. 'Saul, Al, or Leo? And how do we know?'

'I have no idea, Saslow,' replied Vogel. 'Maybe there's even another self.'

'What? Aeolus, you mean?'

'Good point, but no, as well as Aeolus. Look, we have no other record of any crime where his DNA has been found. So maybe our man has been living an apparently normal life outside his three, or four if you include Aeolus, alter egos.'

'Surely nobody could do that, boss,' said Willis.

'I have no idea what this bastard can and cannot do,' replied Vogel. 'He certainly doesn't seem to do limits. If I am right, there is only one thing we know for absolute certain about him: he's mad. Quite mad.'

TWENTY-FOUR

Vogel called DS Clarke straight away.

'Boss, I think I've got something here, but I need help to sort it out,' he said. 'Do you remember that trick cyclist, the one you got to help us tie up the loose ends after the Sunday Club murders, Freda something or other?'

'Do you mean Professor Freda Heath, per chance, Vogel, arguably the most distinguished criminal psychiatrist in the country?'

'That's the one, boss. Could you arrange a meet, soonest?'

'Perhaps, if you were a little more respectful, Vogel.'

'Sorry, boss. Look, I think I may have sussed out something about this raving lunatic we're both after, but I need to be sure I'm not going barmy myself. Can you fix a meet today?'

'Vogel, you don't half push it. It's two thirty in the afternoon already and you have to get here from Bristol. Freda's NHS. Do you expect her to drop everything?'

'I hope you will persuade her too. Yes. We've got three deaths between us already, boss, and barely a clue to go on.'

'She'll want to know where you're coming from, Vogel.'

'Of course.'

Vogel briefly explained his hypothesis. When he'd finished there was a brief silence before Nobby Clarke spoke again.

'So you think our man has, at least three, separate identities and may also believe that he is a figure from Greek mythology. Is that about it?'

'Yes, boss.'

'You don't think this is a theory that may be just a tad off the wall, do you, Vogel?'

'The whole thing is off the wall, boss, but it's all we've got. Anyway, that's why I need to talk to your trick cyclist. Sorry, I mean Professor Heath.'

Clarke let that pass.

'I'll call you back,' she said and, without another word, ended the call.

Ten minutes later she was back on the line.

'Freda says even NHS doctors have to eat. She'll meet you and me both for an early dinner. Six o'clock at Joe Allen. She's giving a talk to the Royal College of Psychiatrists at eight and will need to leave around seven thirty. Don't be late.'

'I won't. Will you be able to stay on? I want to pick your brains more about the Timothy Southey murder and generally compare notes.'

'Vogel, what time did you leave home this morning?' asked Clarke obliquely.

'About a quarter to six. What's that got to do with anything?'

'And you'll be lucky to get home much before midnight. You don't change, Vogel, do you? Can't imagine how your missus puts up with you. You're like a dog with a bone.'

'And you're not, boss?'

'Ummm, maybe, but I don't have a missus.'

'Really, boss?'

'You're so pushing it, Vogel.'

Vogel smiled. DCS Nobby Clarke was notoriously protective of her privacy in many more respects than just that of her name. Nobody in the Met knew anything worth knowing about her private life. There were the usual rumours amongst the good old boys that she was a lesbian, but based more on the fact that she had rarely been spotted with a man, other than a colleague, and always turned up to police functions alone.

In spite of the banter, she was and would always be something of a mentor to Vogel. He welcomed the opportunity of discussing everything with her, almost as much as getting the opinion of an eminent psychiatrist.

'By the way, Joe Allen, that sounds familiar.'

'I'm quite sure it does. You'll be able to find your way all right, I expect.'

'I will indeed, boss.'

He caught the 3.30 p.m. train from Bristol Temple Meads by the skin of his teeth and arrived at Joe Allen in Covent Garden at five minutes to six. He paused briefly outside, remembering his association with the restaurant, known as Johnny's Club at the time, during the Sunday Club murders. Vogel hadn't been there since that investigation. It looked much the same as he remembered it. The same theatrical billboards and photographs. The same piano, albeit with a different, female pianist, wearing a hat.

He was the first to arrive and shown to the table in the far corner, where a plaque commemorating Sunday Club remained on the wall. Clarke and Professor Freda Heath arrived a couple of minutes later. Freda Heath was very tall, very black and very beautiful. She was also very clever and at the top of her profession, which, of course, was the only thing about her which really interested Vogel.

Hands were shaken and greetings exchanged. They quickly ordered drinks and food.

'I asked for this table,' said the DS, waving one hand at the Sunday Club plaque. 'Holds a few memories for us, eh Vogel?'

'Some I would like to forget, boss,' said Vogel.

'We solved the case, that's the main thing.'

Vogel nodded. He would have preferred to have solved it a lot more quickly, before so much damage was done. Now, he was becoming desperate for the Tim Southey, Melanie Cooke and Manee Jainukul murders to be solved, before anyone else was hurt or killed.

'I hear you have a rather intriguing theory for me,' interjected Freda Heath.

'The boss has filled you in then?' Vogel asked, Freda nodded. 'So, am I just as crazy as I believe our killer to be, or does any of this make any sense to you at all?' asked Vogel.

Freda Heath nodded again.

'It does make sense,' she said. 'And it's possible that this could be an extreme representation of Dissociative Identity Disorder. But you may not be aware, David, that there are a number of highly esteemed figures in my profession who don't even recognise its existence.'

'Really? I've done some internet research and I would have thought there were far too many case histories on record for any expert to totally dismiss it.'

'Not totally, perhaps, but it is a reasonable argument to dismiss DID when used as a defence in criminal law as nothing other than a legal ploy. And there are definitely examples of that having been the case in the UK and to a considerably greater extent in the States and then there is the Iatrogenic factor.'

Vogel raised his eyebrows questioningly.

'Cause and effect,' said the professor. 'It has often been alleged that the wide publicity given to people of suggestive personality, combined with the credulity and enthusiasm of therapists . . .' Freda Heath allowed herself a wry smile. '. . . has been responsible for at least a proportion of those claiming to suffer from DID.'

'But you don't go along with that? You believe in DID?'

'Whether or not I go along with the Iatrogenic factor depends on the circumstances,' said Freda. 'There is little doubt it plays a part. But in my opinion, the Iatrogenic factor can detract from the genuine cases out there. Even I am cynical about anything in psychiatry that cannot be clinically proven but, over the years of my work at The John Howard Centre, I have no doubt that I've dealt with several, absolutely genuine and involuntary cases.'

Vogel realised he had no idea what The John Howard Centre was, and neither could he exactly recall Freda Heath's position in the NHS.

Nobby Clarke came to the rescue.

'Freda's professor of Personality Disorder for The East London Trust, and The John Howard Centre is their medium security hospital out at Homerton,' she said. 'I've been there. Trust me. There is unlikely to be any condition of the human mind which hasn't been seen at the John Howard.'

Vogel was thoughtful.

'You referred to "totally genuine and involuntary cases,"' he began. 'Does that mean that someone with DID has no control over which personality they become at any given moment? Because I am not sure how our man could have continued to function, if that is the case.'

'Sometimes they can maintain a certain control,' Freda explained. 'They have their own ways of keeping an unwanted, alternative identity at bay, for example. If they are with people, they may make an excuse like a visit to the bathroom, or feeling ill if more time is needed, in order to prevent an involuntary intrusion.'

'How long can someone keep up this business of being several different people?'

'Much longer than you would think.'

'Is there always a dominant personality, one which takes precedent over the others and maybe has some control over the others?'

'More often that not, yes. What we usually talk about is a host. In the case of your man, whom you believe to have several unrelated identities, Saul, Leo and Al, possibly Aeolus too, there is probably a host. Your subject's behaviour patterns indicate that there is a secretive side to all three of these characters. This secrecy was perhaps obligatory with Al the paedophile, but not necessarily so with the other two, before they turned to murder.'

'But isn't the host Aeolus?' asked Vogel.

'I doubt it. Complicated as this sounds, I would say Aeolus is the driving force. The personality your man aspires to be, rather than the host. We can assume that he has been going about his day-to-day existence in an apparently normal way for a considerable period of time, perhaps years. This doesn't quite fit with being a Greek mythological hero. No. I suspect that there's an unrelated host; someone who appears to be totally normal.'

'So it's the host we should be looking for?'

'Yes. I would say that's correct.'

'Any idea what sort of person might host these disparate characters?'

Freda shrugged.

'I'm afraid not,' she said. 'It's often someone who does not draw attention to themselves. He almost certainly lives alone, because it would be difficult to hide something this complex from anyone you lived with, be it a lover, a relative, or even just a flat mate. He probably avoids making friends too. But he would also contrive to appear pretty normal. It is quite possible that he holds down a job, even a responsible job.'

'Anything else?'

'Well, clinical research shows that DID patients describe severe childhood abuse, physical or sexual or both. Your subject has probably experienced some kind of major trauma but, of course, you wouldn't know that.'

'So are the different personalities aware of each other?'

'Each would have its own memories, behaviour patterns and preferences, including sexual preferences, but none would have access to the memories and thought processes of the other. The host must be aware, to some extent, of the existences of these secondary identities. But when another identity takes over the host, it's usually involuntary, as I explained earlier, though some hosts can develop ways of control, up to a point. However stress and, most importantly of all, an event or incident which could be seen as a threat to one of the identities, is likely to bring that identity to manifest itself.'

'So where would Aeolus come into this?'

'Ummm, a complication, but not unknown. In the case of your subject, it seems likely that the host, almost certainly subconsciously, loathes and has contempt for his alternative identities. But not Aeolus, it is Aeolus he reveres and aspires to ultimately become.'

'Where does that lead us?'

'Well, if someone with DID actively seeks to become a certain personality, they won't be able to control that indefinitely. Extreme pressure or stress will bring Aeolus to the forefront. He will take over and your man – the host – won't be able to stop it. Ironically, the closer you get to him, the more likely it is that he will succumb to his own involuntary subterfuges and believe that he has become Aeolus.

And that, DI David Vogel, is when your killer will get really dangerous.'

Vogel called Hemmings from the 21.15 back to Bristol. The commuter rush was well over and the train was quiet. Vogel was easily able to find a secluded corner, where he wouldn't be overheard. He related his meeting with Professor Heath as quickly and accurately as he could.

'Basically she backs up my theory, boss. I know it probably sounded far-fetched when I came into your office today, but it does make sense. The DNA evidence means it's virtually indisputable that the same man was responsible for all three murders. I don't think there's any other feasible explanation.'

Hemmings remained silent for several seconds.

'Neither do I, Vogel,' he said eventually.

Vogel waited for Hemmings to continue. He understood the senior man's reticence. The next step presented clear risks. It could leave the entire Bristol MCIT team open to ridicule.

'OK, we have to go public with this now, without delay,' said Hemmings.

'I'm sure that's the right thing to do, sir,' responded Vogel.

'Yes,' agreed Hemmings. 'I still don't like it, but we have no choice. The only hope we seem to have of finding this man is through the media and the public. I shall call the Chief Constable straight away.'

'Yes, boss.'

'We now have a picture of the bastard by the way. A photo he emailed to the Thai girl. He'd deleted it and tried to remove all traces of it from his own email account and hers, but the tech boys finally unearthed it.'

Vogel felt a frisson of excitement.

'What does he look like, boss?'

'A pretty ordinary Joe. I'll send it to you.'

'Thanks.'

'Oh and David . . .'

Vogel stiffened. In their almost two-year association, Vogel could count the number of times Hemmings had addressed him as David on the fingers of one hand.

'Well done. Nobody else in the force would have come close to this.'

Hemmings ended the call, leaving Vogel thinking that his superior officer was not wrong about that: which meant that the consequences of going public with the Aeolus theory, whatever they may turn out to be, now rested on Vogel's, not particularly broad, shoulders.

TWENTY-FIVE

A press conference was held at the Avon and Somerset Constabulary's Portishead HQ at 11 a.m. the following morning. It was hosted by Hemmings, as SIO, with Vogel and the force's senior press officer, Jennifer Jackman, by his side.

Willis and Saslow were also present, as Vogel's first lieutenants, in case he wished to refer to them, but they hadn't been asked to sit on the platform.

Vogel suspected that Hemmings may have been hoping this would be one of the conferences the Chief Constable might choose to host himself. But the CC, like most of his rank in modern policing, had become rather more a politician than a policeman. He excelled at covering his own back more than anything else, in Vogel's opinion.

Hemmings, however, gave no sign of any discomfiture he might be feeling and did a more than competent job. He ran through the basic details of the three murders, then revealed that DNA evidence pointed to the same perpetrator in every case. There was a stir of increased interest in a briefing room packed almost to capacity.

On the instruction of the CC, Jennifer Jackman had already indicated that there'd been a sensational development suggesting a strong link between the cases of Timothy Southey, Manee Jainukul and Melanie Cooke. Journalists known to be closely following these cases had been contacted directly. Almost all of those in attendance were experienced crime reporters representing local and national television, and mainstream local and national written press. They understood about profiling and modus operandi. They were as surprised by the DNA evidence as Vogel and the MCIT team had been.

Hemmings turned to Vogel to explain his theory of Dissociative Identity Disorder. Vogel hated doing this sort of thing, but he couldn't avoid it. It was his convoluted brain that had come up with the Aeolus theory and it was only logical that he should be the one to pass on his thinking to the world at large.

By the time he finished the air of quiet excitement and anticipation had turned into near bedlam. The press photographers and news cameramen pushed forward, thrusting their cameras into Vogel's face. Many of the gathered journalists rose to their feet and started to shout out questions. Others were clearly already filing copy.

Jennifer Jackman called for order.

'Neither DI Vogel nor DCI Hemmings will say anything more nor take any questions until everyone calms down,' she said.

'Please take your seats and if you have a question raise your hand.'

Jackman succeeded in her plea for calm, to a degree, but her reward was merely a sea of waving arms.

'Question for DI Vogel,' began the correspondent from BBC Bristol. 'Are you really telling us that we are looking for one man, who thinks he has at least four personalities including a figure of Greek mythology, Detective Inspector? Could you clarify that for me please?'

Bedlam turned to hush.

Vogel blinked rapidly behind his spectacles. He reckoned he would prefer to pull his own teeth out, rather than face the great British press on a charge.

'Well yes, that's about it,' said Vogel.

'Do you have any medical evidence to back this theory up?'

'We have taken advice from a senior criminal psychiatrist, yes, which led us to decide to make this announcement this morning.'

'So do we have three different motives then, as well as three different identities within the same perpetrator? Is that what you are saying, Mr Vogel?'

That was a concept Vogel had considered, but he had so far been unable to come to a properly thought-out conclusion.

'Until we apprehend this man and can acquire detailed psychiatric reports on his state of mind, I'm afraid we cannot comment on his motivation,' he said.

'Exactly how do you plan to apprehend him, DI Vogel? I mean, isn't he really little more than some kind of fantasy figure?'

'Not exactly, we do have a photograph of our suspect,' Hemmings interrupted.

The DCI waved a hand at Janet Jackman, who had her laptop open in front of her. She tapped the keyboard and a large image of the photo emailed to Manee Jainukul flashed up on the big screen above the platform.

Vogel turned to look at it. He'd already pored over the photo on the train as soon as Hemmings had emailed it to him the previous evening and again when he got home and again that morning. He had a feeling that face was vaguely familiar but then, he'd spent so much time looking at it he supposed it would be.

'The experts tell us this image has been heavily Photoshopped,' said Hemmings. 'We have no idea how alike it is to our suspect – whom we believe to be Saul Homer, Leo Ovid, and Al – but it's the best we've got. Please use it to help us find him. He is highly dangerous.'

The media went ballistic.

AEOLUS

I wasn't quite sure what I felt when I watched the news and read the TV reports. In a way I was proud of the attention. Who wouldn't be? My story led the news on every TV bulletin and I was splashed all over every front page. My picture was everywhere, well, the picture they thought was me. It was the same on the net.

Of course, I knew the story was a captivating one. A damned good yarn, the press boys would say. I particularly enjoyed headlines like POLICE PUZZLED AND BEFUDDLED BY TRIPLE KILLER . . ., MYTHICAL MURDERER MAKES MOCKERY . . . and THREAT OF THE THREE-IN-ONE FIEND . . .

I was, of course, aware that merely by working out what I was, the forces of the law had put me at greater risk of discovery. Detective Inspector David Vogel was clever for a police officer, there was no doubt about that, but not as clever as me. I wasn't too worried.

The media asked one question. The same question.

'Who is Aeolus?'

I am Aeolus. I am not the pathetic creature whose picture the police released. I'd used and doctored that picture, for my own ends. It barely resembled me. Nobody would recognise the real me from that picture.

I am Aeolus. I am the ruler of the winds. I have powers the likes of which DI Vogel can only ever dream of.

TWENTY-SIX

The results of the press conference wildly exceeded anything Vogel had ever experienced. Even the coverage of the Sunday Club murders in Covent Garden, which had attracted extensive media attention, paled into insignificance compared with this.

It was approaching mid-morning the following day and Vogel was still trying to get to grips with the sheer enormity of public response to the massive media onslaught, when his phone rang. Bill Jones, the duty sergeant at Trinity Road – the police station which covered the St Pauls district, where the body of Manee Jainukul was found – sounded unusually animated.

'Woman just walked into the front office here. I think you should see her personally, sir,' said Jones. 'Claims she had an internet relationship with your Saul. Got a feeling about this one, sir.'

'You've talked to her yourself?'

'Briefly, sir.'

'All right,' said Vogel.

He respected Sergeant Jones and was pretty sure the man wouldn't bother him directly with anyone likely to turn out to be a nutter. If Jones thought this woman was worthy of Vogel's personal attention, then she almost certainly was.

But, for once, even Vogel didn't dare leave his office. He really had to remain at the hub of the investigation of which he was DSIO. Hemmings was not going to stand for anything else.

'Look, there's no way I can come over to you,' he told Sergeant Jones. 'Would this woman be prepared to come here, do you think, if you got a uniform to drive her?'

Sergeant Jones replied that he reckoned that could be arranged.

Miss Sonia Baker arrived less than half an hour later. Vogel had her brought straight to his office. She was now sitting opposite him, a fair-haired woman, probably in her late thirties, just a little plumper than she might like to be and well dressed, in a rather old-fashioned sort of way. Discomfort oozed from every pore of her body. A handkerchief was clasped tightly in her left hand. She looked as if she may have been crying.

Vogel introduced himself, offered Sonia Baker coffee or tea and tried to do everything he could to make her feel less ill at ease. The woman attempted a weak smile. He noticed that her lips were trembling, but he needed to start questioning her swiftly in order to ascertain whether she really was the genuine article or just another time-waster.

'Could you please begin by telling me what you told Sergeant Jones at Trinity Road,' he said.

Sonia, in spite of being so upset, related clearly how she had met Saul Homer on line, through *marryme.com*, how they'd corresponded in detail for some time and had eventually arranged to meet.

'And you are sure it's the same Saul Homer we are now looking for?'

'Oh yes. Well, it's an unusual name, of course, but that's not it. As soon as I saw the picture on the TV this morning, I recognised him at once. It's the same photo he posted on *marryme. com*. It's not there now though, I checked. But I have a print-out.'

Sonia Baker reached into her handbag, removed a sheet of A4 paper and put it on Vogel's desk. Vogel glanced down. The bespectacled face, which had been haunting him for a day and half now, was before him. It was the same Saul all right.

'So did you ever meet him, Miss Baker?' he asked.

'No, he didn't turn up, you see,' said the woman 'I stood on the railway station at Bath like a total idiot. He was supposed to be arriving there from Swindon, where he said he lived. I looked all along the train he was supposed to be on. I even thought I saw him. There was this man who was about to step out of one of the carriages and then turned away and went back in. I thought it was him at first. There was definitely a similarity, although it might just have been that he was wearing tinted glasses like Saul's. I caught a glimpse of him again, looking out of a window. Straight at me, I thought, but he wasn't my Saul, obviously. My Saul never arrived. I waited for the next two trains from Swindon. We'd spoken on the phone a couple of times. He had this quite gentle voice, with the hint of a rural Wiltshire burr. I thought he sounded so nice. What a fool. I couldn't phone him from the station. He said he'd lost his phone, a lie obviously. I realise now how stupid I was, but he seemed to want all that I wanted. He must have told the same sort of story to this poor woman from Thailand. It still upsets me, which is ridiculous really because I could be dead, couldn't I, Mr Vogel? I could have been another victim. It all fits.'

'If you are right and I suspect you are, then I think you may have had a very lucky escape indeed, Miss Baker.'

Vogel asked the woman if she would make a full statement and she agreed to do so at once. He said he would arrange for someone to go through the procedure with her and asked her to accompany him to reception. In the corridor, they met Willis and Saslow, clearly on their way out.

Vogel asked Sonia to wait a moment and took Saslow to one side.

'I need a word with you two, where are you off?' he asked.

'They've had a walk-in at Avonmouth nick. Character who claims he's Aeolus.'

'Ah, the first and almost certainly not the last.'

'I know boss, but apparently he's pretty convincing. Hemmings wants us over there pronto, just in case.'

'All right, Saslow, let me know how you get on.'

Saslow hurried after Willis, who had barely paused and was virtually out of the door. Typical, thought Vogel, not disapprovingly, Willis was always completely focused on the job in hand.

Sonia Baker took a step towards the DI and touched his arm lightly.

'Mr Vogel, who were those people?' she asked.

Vogel told her.

'Then you are probably going to think I'm crazy, Detective Inspector, but I have something to tell you.'

As soon as Sonia Baker left, Vogel picked up his phone to call Saslow and Willis. Then he put it down again.

He had questioned the woman thoroughly and the more he'd questioned her, the clearer it seemed that she was not entirely sure of the quite startling information she had given Vogel. Indeed when the DI had suggested that she make a formal statement on the matter she'd declined at once.

'I wouldn't like to do that, not until you have checked it out and tried to discover whether it might be possible or not,' she said.

She could be letting her imagination run away with her, Vogel told himself.

But he'd seen, many times, how a clever barrister can destroy a witness in a court of law; making someone, who had previously been quite sure of their evidence, seem inept and full of doubt. He'd always thought that sort of lawyer to be too clever by half, and maybe that's how Vogel himself had just been behaving to Sonia.

On the other hand, Sonia Baker had said that she couldn't be sure, not absolutely sure, anyway. Then again, Vogel had never been the kind of policeman who would only believe what he wanted to believe. He was a meticulous man, who made sure that he or his team checked and double checked every lead, however obscure. However unlikely. However ridiculous.

And this was ridiculous, surely.

Quite ridiculous.

He should certainly do a little elementary checking before alerting others. He didn't want to be guilty of a false alarm on a matter of this enormity.

It was always a good idea to check dates and opportunity before wreaking havoc. To at least discover if a possible suspect had a solid alibi, like being aboard an aircraft in the middle of the Atlantic or picked up on CCTV at the other end of the country. He switched on his computer and called up a file, which would give him the information he needed.

Involuntarily, he raised one hand to his lips. It was as he'd feared. He knew his breathing had quickened. So far, everything matched. He was pretty sure of that. But it couldn't be. It just couldn't be.

He made himself take extra special care. He knew he must be as sure of himself as humanly possible before proceeding. He closed the file and opened another containing the Met's report on the murder of Timothy Southey in London, sent over by Nobby Clarke's team.

He needed to double-check that the dates matched.

They did.

Vogel leaned back in his chair and closed his eyes for a moment. An occasional habit when under stress or in shock. He clasped his hands and rested them on his chin. His palms were clammy.

He told himself it could still be nothing. All of it. On the other hand, he thought, better safe than sorry.

He sucked in a gulp of air, filling his lungs, then he leaned forward and picked up his phone again to call Dawn Saslow.

AEOLUS

I knew the net was closing in at last. I suppose it was inevitable. Even so, it was probably a stroke of silly, bad luck that was going to bring me down, rather than any mistakes I had made. The events of the last few minutes had been disturbing; an unlucky coincidence that could destroy me. I might get away with it, yet again, or I could be wrong. It may not have mattered at all. I told myself to stay calm.

I was the one who would have to clean up the mess that Saul left behind in his foolish wish to meet Sonia. But, no matter, I was strong. I was clever. I could handle this. I'd handled everything else, after all. I controlled the winds. I could whip up a hurricane. I was all powerful. These people would never understand me. Never get close to me or be able to guess what I was capable of. They would never get inside my head.

I had always known, I suppose, that I would have to reveal myself one day. Show them who I was. I was proud of what I was capable of. Proud of what I had done right under their foolish noses. In some ways, I wanted it out there. I wanted the world to know who I really was. And there were people in my life I would quite relish bringing down with me too. Smug bastards who thought they were smart but, compared with me, they were stupid.

So it annoyed me immensely that they could now take credit for having brought me down. I had always imagined that I, and only I, would decide how and when to show myself. That I would reveal myself on my own terms, as I pleased and right now I wasn't ready. Not yet.

I had to remind myself that it still might not happen. Not any of it. They had all repeatedly shown how slow they were. How clumsy their thought processes were. I told myself I was quite likely to continue to get away with it. They could not unmask me. I was Aeolus. I governed the winds. I governed a force that made all the sources of power and energy created by man look as pathetic as they really were.

It was at that moment that the phone rang.

TWENTY-SEVEN

Saslow was mildly surprised at Vogel's instruction, not least because the DI was overriding a direct order from DCI Hemmings, but she wasn't in any way alarmed. That's how it was with policing. People kept changing their minds, particularly senior officers, it seemed to her.

'I need you and Willis back here sharpish,' said Vogel. 'Something urgent has come up.'

'Right, boss,' said Saslow. 'Are you sure you don't want us to check out the Avonmouth Aeolus first? We're nearly there.'

'I said it was urgent,' snapped Vogel. 'Please don't argue with me.'

'I-I wasn't, I mean, uh, sorry boss,' said Saslow, stumbling over her words.

She was surprised and curious. This wasn't like Vogel. He was almost always measured and quietly spoken.

'Who's driving?' asked Vogel

'Willis,' replied the detective constable. She was really curious now.

'Are you in his car?'

'Uh yes, it was parked right outside, so . . .'

'Of course,' responded Vogel.

Saslow felt he was making an effort to sound as if everything was fine, when it wasn't. Whatever he wanted her and Willis for, was something major, no doubt about that.

'All right, well ask him to turn around soon as he can and get back here, OK?'

'OK boss, will do,' said Saslow.

She was aware of Willis glancing at her sideways.

'What was all that about?' he asked, turning his attention to the road again.

'The boss wants us back straight away,' Saslow told him. 'Said something urgent has come up.'

'Did he say what it was?'

'Nope. Think it's something big though. He practically bit my head off when I suggested we check out this alleged Aeolus first. After all, it was Hemmings who dispatched us . . .'

Saslow paused, suddenly aware that Willis had made no effort to find a place to turn around or even to slow down. In fact, he seemed to have speeded up.

'Come on, John,' she said. 'We'd better get back there. The boss is in no mood to be messed about, I can tell you. In any case, I want to know what the hell is going on.'

'Of course,' said Willis. He aimed a smile at her, began to slow down and swung his vehicle into a side street, which appeared to lead only to a row of deserted lock-ups.

'This will do,' he said, putting the car into reverse.

Saslow was still musing about Vogel's manner.

'He sounded really stressed out,' she said. 'I've never heard him quite like that . . . just can't imagine what's got him going. He's usually so bloody cool . . .'

They slowed to a halt. Willis switched off the engine.

'For God's sake, what are you doing now?' asked Saslow.

'I think I need a slash,' said Willis.

'Well hurry up then . . .' began Saslow.

She managed no more words. Willis's fist caught her full on the right side of her head. It was a good punch. He was a fit man and he'd trained as a boxer, earlier in his police career. Saslow wasn't knocked unconscious but she was stunned.

By the time she became fully aware again, she realised that Willis had used his handcuffs to fasten her hands behind her back, then pulled her seatbelt tight around her. Too tight. Her hands and arms were twisted uncomfortably. She was aware of shooting pains in her shoulders and her chest. It felt as if she could hardly breathe.

She began to shout and struggle, kicking out at the man she'd thought was just another colleague. The one she spent the most time with.

'Stop that,' Willis commanded. 'If you do not stop I will kill you, here and now. If you do as I tell you, there is a chance that you might live. I have no wish to hurt you. I am not a common murderer. I need to protect myself, that's all.'

His voice was very calm.

Saslow was afraid she was going to be sick. She'd heard and used the expression sick with fear, but she didn't think she'd ever really understood what it had meant before now. She stopped struggling. She would do as she was told. Maybe he was going to hold her hostage. She had been trained for hostage situations but nothing, she thought, could ever prepare you for the real thing. The very thought of it terrified her even more, but she guessed it was her best chance of survival.

She stared at him. The man she knew only as DS John Willis. His eyes were dead and his lips were contorted. His voice sounded different. The tone was deeper than usual and he spoke with the hint of an accent she could not quite recognise. It could have been Greek, or perhaps Latin. Although Saslow, like most people, had never heard much Latin spoken. She wondered how she could not have seen something in that face, heard something in that voice before to make her at least suspicious of John Willis But she never had.

'You are Aeolus,' she murmured.

It was not a question, just a statement of fact, which she now accepted with a terrible, clear finality.

'I am.' He hissed the words at her, his face close to hers. 'I am the ruler of the wind. I can dictate the direction the world will take. I can be whomever I want and I can do what I want, just as I have always done. You cannot stop me. No one can stop me.'

His eyes were quite mad. Dawn could not understand how he had been able to hide his obvious insanity so well that neither she, nor Vogel, nor anyone else had suspected anything. How could they have missed it and for so long?

His words were those of a madman too. A madman who had killed three times. At least three times. How many more times might he have killed in his crazy mixed-up life, she wondered?

Her mouth was dry. Her throat was dry. There had previously been frightening moments in Dawn Saslow's time as a police officer, but she had never before experienced blind terror.

So this was what it felt like.

Almost involuntarily, she began to scream. The uncontrolled wailing of a creature suddenly aware that it is in mortal danger. A sound common to all living things.

He hit her again in the side of the head. It was an even more powerful blow than before.

Afterwards there was nothing.

TWENTY-EIGHT

Sonia Baker had told Vogel that she thought it was Willis she had seen at Bath railway station, the day she had gone there to meet Saul.

'He's the man I thought was my Saul, I'm almost sure of it,' she said. 'The man who nearly got off the train, then seemed to change his mind. There wasn't much resemblance to the photograph he'd posted online, but there was something about him. And then there was the way he peered along the platform, as if he were looking for someone. Our eyes met. I was convinced I saw recognition in them.'

Already shocked, Vogel had pressed her, pressurised her even, and it was then that she had said she couldn't be certain.

'Not a police officer, surely?' she'd queried. 'I mean you work with this man, Mr Vogel. How could it possibly be him?'

'I don't know, Miss Baker,' Vogel had replied. 'I certainly hope you are mistaken, I know that.'

'Well, I probably am,' she said then. 'After all, surely you'd know if someone you were close to was capable of such terrible things. We'd all know, wouldn't we?'

'Well, we'd all like to think we would,' ventured Vogel cautiously.

'Yes,' said Sonia Baker. 'Yes, of course. Oh, take no notice of me, Mr Vogel. I'm just a silly woman approaching middle age still looking and hoping for love. I get everything wrong.'

But Vogel had taken notice, and his antennae had begun to waggle, even though he didn't really want them to.

The first file he had looked at on his computer, just after his conversation with Sonia, was the attendance record of MCIT officers. He then double-checked that his immediate suspicions were correct. Timothy Southey had been murdered at the Leicester Square Premier Inn on the same day that Willis had so apologetically requested leave, because his younger child had been taken ill and rushed to hospital. And Vogel clearly remembered Willis going home with a migraine on the day that Melanie Cooke was killed. An excuse to disappear because he could not control one of his identities perhaps, a scenario presented by Professor Heath.

None of this was conclusive and Vogel sincerely hoped he had summoned Saslow and Willis back to Kenneth Steele House quite unnecessarily. It could all still be coincidence and he could be quite wrong in his suspicions.

He decided to call Willis's ex-wife, now Mrs Vera Court, before alerting DCI Hemmings. Fortuitously, she remained listed as Willis's next of kin. She was the mother of his children after all and luckily retained an unchanged mobile number.

Vogel opened the conversation by asking if her children were well.

'Uh yes, very well, thank you,' Vera had replied. 'But why are you calling Mr Vogel? Has something happened to John?'

'No, no,' Vogel reassured her, thinking to himself that, really, he had little idea what may or may not have happened to John Willis.

'No, nothing like that,' he continued. 'It's just that I need to check something. Has your son been taken to hospital recently?'

Vera Willis giggled in a nervous sort of way.

'Our Sam? Fit as a flea, that one. Can't remember when he was last ill and he's never been to hospital in his life. Oh, except when he broke his toe playing football, but he wasn't kept in or anything . . .'

She paused.

'What's this all about, Mr Vogel?'

'Oh, I'm just checking out attendance records here, that sort of thing,' Vogel responded, trying to keep his voice light. 'About a month ago, John suddenly asked for leave, because your son had been taken to hospital. He said it was very serious and he needed to be there. Do I take it that wasn't the case?'

'Absolutely not, Mr Vogel.'

'Was he with you at all around that time?'

Vera Willis laughed, more genuinely this time, albeit with some irony.

'I can't remember when I last saw John, Mr Vogel,' she replied. 'He's not visited the kids in years, rarely bothered since we parted. I doubt he'd turn up, even if one of them was rushed to hospital. I doubt it very much. He pays his child maintenance regularly on a direct debit, always has done. But he made it pretty clear, years ago, that was it as far as he was concerned. He would do his legal duty until they were eighteen, but he wanted nothing to do with any of us.' She paused. 'What's he done, Mr Vogel? What's that bastard done?'

Vogel was surprised at the bitterness in her voice and the note of resignation.

She spoke again, before he had chance to.

'Nothing would surprise me,' she said. 'You should know that. I've always thought there was no limit to what he might be capable of.'

'Why do you say that, Mrs Court?'

'I lived with him didn't I? I had his children. I'm not sure John has ever allowed anyone to get to know him, really get to know him, but if there is anyone in the world who does, then that would be me.'

Vogel felt his nerves jangle as the woman spoke.

'Come on, Mr Vogel,' she continued. 'Anyone who's lived with a copper knows DCIs don't check on attendance records.'

She was right there, thought Vogel, but he couldn't tell her any more, not yet.

'Look Mrs Court,' he said. 'I'll not insult your intelligence. It is possible that John may be involved in something very serious. But I'm not sure yet, so, for the time being, I can't discuss it with you and certainly not on the phone. I wonder, you couldn't pop along to Kenneth Steele House later on today, could you? I wouldn't ask you if it weren't important. Also, by the time you get here I should know more.'

'You're beginning to frighten me, Mr Vogel.'

'I'm sorry. I can assure that's not my intention. Indeed, it is still quite possible that I might be wasting your time.' Vogel paused and took a deep breath. He no longer believed what he was saying. It was both extraordinary and terrifying, but everything was leading to Willis. 'Could you make it in about an hour?' Vogel continued. 'I could send a squad car to pick you up, if that would help.'

'No. I'll drive myself. The last thing I want is a cop car pulling up around here. I'm fairly free during the day, as the kids are at school, but I shall have to be back well before three, when they get home.'

'We shouldn't keep you long,' said Vogel, who actually had no idea at all whether that was true or not.

'All right. I'll see you in an hour or so.'

'I'm most grateful, Mrs Willis,' responded Vogel. 'There's just one thing more. Please make no attempt to contact John directly. This whole matter is highly delicate and highly confidential. So please don't try to phone him.'

'Phone him?' queried the woman. 'I couldn't damned well phone him, even if I wanted to. Bastard changed all his phone numbers years ago and he's certainly never given me the new ones. He doesn't want me in his life and I can assure you, Mr Vogel, I certainly don't want him in mine.'

Vogel put the phone down with Vera Court's voice ringing in his ears. What she had told him made it even more likely that Sonia had been right and that her online suitor had been a disguised Willis. Or, if Vogel's Aeolus theory was correct, a Willis alter ego, which was far more frightening. Not only was there evidence that Willis had lied about his whereabouts at the time of Tim Southey's death, but Vera Court's view of him, of a man who she thought had "no limit to what he might be capable of," shed a disturbing new light on Willis's character. Vogel reminded himself that husbands and wives often had low opinions of each other after an acrimonious break-up. None the less, this, on top of the accumulating evidence against Willis, led him to accept that an urgent investigation into the detective sergeant was now called for. And the time had come to make a full report to DCI Hemmings.

Vogel just hoped he had done the right thing, in attempting to quietly recall Saslow and Willis. But perhaps he should have had Saslow's phone tracked and sent an armed response unit straight-away to intercept the two officers. He had chosen what he had considered to be the course of action least likely to bring about a violent outcome. If Willis had been confronted by armed officers, he would have known at once that he was a suspect. Dawn Saslow was with him and if he really were Aeolus, which was beginning to seem more and more likely, then God knows what he might do to her before he was apprehended.

Aeolus was totally ruthless.

He was supremely arrogant, too. The manner of his killings made that quite clear. Aeolus believed he was cleverer than anyone else and that he could do just what he wanted, that he was untouchable.

He was also totally mad.

Was Willis mad? Vogel couldn't get his head around it. Could he be that mad and none of them aware of it? He remembered how closed up Willis had always been, how he'd rarely smiled or engaged in conversation about anything other than police business. Willis made Vogel look outgoing and open.

Professor Freda Heath had told him about people suffering from multiple personality disorders being totally convincing, but could anyone be *that* convincing? Vogel was still clinging to the hope that nobody could, that his suspicions were unfounded and that Willis was the socially awkward but professionally excellent copper he had always been, nothing more or less.

That could still be, yet Vogel's every instinct was beginning to tell him it wasn't and that, however extraordinary, Willis was Aeolus.

He checked his watch as he walked along the corridor towards Hemmings's office. When he'd asked her and Willis to return to base, Saslow had said they'd been nearly at Avonmouth. They could not possibly have got back yet, but there was increasingly less and less doubt in his mind that Dawn Saslow was in very great danger. He was going to be right on edge, until she and Willis returned. If they returned. He preferred not to think about that.

All he could do was to continue to hope that his decision to make a softly, softly approach had been the right one and that Willis/Aeolus was arrogant enough not to be alerted to impending danger.

AEOLUS

How dare they insult my intelligence like this? Did David Vogel really think for a moment that I wouldn't realise what his urgent new development was? Did he really think I wouldn't act to protect myself? I have always had a contingency plan. A number of contingency plans, actually. I have always been ready to deal with any eventuality. After all, I am Aeolus.

People like Vogel and the Saslow girl are just minor inconveniences to me. I knew what I had to do as soon as Saslow received that call. It wasn't going to be difficult for me. I, more than anybody, know how to make myself disappear.

First, I had to deal with the Saslow girl. Then, I would give my orders to Vogel. He would have no choice but to obey me. The wind obeyed me. I am the ruler of the wind. I have the power of the wind. I can raise a hurricane with a blink of an eyelid. Saslow was still unconscious from the second blow I dealt her. I made sure she would be under my control when she came around. Her upper body was restrained by the seat belt. Her wrists were still cuffed. I used her own handcuffs on her legs, clamping them around her ankles. She would not kick me again.

Saslow was a small girl. Nonetheless the cuffs were not quite big enough, when I pressed them shut they dug into her flesh. I didn't care about that. I never deliberately set out to hurt anybody. But when people challenge me, I must eliminate them. I always triumph. I am Aeolus. I must never allow such paltry outside forces to try and threaten me.

I let Saslow's head fall onto my shoulder. Anyone we passed, who might glance into the car, would almost certainly think she was sleeping.

The girl was now the key to my survival. She would make it possible for me to move on to the next stage of my life.

I needed to get away. I needed to go to another country. I knew what my choice was. I needed to be somewhere where cooperation with the United Kingdom was rarely an option. Somewhere I already had contacts in organisations which would welcome my special abilities. I had money. Not a lot, but enough to keep myself while I rebuilt my existence.

And I had my people, many more than Saul, Al and Leo. I could not always summon them at will, nor could I always deny them when they came to me. Sometimes I could make them wait. Other times I had to allow them to take me over at once. When they come to me and I become them, sometimes it is I, Aeolus, who has summoned them. Called them up at will. But sometimes it is as if they summon me and I have answered their call. They are my people.

As for Willis, poor Willis, he was never more than the cloak within which I wrapped my real selves.

If he disappears for ever, he will be no loss.

I am Aeolus.

TWENTY-NINE

Hemmings stared at Vogel.

'No,' he said. 'No.'

'Well I can't be sure, sir . . .'

'I think you are, Vogel, you know it in your gut, don't you, man?'

'I feel it, that's for certain, sir,' said Vogel.

'What about DNA and fingerprints? Willis's will be on record like every serving police officer in the UK. If he's our killer then his DNA would have come up as a match on the national data base straight away, wouldn't it?'

'Apparently not and I can't explain that, sir. Not yet. We'll have to look into it. Meanwhile, I think we need to take every precaution. All being well, Willis and Saslow should be back within fifteen minutes or so.'

Involuntarily, he glanced at his watch again. If they are coming back, he thought. If Willis was still sticking to his reliable copper personae and hadn't totally transformed himself into Aeolus. It didn't bear thinking about. If anything happened to Saslow, Vogel would hold himself responsible for the rest of his life.

Hemmings was speaking. Vogel heard him from afar. He made himself listen properly. He and Hemmings could only deal with the situation as it now was.

'So let's get an armed response presence here, right away,' Hemmings was saying. 'Low profile, keep them out of sight. Then as soon as Willis and Saslow are in the building we separate them. Get Saslow out of the firing line, before the armed response boys do the arrest. Got it?'

Vogel had it.

'I'll call them in,' said Hemmings.

He did so at once on his desk phone.

'They'll be here within twenty,' he said. 'We may have to play a holding game for a bit, if Willis and Saslow get here first. Keep Willis sweet. String him along a bit.'

Vogel stared at Hemmings in silence for a moment.

Sometimes, just sometimes, he thought the detective chief inspector was from another planet. Keep him sweet? String him along a bit? This could be a man who had killed three times in cold blood and those were only the killings they knew about. This could be a man who did not know who he was from one day to the next, and who, if Vogel had correctly understood Professor Freda Heath, could swing in and out of his various murderous identities almost by the minute. Vogel felt totally out of his depth and that had never happened to him before.

'You know what sir, I'm not sure if that's going to be possible . . .' he began.

'If he comes back here with Saslow, then surely it will be,' said Hemmings.

Vogel did not entirely agree, but saw Hemmings's logic.

'It's if he doesn't come back with Saslow that we need to really worry,' the DCI continued.

Vogel didn't need telling that. He was already desperately worried.

When Saslow came round, she had no idea where she was. For just a split second, she could not even remember what had happened to her. Then she saw Willis and she remembered it all. That's when the pain hit her, surging though her body. The second blow had been much harder than the first. She realised she'd been concussed, more than that, she had been rendered unconscious.

He was standing at a table and seemed to be sorting through the contents of a box. He had his back to her. She tried to speak. Her head hurt, a lot. Her right cheek hurt worst of all. Without thinking, she tried to raise a hand to touch it. She was still handcuffed behind her back. Her ankles were handcuffed too. She realised she was half-sitting, half-lying on a concrete floor, with her upper back against a wall. She wriggled, involuntarily struggling to move, but she was chained to the wall. Willis had looped one of the cuffs on her wrist through a thick, metal chain.

She looked around her. She was in some sort of dimly lit room without windows. This was her prison now. The air was dank and heavy. She wondered if it was underground.

She wondered if she would die there.

She was finding it difficult to breathe. It felt as if her nose and throat were blocked. She tried to speak again, but was aware only of a gurgling sound. Willis turned around then. Only, she could barely recognise him as Willis. The man she'd thought of, not really as a friend like some of those she worked with, but certainly as a close colleague, perhaps her closest colleague. Someone trustworthy upon whom she could rely. This was not Willis. This was some madman, with eyes cold as ice.

He moved towards her. Willis was tall, a good six feet, and the celling in the room was low. He couldn't quite stand up fully. So he walked with his head slightly bowed and when he stood above her, his bent upper body loomed over her. He reached out with one hand. Saslow was absolutely terrified. Was this it? Was he going to kill her? She cowered away from him, as best she could given her handcuffed hands and feet.

'Don't worry, you snivelling bitch, I can hardly bare to touch you,' he hissed at her. Then she saw he was carrying a plastic bottle of water. He placed the neck of it between her lips and tipped. She gulped down as much as she could, desperate for it. Her throat seemed to clear. Then water began to dribble down her chin. She couldn't take any more. Mercifully, he removed the bottle before she choked. She gasped for air. Her breathing seemed a little easier, but she could barely speak. Her voice was little more than a whisper.

'What are you going to do with me?' she asked.

'That depends on your friends, your police friends,' he said. 'If they follow my orders, I will tell them where you are. Then they will come for you, I suppose. If they disobey me, well, you will die, eventually.'

She heard herself begin to sob.

'What did you expect?' he asked coolly. 'You aren't a total fool, are you?'

Saslow was suddenly aware that she was losing control of her bladder. She knew that fear did that. She had seen it happen, but never thought it would happen to her.

'I need to go to the toilet,' she said. 'Quickly.'

He shrugged.

'There is no toilet here,' he said.

She heard herself pleading with him.

'Please, I need to go. I can't hold it much longer . . .'

He shrugged and turned away.

She couldn't help it. She began to urinate. The liquid poured from her, seeping through her clothes and leaking on to the floor. He turned back to face her.

'You filthy, filthy bitch,' he growled.

Then he stepped towards her and slapped her twice across her already battered face. She screamed with pain. He stepped back and just stared at her.

'I couldn't help it,' Saslow stammered, aware that anything she did which offended him, would only make him more dangerous. 'I told you I needed to go. I couldn't stop it.'

He stepped towards her again and began to unlock the hand-cuffs on her wrists.

'If you try to struggle I shall hit you again,' he said. 'And this time I shall not be so gentle. If you want a chance of living, do not resist me. Never resist me.'

He removed the handcuff on her right wrist. The one on her left was still fastened to the chain, which attached to the wall.

'You are alive only because you are useful to me,' he said. 'I am not a common criminal. I do not kill or cause pain unless I have to. I am Aeolus, I am the ruler of the winds. I am honourable. I now seek only safe passage. If I am given it, I shall tell them where you are. If not, I shall never reveal your whereabouts and you will not be found, Dawn Saslow. I am telling you this because I want you to know that, if that is what happens, it will not be my fault. It is not part of my plan that you should die.'

He then fetched a bucket from the far side of the room, which he placed beside her.

'Your toilet, madam,' he said. 'Although it seems you know how to do without one.' His lips curled with distaste.

He went back to the table and brought to her the box he had been sorting through. In it were some basic supplies: packets of biscuits, tins of meat, baked beans and two more bottles of water.

'You have provisions here to keep you alive, until they get to you. There's probably enough for a week or so. I would expect them to get to you before that, long before that. Indeed, if they don't, I suggest you conserve your rations, because that means they have double-crossed me. If they double-cross me, I shall tell them nothing and your life will end here.'

He leered at her. She made herself try to think. What could she say, what could she ask for that might help her?

'Why don't you unchain me and free my legs?' she asked. 'The handcuffs are too small for my ankles. My feet have gone numb. After all, you said you didn't want to cause me unnecessary pain. You said you were honourable. And what am I going to do? I accept what you say. I will never be able to get out of here, once you have gone, unless they come to get me.'

'I do not take unnecessary risks,' he said. 'You will remain cuffed and chained. You will just have to hope that Vogel does not try to be clever, that he does my bidding. Then you will be freed. Then and if.'

She made one last attempt to talk to him. He was Willis after

all. The man she had worked alongside for almost six months
– or at least that was one part of him. Perhaps, if she appealed
to that part of him, she might get through.

'John,' she said. 'C'mon. You and I have always been chums.
I would never do anything to harm you. Set me free and I'll try
to help you.'

'Who is this John?' he asked. 'I know no John.'

As he spoke, she realised it was hopeless. He turned and
walked to the far side of her prison. She watched him pick up a
suitcase, clearly pre-packed. Ready for this eventuality, presumably. She realised he was now going to leave her. He took a small
torch from his pocket and turned it on. Then he flicked a switch
on the wall. The terrible, little room was plunged into darkness,
apart from the narrow beam from his torch.

She lost control again then. She'd done her best to engage him
and failed. It was over now, probably for good. She began to
scream. She could no longer see his face, but she could hear his
voice all right. That awful, hissing apology for a voice, half-
pompous and half-threatening, the voice that was not Willis any
more. The voice that was Aeolus.

'Make all the noise you like,' he said. 'Scream and scream with
all your might. You will not be heard. Nobody will hear you.'

She was lying in her own urine and she could feel her bowels
beginning to move. She had no control at all over her body any
more. She was aware of him leaving though, and the sound of
some sort of very heavy object sliding across the floor. Then he'd
gone and there was only darkness.

She was quite alone in her stinking, black prison.

THIRTY

As promised, the armed response boys arrived within
twenty minutes and concealed themselves strategically,
both in the car park and inside the building.

Willis and Saslow had yet to return.

Vogel was beginning to get very nervous indeed. He tried to

make use of the waiting time by studying Willis's file and collating everything he knew about the DS. It wasn't a lot. Willis had graduated as a mechanical design engineer at a Manchester college and worked briefly in construction, before totally changing tack and moving to Bristol to join the Avon and Somerset Constabulary. Vogel had been vaguely aware that Willis had an engineering background, but he had little knowledge of the DS's early life. After all, Willis barely talked about it.

It had never occurred to Vogel to question Willis's career switch. Many officers joined the force from very different walks of life. But, if Willis was Aeolus, why on earth had he decided to become a policeman? Vogel had no idea.

An alert had been put out for Willis's vehicle, with an instruction that no approach should be made, but any spotting reported at once to MCIT. The region's CCTV units were also alerted, but results from this source would not be immediate. Footage had to be collated and checked. As the minutes passed, Vogel continued to wait uneasily for the return of Willis and Saslow or news that the vehicle had been spotted. The tech boys were swiftly able to identify the location from which a signal had last been picked up from Saslow's phone. It was an industrial cul-de-sac just off the Avonmouth Road.

A squad car, already located nearby, was sent to investigate cautiously. They called in within minutes. To Vogel's dismay, they reported that there was no sign of Willis's vehicle or either officer believed to have been travelling in it, but they did have some disturbing news.

'We've found a phone,' said Constable Jamieson. 'It looks as if it was thrown against a wall. The screen's smashed and the back's fallen off. The sim card's been removed and it's dead as a Dodo.'

'Is it an Iphone seven plus, with a blue, sparkly case?' asked Vogel with trepidation. He and Saslow had the same phone, only hers had that sparkling case on it, and she'd actually once threatened to get the pink version for Vogel. They were both Apple devotees and liked to have the latest technology.

'Yes, sir. We found a case like that, too.'

That was not what Vogel wanted to hear. Clearly this was Saslow's phone. He slumped in his chair behind his desk. This was the calm before the storm. There was no point in waiting and hoping any more. Willis and Saslow were not returning. Vogel steeled himself to take control of the situation and be ready for the next course of action.

He stood up and headed for the incident room.

It was then that his mobile rang.

The caller was Willis.

Vogel felt his heart thumping in his chest.

He pushed the green button and spoke, in as level a voice as he could manage.

'John,' he said.

The voice which responded didn't sound like Willis at all.

'If you do exactly as I say, nobody will be hurt.'

It was the voice of someone who expected to be obeyed. It was confident and clear as an English public schoolboy's, but with more than a touch of a rarely heard accent. Latin, thought Vogel.

'Go on,' he said, struggling to keep his voice level.

'I need to leave the country,' Willis continued. 'I shall not trouble you again. I have a place to go. I have a plan. I always have a plan.' There was a pause. 'I am Aeolus. I do what I wish, when I wish.'

Vogel's heart seemed to do somersault inside his chest. He could barely breathe. He waited. There was only silence.

'Go on,' he said again.

'I need no help from you, not any of you. Alone, I am enough. I need only for you to clear a passage for my journey and not to stand in my way. You may well spot me, on the road or elsewhere, as I begin my journey. You may well spot me as I board an aircraft or a ship or a train. *Yet you will not apprehend me. You will do nothing to hinder my passage.*'

The last two sentences were shouted at the top of the caller's voice. It was filled with menace. Then Willis continued, softer, quieter and even more threateningly.

'If you hinder my progress in any way, you and your people will never see Saslow alive again. I have her safe, but you will never find her without me and, if you hinder me, I will never tell you where she is. But if you allow my safe passage to another place and another life, then I will contact you. Only when I know that I am free again, will I tell you where she is.'

'Look, Willis, I will do everything in my power to assist you, you must know that . . .' Vogel began.

'*I am Aeolus,*' the voice boomed. 'Willis is my *servant.* Willis is nothing, Aeolus is everything, all-seeing and all-powerful. All you have to do is obey the orders of Aeolus. If you do not do so, then Dawn Saslow will die and it will be a terrible death. A death decreed by the Gods. So you will obey. You must obey. Aeolus has spoken.'

Vogel's heart now felt as if was no longer ticking. This was his worst nightmare.

An all out operation was launched to search for Saslow and Willis, with a warning that Willis, must not on any account be approached, apprehended or alerted in any way. The CCTV team pulled out all the stops. They scoured, as a matter of urgency, footage within a five-mile radius of the cul-de-sac where Saslow's phone had been found. One camera had picked up Willis's vehicle proceeding north up the B4057 along King's Weston Road. The shot was such that it was unclear whether or not there was a passenger in the car.

It was Hemmings, who knew Bristol like the back of his hand, who spotted something Vogel never would have done.

'Hang on a minute, doesn't Willis live out that way?' he asked.

Vogel had Willis's address to hand. A team had already been sent to the detective sergeant's home, as a matter of routine.

'Henbury, BS10,' said Vogel, who had little idea exactly where that was.

'And his vehicle hasn't been picked up since?'

'Not yet, boss,' said Vogel.

'The bastard was heading home!' said Hemmings. 'If he plans to leave the country, whether we do his bidding or not, he needs a passport, doesn't he? Does he carry his passport? I don't know. Most of us don't, not that he's most of us. He probably has a selection of passports, I shouldn't wonder, one for each of his many identities. Well, whatever identity he has chosen for his great escape he'll need a passport and money. We already know he has at least two bank accounts, his own, and one in the name of Richard Perry. He quite likely has more. If he's capable of murder as he appears to be so casually then he's surely capable of embezzlement and theft on a massive scale. He told you he had a master plan, Vogel, and no doubt he does. It makes sense that he headed home to sort himself out, before taking off.'

'It makes total sense sir,' said Vogel. 'But the team already at his house have found no sign of him or Saslow. They're searching the place as we speak, but so far they've discovered nothing untoward.'

'When did they get there?'

'About five minutes ago,'

'So Willis would have had time to do whatever he wanted to do there and leave.'

'Yes, but what's he done with Saslow? He said he'd hidden her somewhere we'd never find her. Surely not at his home?'

'Just make sure the place is torn apart, Vogel.'

'I will, boss.'

'And keep checking Willis out. I want to know how we've missed this. It just doesn't seem possible.'

No, thought Vogel, but we damned well have missed it. We've been working alongside a crazed murderer for years and we didn't have a clue.

AEOLUS

I knew exactly what would be happening within MCIT. I had specialist knowledge of similar investigations. Nothing on this scale, of course, nothing like the havoc I, Aeolus, have wreaked. But I knew I could second-guess the lot of them.

There would already be a call out for Willis's vehicle. They had probably already spotted me at least once or twice. Sooner or later, they would pick up on the direction in which I was now travelling. They would have already sent a team to search Willis's home.

That didn't matter. They would find nothing there that would lead them to be able to apprehend me. Nothing which would shed any light on what I had done in order to protect myself. I was

Aeolus and I could not be harmed. I must not be harmed. I still had another life awaiting me in another land.

Perhaps they would work it out in the end, but that's probably giving them too much credit. Anyway, by then, I would be clean away. After all, how would they dare stop me, when my freedom was the price they must pay to allow poor, little Dawn Saslow the chance to survive?

Not that the chance was all that great, fifty-fifty probably. Sure, I'd left her food and drink, but she probably needed medical attention from the blows I dealt her.

I wouldn't expect her to last long. Her only real hope for surviving was if nobody got in my way and I reached my destination safely and quickly. Otherwise, she would die.

I felt no animosity towards Saslow. Indeed, she had been probably the least annoying of my alleged colleagues within the Avon and Somerset Constabulary.

But neither did I feel anything else for her. No affection. Not even professional regard. It is impossible to feel such things, when her abilities were so much more inferior than mine.

I wished her no harm. But if she died, then she died. I did not care. I was Aeolus. I had to protect myself.

THIRTY-ONE

Vogel was on his way back to his office when Willis's ex-wife arrived. So much had happened since his phone conversation with her, that he'd practically forgotten that Vera Court had agreed to come in.

Vogel had never met Vera. He'd transferred to the Avon and Somerset only relatively recently, long after Willis and his wife had parted. In any case, he doubted that Willis would have ever included his wife much in his working life. Vogel, being a private man himself, hadn't even considered that there was anything odd in Willis's reticence concerning anything personal. He kicked himself now. Willis was right, he thought, he was supposed to be so damned clever and yet he'd spotted nothing amiss. He chastised himself. Another, more outgoing officer might have been so much more aware. Although, of course, Willis had somehow or other kept up his front within the force for many years. And nobody came close to guessing what lay beneath his calm exterior.

Vera Court was a surprise. Vogel didn't know why she should be, but she was.

She was tall and thin, with spiky blonde hair. She was dressed young and streetwise, sporting stonewashed jeans, boots and a funky, leather jacket. She appeared to be neither mumsy nor downtrodden ex – nothing like the rather cliché-ridden image he had imagined.

She and Vogel walked together through the incident room, en route to his office. Vogel could see her looking around at the photographs and charts lining the walls. She no doubt watched the news on TV and read newspapers. Vera Court had already made it clear on the phone that she was no fool.

'Is this about these murders?' she asked. 'The serial killer with different identities?'

Vogel dodged the question as he gestured for her to take a seat.

'Look, please bear with me,' he said. 'I just need to ask you some more questions. First of all, can I ask you if John was ever violent towards you when you were together?'

Vera Court looked stricken.

'Why are you asking that?'

'Please, Mrs Court, I know this must be very disconcerting, but could you just answer my question. Was John ever violent towards you?'

Vera Court answered quickly then.

'Once,' she said.

Vogel was mildly surprised. Not that Willis had been violent towards his ex-wife, but that it had only been once. He studied the woman carefully. Was she telling the truth? He was almost sure she wouldn't lie. She'd already worked out how serious this all was.

It was just that, in his experience, if a man was violent towards his wife once, he almost always was again. And again. This was unusual. But then, everything was unusual in this case. John

Willis thought he was a figure out of Greek mythology. No. He didn't think he was, Vogel corrected himself, he became a figure out of Greek mythology in his own head. Freda Heath had told him that people with DID actually did become their alter egos.

'It was the beginning of the end really, Mr Vogel,' Vera Court continued. 'In more ways than one. He nearly killed me.'

She paused. Vogel waited in silence for her to begin again.

'He tried to strangle me. He put his hands around my neck and squeezed. All the while, it was as if he were not seeing me. We were in bed. I was asleep. Can you imagine that, Mr Vogel? I woke up to find him on top of me. I was gasping for breath. I couldn't speak and, in any case, I instinctively knew it would make no difference. There was a pair of scissors on the bedside table. I grabbed them and lashed out. I stabbed him in the shoulder. It wasn't very deep, but then he went really crazy. He started to hit me in the face. He dragged me out onto the landing and pushed me down the stairs. All the while he didn't speak. I fell awkwardly. I broke my ankle and my left wrist. He just walked casually down the stairs, stepped over me, opened the front door and left the house.

'I didn't hit my head thank God. I was in horrible pain, but I remained conscious. The children were in the house. The eldest, Sam, he was five and little Lucy just three. They both woke up. There'd been such a commotion. Sam came on to the landing. I told him I'd been a silly mummy and fallen down the stairs. I said would he go to the phone and bring it to me. I dialled 999. I also told the emergency services I'd fallen down the stairs. I don't know if they believed me.

'I'm sure they didn't at the hospital. They kept asking me about the marks on my neck, then questions about my husband. I did what so many wives do, even nowadays. I told them nothing and made excuses. I said my husband locked up men who beat up their wives, that he was a police officer. They backed off a bit then.

'I should have told the truth but, apart from anything else, I was in shock. John had never laid a finger on me before. Although sometimes, if we'd just had a silly row, only like husbands and wives do, he would look at me as if he hated me. Stare at me and not say anything. I'd sometimes thought he might attack me, but he just used to back off in silence and go to the spare room. Afterwards, he would seem to be perfectly normal again, in as much as John was ever normal. He always blamed his migraines.' She glanced up at Vogel. 'I expect you know about the migraines?'

Vogel nodded. The times, albeit not that often, when Willis had simply said his head had gone and he had a migraine. Like on the day Melanie had been killed, he would always leave at once. Wherever they were, at Kenneth Steele or out on inquiries. Usually, he would drive himself home. Vogel had occasionally wondered about that. How could a man drive in that condition? Vogel had never suffered from migraines, but his mother had. During her brief yet severe bouts, she'd been incapable of functioning at all, let alone driving a car. Now it was all beginning to make sense.

Willis hadn't been battling migraines. He'd been battling the multiple personalities, which lurked within him and surfaced at times without him wishing them to. Freda Heath had called them 'involuntary identity switches.'

'Anyway,' Vera continued, 'John eventually turned up at the hospital full of concern. He actually asked me how it had happened and said he was so sorry he hadn't been with me. Then muttered about that being the trouble with being a policeman. I just took it, but when the nurse had gone I turned on him. Told him he was a terrible hypocrite and a vicious bastard. He'd done this to me, he had tried to strangle me, then he had pushed me down the stairs. No, half *thrown* me down the stairs. I was lucky to be still alive.

'He was so calm, eerily calm. He said I must have had a really bad knock on the head. I was confused. Surely I knew he would never hurt me, not with his history. I kept saying I hadn't knocked my head and he bloody well knew what he'd done. He wasn't kidding me, but he insisted that he hadn't touched me. And you know, I found myself believing that he really didn't know that he had attacked me. Let alone why and that was all the more frightening.'

'What did he mean about his history?'

'Oh, both his father and his stepfather used to knock his mother around. The stepfather used to hit him too. That's what he said anyway. I never knew what to believe.'

Vogel remembered then Willis's remark on the day after Melanie Cooke's death, concerning violence that he had experienced in his childhood.

'His father was a philanderer too, apparently. He walked out when John was five or six, then his mother took up with another bastard. Or so he said. She was following a pattern like a lot of women do, he told me. Almost as soon as we met – it was a year or so after he came to Bristol – he told me that I could be sure he would never stray and that he would never hurt me. Because of his childhood. I believed it too and that's part of the reason I stuck with him, even when he became so peculiar and distant.

I thought, well, a lot of women have it worse. I had a husband who brought home a decent wage, provided a nice home, wasn't violent – until that one awful time – and never strayed. Although he was absent from home so much, I did begin to wonder about that. But he always blamed police business, what a great excuse for a double life, eh?'

Vogel smiled weakly. A double life, he thought. That, he feared, was something of an understatement.

'What happened after he attacked you? What did you do?'

'I had two young children. I did what so many women do. I just went home and got on with it, but it was eerie. Uncanny. I tried to talk to him about what had happened. He shut down. He said that I must try to forget about it, try to move on and be thankful I wasn't more badly hurt. That he wished we knew what had caused me to fall down the stairs, then it would be easier for me. That I must stop this ridiculous thing of saying that he'd done it. He was my husband. He would never hurt me. I almost came to believe it in the end. Crazy, I know, but he was so certain and so calm, quite kind too, albeit distant. I told myself perhaps I really had imagined the whole thing . . .'

Vogel felt as if his whole body were chilled. The picture emerging of John Willis fitted pretty damned exactly the profile of Aeolus provided by Freda Heath

'You hadn't imagined it, though, had you?' he asked, although it wasn't really a question.

'Of course not.'

'And he really never did it again?'

'Well, no.' Vera Court hesitated. 'But I carried on thinking he was going to, so I couldn't sleep properly. I was sharing a bed with him. What if he attacked me again in my sleep? Then, one night, I woke up to find him looming over me, arms outstretched, as if he were preparing to put his hands around my neck again. I think I'd only been dozing, because I woke so quickly and I suppose I was half prepared this time. I slapped him hard across the face and he just rolled off me onto his side of the bed. I jumped up. I was terrified he was going to hurt me badly again. But there he was, lying there, looking every bit as if he'd just woken up or, actually, had been woken up by me. "What's up love?" he asked. "Can't you sleep?"

I'd hardly been able to believe my ears. I didn't challenge him. I was too afraid. I was beginning to think he was quite mad. The next day, he left for work early, as usual. I kept our Sam off school and just walked out with him and the little one. I went straight to my mum and dad's place. I'd eventually told them the truth about what John called "my accident" and my mum had begged me to leave him then. But like I said, there were the children. Two lovely kids. Mind you, they were a miracle.'

'Why?' Vogel asked. 'Why a miracle?'

'John was virtually impotent. With me anyway. I read some-where that impotent men often have a very high sperm count. God's way of compensating. He could only . . . I'm sorry. This is embarrassing. Do you really need to know?'

'I would appreciate it,' said Vogel. 'It could be relevant.'

'To what? To the profile of a serial killer?'

Vogel tried to look non-committal.

'I really would appreciate . . .' he began.

'All right. Well, I could coax him into an erection, but, uh, almost as soon as he tried to enter me he would lose it, sometimes ejaculating, sometimes not. Well, I suppose it only takes one of the little buggers,' she said with a wry smile.

'Have you met John's mother, the father or the stepfather?'

Vera Court shook her head. 'His mother died when he was in his late teens, he said. He wasn't in touch with either his father or his stepfather. He said he hated them both.' Vera paused.

'There's something else?' Vogel enquired.

'John's mother had another child with her second husband. John's half sister was born when John was eleven or twelve I think. The girl died, drowned in the bath. Her father, John's stepfather, was bathing the little girl, claimed he'd gone to answer the phone or something, and the child had slipped underwater and drowned. But there was some question of unexplained bruising on the child's body and both parents were questioned. Her father several times, not just concerning the drowning, but also on suspicion of having abused the little girl.

'There was no real evidence and John's stepfather was never arrested or charged. But John said his mother always suspected the stepfather might have been abusing the little girl in the bath and then killed her, even if accidentally, when she struggled. Unsurprisingly, the marriage broke up. That was John's story anyway, and he made it quite clear he was glad to see the back of his stepfather. Same with his father. He adored his mother, though. The only time I ever saw him show any real emotion was when he spoke about his mother.'

Vogel could hardly believe how well everything Vera Court said fitted in to the shocking scenario now unfolding.

According to Professor Heath, this was an almost classic background for someone suffering from Dissociative Identity Disorder. John Willis's colleagues had just accepted Willis as a socially awkward man, who didn't like to be drawn on anything personal, but was a damned good copper. What a joke that assessment was proving to be.

Vera Court began to speak again.

'Mr Vogel, I'm right, aren't I? You think John is this crazy killer, this Aeolus?'

Vogel felt the time had come to be honest. He needed more help from Vera. Willis had Saslow. He didn't suppose anyone could second-guess the man who thought he was Aeolus, but Vera had some insight that nobody else did. At that moment, she seemed the only hope he had.

'Yes Mrs Court,' he said. 'I am afraid there is no longer any doubt.'

'Oh my God,' she said. 'I've thought for years he wasn't right in the head. But this? Nothing like this.'

The woman may have already guessed, but now that Vogel had confirmed her suspicions, she seemed totally in shock.

'Mrs Court,' continued Vogel gently. 'There's more. It appears that John is holding one of our officers hostage. We have grave fears for her safety. We need to find her, and John, as quickly as possible. Have you any idea where he might go, where he might take someone in a situation like this?'

Vera Court shook her head.

Vogel persisted.

'He didn't have another property. A lock-up anywhere?'

'No, not that I know of, anyway.'

'Was there any place, I don't know, somewhere remote, where he might hide, or hide someone else?'

Vera Willis shook her head again.

'Mr Vogel, I lived with John for nearly seven years, and I realised long ago that I didn't really know him at all. I have no idea where he might go, or where he might take someone, but I dread to think what he might do to that someone.'

Right after Vera Court left, Vogel called forensics to see if there'd been any results yet, following his request for an urgent check on the DNA and fingerprints on record for Willis. He wasn't surprised to learn that there were still no matches found for Willis's DNA.

'The fingerprint record on file has just been checked and found to be unidentifiable,' the forensic technician told Vogel.

'What does that mean?' Vogel asked.

'Well, it's not a properly obtained record,' came the reply. 'The prints are distorted.'

'Distorted?' queried Vogel. 'How?'

'Simple really,' said the forensics technician. 'You only have to drag your finger a fraction of a centimetre and the prints are rendered useless. Of course, with members of the public, who are on suspicion of offences, the results would immediately be thoroughly scrutinised by the officer in charge. But with a copper? Well, you know . . .'

Vogel did know. The taking of a new police officer's finger-prints was just a matter of routine. Nobody was likely to check them very thoroughly. As for DNA, Vogel thought back to his own experience. Samples were usually taken during a recruit's training. In Vogel's day, the instructing officer was inclined to build the taking of such samples into training procedure. Vogel remembered being teamed up with another young copper. They took samples of each other's saliva using a swab. That way, not only was their DNA put on record as required, but they learned the procedure of doing so.

It seemed clear that Willis had falsified his own records one way or another. Unfortunately, Vogel could see only too clearly how it might have been done. Advanced technology and tighter regulations had combined to make it increasingly more difficult for anyone so inclined to do such a thing, but John Willis had joined the force thirteen years previously.

One of the most frightening aspects of this was why had he falsified his records all that time ago, long before the recent spate of killings that he was almost certainly responsible for? The obvious answer was that Willis had already committed some kind of serious crime, most likely a murder or murders. At the very least, he was covering his tracks for the future.

Vogel thought it was probably both.

He clicked into Willis's file again to see who his training officer had been, the man who would have overseen his DNA testing and finger printing. DI Phillip Marcus was long retired, but his contact details were all there. Marcus answered his phone straight away. He sounded surprised but not alarmed.

No, he didn't remember John Willis in particular. But yes, he always used to ask recruits to take each other's DNA samples. Two training jobs got done at once that way. And yes, of course he'd always checked that recruits' fingerprints were identifiable. Only when pressed by Vogel, did Marcus finally admit it.

'Well, no, I was probably not as thorough as you would be with a suspect. I don't think anyone was. Not in my day, anyway. I mean, you're dealing with police officers and it's a routine process.'

Marcus told Vogel nothing he did not already suspect. Things were going from bad to worse. The DNA must have come from a real person and someone not on the PNC or the national data base. Various scenarios came to mind, all of them chilling. Vogel had read of a case in America where a suspect had paid a down-and-out to allow him to take a DNA sample, which he later substituted for his own. Vogel had no knowledge of any suspect having manipulated DNA that way in the UK, but it would clearly be much easier for a trainee police officer to do so.

Which led Vogel's train of thought onto the muddle over

Melanie Cooke's father's DNA. They'd put it down to a rare forensics cock-up. Now it seemed likely that Willis had deliberately substituted his own, previously unrecorded, DNA and prints for Terry Cooke's. He'd almost certainly done something very like it before.

Willis, at Vogel's own request, had gone to Patchway to babysit Cooke's processing. More than likely he took over, thought Vogel. The custody boys wouldn't have questioned an MCIT sergeant.

Of course, Willis would have known that, sooner or later, it would be discovered that the samples he submitted were not Cooke's. So why would he do it? Vogel remembered the absolute loathing Willis had expressed for Cooke, the alleged wifebeater. As the son of a mother who had been beaten, that alone could have been Willis's motive for framing Terry Cooke. Or Willis may have been playing for time, trying to wrong-foot his own team, which he certainly succeeded in doing. Vogel wasn't sure, but he reminded himself that Willis was mad. He might have switched the samples just because he could.

Whilst he was still contemplating this latest piece of news, PC Polly Jenkins knocked on the open door to his office and entered.

'Boss, traffic have spotted Willis heading out of the city and onto the M4 towards London. The boys want to know what to do. They are currently following but keeping their distance. They think Willis has spotted them, but he doesn't appear to be reacting.'

'Tell them to back off,' said Vogel quickly. 'The car's on a motorway. We can track it without physically following it, make sure we do and make sure everyone knows that no approach must be made.'

'Right boss.'

'Most importantly of all, could the boys see if there was anyone else in the vehicle? If Willis still has Saslow with him?'

'We asked that straight away, boss. They couldn't say for certain but, if Dawn is in the car, they're pretty sure she's not sitting next to him in the passenger seat.'

Vogel grunted. Jenkins looked as concerned as he felt. He knew what the young woman was thinking. Dawn could be lying on the back seat out of sight of the cameras. She could be locked in the boot. She could be unconscious, or already dead.

Vogel shook himself out of it. She could be alive and secreted somewhere Willis/Aeolus was confident she would not be discovered, as the man himself had said on the phone. Aeolus wouldn't lie, would he? He wouldn't see the need to lie, Vogel told himself. They just had to find her.

But where was she?

Thanks to the CCTV cameras along the B4057 and Hemmings's local knowledge, it was strongly suspected that Willis had driven straight to his home, after being alerted by Vogel's phone call to Saslow. It was reasonable to assume, from the timeline, that Saslow had still been with him and quite probably still with him when he arrived at his home.

Vogel struggled to keep calm. Not for the first time he was glad that he wasn't naturally an emotional man. Nonetheless, when the life of a fellow officer was at stake, it was difficult even for him to remain composed, and this wasn't just any officer. This was Dawn Saslow. His Dawn.

He had to remind himself that he didn't even know for certain yet that Willis had gone to his home, let alone taken Dawn Saslow there. But every instinct, coupled with Hemmings's irrefutable logic, told him that's what had happened. If Saslow was no longer with Willis in his car, or heaven forbid, lying dead or injured on the floor or in the boot, then she could still be at the house.

But Willis lived in an ordinary suburban semi. A cursory search had already been completed and the CSIs were now going through the place with a fine toothcomb. Vogel knew all about deficiencies in police searches. The Tia Sharp case came to mind; the twelve-year old's body, concealed in the attic of her grandmother's East London home, was missed twice by police searching the premises. Vogel had personal knowledge of CSIs failing to notice an obvious murder weapon, even a bloodied knife, at a crime scene. But this time they were looking for a fellow police officer. Everyone involved was on red alert and hopefully Dawn Saslow was alive. Surely her presence in a three-bedroomed semi couldn't be overlooked.

Vogel called Vera Court on her mobile. The woman had not quite reached home. She still sounded in shock. Her life was going to change, thought Vogel obliquely. She mightn't still be married to this monster, who had fooled so many, but she had been once and their children still bore his name.

'Look, this might seem crazy,' Vogel began. 'But is there anywhere at your old, marital home where a person could be hidden? A place that we wouldn't find, unless we knew it was there?'

'No,' replied Vera at once. 'It's just an ordinary, small house. I mean, there's an attic, not much space up there. Then there's the garage. John was always very protective about the garage. I called it his man cave. Nobody else had a key to it and the kids weren't allowed in. He kept stuff in it for tinkering with the car, for the garden, just ordinary things. I hardly ever went in there. He kept the car in the garage, but if we were going out together he'd fetch it and drive round the front to pick me up. But I'm sure your people have looked in the garage by now, haven't they, Mr Vogel? And I expect it was as tidy as ever, too. Not much of a hiding place.'

Willis muttered his agreement.

'You really can't think of anything else?'

'No. Well . . . just something, but it's probably nothing . . .'

'Go on, Mrs Court.'

'Well I remember one of the elderly neighbours there, old Willy Fox, who used to talk about playing in the air raid shelter, which was built in his garden just before the war. I suppose it would have been used when the docks were bombed in Bristol. Our house didn't have one as far as I know. John never mentioned it certainly, nor anyone else, but it's just a thought . . .'

Vogel sat up straight in his chair.

'John lived in the house before you were married, didn't he? Might he have known things about the house that you didn't?'

'I suppose so, but he couldn't hide an air raid shelter from me and the kids, surely?' said Vera.

'I don't know, Mrs Court,' responded Vogel. 'I do know that he appears to have hidden multiple identities and multiple murders from all of us. You said you thought John was capable of anything. He thinks that too. He thinks he is super capable, super clever and that the rest of us pale into insignificance by comparison. That may be his only weakness.'

As he ended the call, Hemmings walked in.

'The CSIs have been on again to say that there's nothing at all at Willis's house,' said the DCI. 'A neighbour saw him pull out of the back alley leading from the garage about an hour ago, but couldn't tell whether there was a passenger in the car. Indeed, they couldn't actually see Willis, but just assumed it was him. Nobody, that we know of so far, saw the car arrive. There's no sign of any hurried packing or anything like that and certainly no sign of DC Saslow. They found his passport, in the name of Willis, but we know he has at least one other in another name . . .'

Vogel was barely listening. He interrupted Hemmings to repeat what Vera Court had just told him.

'There could be an old air raid shelter at Willis's place, and I'm banking on it being beneath the garage. Aeolus' lair. He's hidden Dawn at that house somewhere, I feel sure. He just wouldn't have had time to do anything else. And the bastard believes she's too well concealed for us to find her. I'd like to go round there myself. I know Willis.'

'Umm,' muttered Hemmings, 'Not as well as you bloody well thought, it would seem.'

Vogel couldn't argue with that. He said nothing.

'What makes you think you can find something the search team haven't?' Hemmings persisted.

'I'm gonna dig, boss,' Vogel said. 'Aeolus think's his lair is safe. Thing is, I don't remember any mention of pneumatic drills in Greek Mythology.' Vogel almost made himself laugh. It must be the onset of hysteria, he thought. 'I want to get some hairy-arsed, construction workers out there, sir,' he continued.

'If you think you're onto something, go for it.'

'Yes, boss, if I'm right and he's made some sort of a den out of an old air raid shelter, we don't even know what ventilation system it has. We need to find Dawn fast, whilst she's still alive. If she's still alive.'

THIRTY-TWO

Vogel took Polly Jenkins with him to Willis's home. He knew she and Dawn Saslow were friends. If they found the DC there, he had no idea what state she might be in, and he felt that Jenkins' presence could only help.

As soon as they arrived, they both suited up and joined the search team already at work in the detached, double garage at the top of the small back garden. It contained a mechanics inspection pit, which clearly demanded close attention. In spite of assurances from the CSI team that they had checked out that area thoroughly, Vogel clambered down, armed with a lump hammer which he smashed with all his strength against the walls and floor of the pit.

'Careful, sir,' admonished a young woman CSI.

Vogel glowered her.

'We have an officer missing,' he growled. 'Our first priority is to find her. We can worry about forensics after that.'

'Yes sir, of course, sir,' said the young woman. 'But you should know we've done more or less exactly what you're doing all over the garage. Everything is solid as a rock. There's no false floor or anything like that. We're sure of it.'

'Some of these wartime shelters were five, or more, metres below ground level,' muttered Vogel.

'Yes sir, but they had to have an entrance. We've found no sign of anything.'

Vogel started to climb out of the pit. As he did so, the workmen he'd asked for turned up; two of them, both carrying heavy-duty, pneumatic drills.

Ignoring the obvious disapproval of the CSIs, Vogel ordered them down into the pit and told them to dig.

The noise, in a confined space, was overwhelming.

After a few minutes, the workmen paused.

'We're down three feet and it's still solid concrete,' reported one.

'Three feet of concrete?' queried Vogel. 'Isn't that odd?'

'Well yes. Unless it's the roof of an old shelter which no longer has an entrance at all.'

'It must have an entrance.'

Vogel was adamant.

'Try drilling down the sides.'

They did so.

'Anything?' yelled Vogel after a few minutes.

The men switched off their drills so that they could all hear themselves speak.

'Well, there does seem to be the narrowest of gaps around three sides of the pit and down the centre,' reported one of the workmen. 'Hair's breadth. But then, concrete is sometimes laid like that – well, it's always laid a bit like that, in blocks, to stop it cracking as it sets. Do you want us to carry on digging, mate?'

'Hold on a minute.'

Vogel lowered himself into the pit and bent over to examine closely where the men had been drilling around the edges. He asked to borrow a screwdriver with which he prodded and probed.

'This couldn't be some kind of giant plug, could it?'

'A plug, mate?'

'Yes, exactly that. A plug made to fit precisely into a bloody great hole. '

'Well if it is, then it looks to be permanent.'

'It can't be permanent. It has to move. The only question is how it moves.'

Vogel hauled himself up and began to root around the garage.

'What's that,' he asked, pointing at a large piece of machinery propped in a corner. 'Isn't that some sort of hydraulic pump?'

'Well yes, but it's just the sort of stuff that ends up in a garage, isn't it?' said the same young woman CSI.

'Is it?' queried Vogel. 'Look, you can see it's in decent working order. No dust. Could have been used recently. Hydraulics can be channelled to move large objects. Did nobody think of that?' The CSIs exchanged uncertain glances. 'If this is what I think it might be, that pump must connect to something,' muttered Vogel.

Jenkins spoke then, pointing to a cupboard over to Vogel's left.

'Look at that, boss,' she said.

The door to the cupboard was slightly ajar. Vogel could just see a wheel inside, fitted to the wall, and a complex of pipes emerging from the floor.

'Have you checked that out?' he asked the CSIs.

'Probably some sort of old water supply,' replied one of them. 'We did look at it, yes . . .'

His voice tailed away as he glanced back from the cupboard to the pump.

'Bloody hell,' he muttered.

'Let's get on to it,' snapped Vogel.

'You guys.' He turned to the workmen. 'Either of you two know any more about engineering than this lot seem to?'

'A bit, I've worked in mining in South Africa,' said one of them, a big man with an abundance of red hair that matched his complexion. 'We used hydraulic rams over there. I'll have a look if you like.'

'Good, get on with it.'

Vogel turned to the second workman. 'And you, clear all that rubble away in the pit. They'll help you.' He gestured at the less-than-thrilled-looking CSIs. 'If I'm right, we need to make sure there's nothing down there that might impede smooth movement.'

The redhaired workman was already at work.

'The pump's petrol driven and its tank's half full,' he reported. He moved the pump close to the cupboard. Vogel was no longer surprised when it became apparent that the pipe-fitting connectors in the wall cupboard and on the pump itself matched perfectly.

The workman was able to attach the pump with little difficulty.

'Shall I fire her up?' he asked.

'Quick as you like.'

The man paused.

'You know, it would be quite an engineering feat to construct anything like this. Can't be many people capable of it.'

'No,' agreed the DCI, thinking about Willis's background as a mechanical design engineer.

'Just the one,' he continued. 'But he is Aeolus.'

The man looked confused, perhaps he was one of surely only a handful of people in the country who'd managed to avoid the massive media coverage.

'Just get on with it,' instructed Vogel.

The pump fired at the third attempt.

The workman then began to turn the wheel within the cupboard, at first with no apparent result. He tried again. There was a grinding noise, followed by a shuffling sound, which came from the foot of the inspection pit. Vogel swung round, lurched towards the edge of the pit and lowered himself down in one clumsy but effective motion.

Part of the base of the pit was moving; a section of concrete was sliding slowly to one side. But the giant plug, as he had rather aptly described it, was moving too slowly for Vogel. As soon as a big enough gap had been created he leaned through it, hanging on precariously in a crab-like position, with one arm and one leg still on the stationary part of the pit's base.

As soon as he got his head through the gap, he could tell there was a considerable space beneath him. But it was very nearly pitch black, barely illuminated at all by the light behind him. He yelled for a torch which was thrown down by a CSI. He shone it into the space.

Dawn Saslow was just a few feet away, sprawled on the floor and chained to a wall, the way Willis must have left her. Even in the dim light of the torch, it was immediately apparent that she had been badly beaten. Her face and clothes were covered in blood. One cheek was little more than a swollen, black mass. Vogel could also smell the sweet stench of human excrement. Oh my God, he thought, were they too late? Then Dawn lifted one arm, just a little, almost like a weak wave of greeting.

She was alive.

'It's all right, Dawn, it's all right now, we're here,' he shouted.

She seemed unable to speak. He couldn't tell yet how bad her injuries were. But Dawn Saslow was alive. The massive block of concrete continued to shift. Vogel let himself drop to the lower ground level. He ran to Dawn, scrabbling hopelessly at the cuffs around her legs and the chain which restrained her. PC Jenkins followed Vogel down through the inspection pit and was quickly beside him.

'Sir, gently, sir, you could hurt her,' she said.

She let her fingers brush lightly against Dawn Saslow's good cheek.

'Hang on in there, sweetheart,' she said. 'We've got you now and we'll have you free in a jiff.'

It was probably the gentle touch and the kind words which caused the tears that began to run freely down Saslow's damaged face.

The workmen had come well prepared. On cue, one of them jumped down wielding a pair of heavy-duty bolt cutters. Vogel gestured him forwards and he began at once to cut through the cuffs and the chain restraining Saslow. She grunted with pain as the man attacked the cuffs around her ankles, which had bitten deeply into her flesh, but, although clearly shocked to the core, he was admirably quick and efficient.

Once Dawn was free Vogel wrapped his arms around her and held her close.

'It's all right, baby,' he said. 'It's all right.'

He could feel the young woman's body heaving, her sobbing now quite out of control. But she was alive, bless her, she was alive. Vogel felt relief flowing through every vein in his body. Eventually Dawn's sobbing began to subside, then she spoke. Her voice was weak, little more than a croak, but the message was clear enough.

'Just get the bastard, boss,' she said.

The paramedic team were still checking out Dawn Saslow, before carrying her from the prison that had nearly become her grave, when Hemmings called Vogel's mobile. He said that Willis/Aeolus had been duly tracked up the M4 and spotted swinging off towards Heathrow.

A simple check of flight information had already revealed that he'd booked himself on a flight to Moscow under the name of Richard Perry, whose passport and driving licence he presumably had with him.

Well, he didn't think he had anything to fear, did he?

After all, he'd been quite confident that Dawn Saslow would not be found, unless he chose for her to be.

The airport police, a branch of the Met since the 70s when airport security concerns had begun to seriously escalate, had been alerted. Yet, so far, they had been told to keep only a watching brief. They, and just about every cop in the country, had been informed of DC Saslow being missing and instructed that her recovery was first priority. Now she was safe, their priorities had shifted. Heathrow's highly trained specialist police unit were fully armed and programmed to handle major terrorist situations. Vogel thought they were just the boys to deal with bloody Aeolus.

'Dawn's safe, boss,' he said. 'We've just found her and she's alive. You can tell the Heathrow lads to move in on Willis, or whatever he's calling himself today. And they can move just as hard as they like.'

The relief was clear in Hemmings voice when he spoke again. 'Thank God,' said the DCI.

'But please boss, can you make sure I'm the one to talk to Willis first?' asked Vogel.

'He's yours, David,' said the DCI.

THIRTY-THREE

W illis was arrested on suspicion of three counts of murder and brought straight back to Bristol, where he was processed at Patchway and held in a police cell.

Within four hours of Dawn Saslow being found, Vogel – backed up by Polly Jenkins – was ready to conduct the first interview. Freda Heath, whose expert opinion was much-needed, had dropped everything to make the journey from London as soon as Vogel contacted her. She might be NHS and overworked, but she wasn't going to miss this opportunity.

'You do realise this is psychiatric history in the making,' she told Vogel excitedly.

'It wasn't my first thought,' responded Vogel drily.

DS Nobby Clark travelled to Bristol with the professor. After all, the extraordinary suspect now in custody had murdered on her patch too.

Willis was already sitting in an interview room, when the four entered. Vogel studied him carefully while PC Jenkins made the usual formal pronouncement of date, time and those present, for the video record.

Willis looked like, well, he looked like Willis, thought Vogel. Nothing more or less. Albeit Willis in a custody suit. Other than that he looked pretty much as usual.

It was Willis who spoke first and it really was Willis, or as near to Willis as was ever likely to be seen or heard again. Willis's voice with more than a hint of Lancastrian.

'I don't understand boss, what's all this about?' he asked, as he straightened the sleeves of his suit and turned them back so that they formed neat cuffs of equal size. 'I was heading off with Saslow, to see that walk-in at Avonmouth, and the next thing I knew I'd been arrested.'

'Is that really your only memory of today, Willis?' asked Vogel.

'Yes, boss. Of course it is.'

'Do you remember where you were arrested.'

'Course I do. I was in my car. A load of armed heavies pulled me over. They were none too gentle, either.'

'Yes. But do you remember the location of your car at the time you were pulled over?'

Something flitted across Willis's eyes. One of those involuntary events Freda Heath had described to the DI, perhaps.

'Uh no. Not exactly.' Willis suddenly seemed confused. Unsure.

Vogel glanced towards Freda Heath. He'd already asked her to intervene and indeed to take over the questioning, if she felt he were muddying psychiatric waters. She shook her head very slightly and gestured for him to continue.

'Do you remember if anyone was with you in the car?'

Willis frowned. He seemed to be really concentrating, making an effort to answer truthfully.

'I'm not sure. Uh, yes. Dawn Saslow was with me, wasn't she? But . . .'

Was there a kind of panic in Willis's eyes. Vogel couldn't tell for certain.

'But . . . she wasn't there when I was pulled over.' Willis clenched both his fists and held them briefly in front of his mouth, before lowering his hands and placing them on the table before him.

'Why was that?' he asked, almost curiously. Vogel glanced at Freda Heath again.

'Might you have left Dawn somewhere?' Freda asked in a level tone.

Willis looked at the professor as if seeing her for the first time.

'Why would I have left her anywhere?' he asked, sounding bewildered.

'Could you have hurt her, perhaps? Might you have done that, DS Willis?'

'What? Hurt Dawn? Why would I do that?'

The words sounded normal enough, but Willis's eyes no longer seemed focused on anyone or anything in the room. His chest began to heave, as if he were having trouble breathing or as if he were struggling to control forces within himself. His eyes rolled back into their sockets. His tongue protruded slightly from his mouth. He lifted his hands from the table and let his arms fell loosely by his side. Then he sprang to his feet and threw both arms in the air.

The two uniformed constables on duty by the door stepped forward. Vogel and Nobby Clarke both indicated that they should hold back.

'I am Aeolus,' said the man, who had previously been known to them only as Willis. 'I am Aeolus. I control the winds. The winds of fortune. The winds of change. I am all powerful. This Willis is merely my servant.'

The voice was immediately different, more educated and with the hint of Latin accent that Vogel had noticed on the phone. His eyes blazed. If Vogel hadn't known better, he would have thought it was with a kind of righteousness. So, when Willis was Aeolus, he was aware of his other identities. Or at least some of the time he was, at any rate. Freda Heath had suggested that might be so.

'And the others, Leo, Al, Saul, are they also your servants?' Vogel continued.

'When I call upon them they are there.'

'But why, you Aeolus, so powerful, why do you call on these . . .' Vogel paused, wondering how far too push this. Again he glanced towards Freda Heath. The professor gestured for him to continue. Was she reading his mind, Vogel wondered? Well that's what psychiatrists were supposed to be able to do, wasn't it? Or was it? Vogel didn't have the faintest idea. He went for it anyway. The man he had thought to be a perfectly ordinary police detective was staring at Vogel. Silent. Expectant. Challenging?

'Yes?' he queried.

'. . . these pathetic apologies for men,' Vogel continued. 'A serial paedophile, a twisted closet gay, an inadequate sexual misfit, who dreams of having a family but cannot even perform the sexual act . . .'

It happened very quickly. Again there was the moment of

almost total muscular relaxation. Then the man, who had once been Willis, threw himself across the desk that separated them and tightened his hands around Vogel's neck.

'You think you are better than me, you jumped-up piece of filth,' he yelled. 'You think you're the special one. I can have any woman I damned well want. They flock to me. I know how to court them. I know what they want . . .'

The two uniforms leapt forwards, grabbed the suspect and pulled him off the DI. This time nobody protested. They pushed him back onto his chair and now stood on either side of him, each with a hand on one shoulder.

Willis slumped in his seat. Vogel coughed a couple of times and took a drink of water from the one glass that had survived the unexpected onslaught. The voice Willis had just used had held more than a trace of Wiltshire. A rural burr. That must have been Saul speaking, Vogel thought, just as Sonia had described him.

'Yes, but you can't give it to them though, can you?' Vogel remarked, continuing to pressurise. 'That's your problem, isn't it? You can't do it. You can't fuck.'

Willis/Saul/Leo/Al, the man who believed he was Aeolus, raised his head and stared at Vogel. There was ice in his eyes. Vogel wondered if he would try to attack again, but he didn't. Instead, his lips cracked into a kind of leer.

'They have to be the right age,' he said. 'If they're young enough I can do it.'

The accent was now Scottish. Melanie Cooke had told her friend, Sally, that Al spoke with a Scottish accent. So this was Al, Vogel thought. Vogel watched him pull repeatedly at the collar of his suit, at the back of his neck. What was he doing, Vogel wondered? Then he realised. He was trying to put a non-existent hood over his head. Al was always hooded, even in the summer. All the reports about him indicated that. This was Al all right.

'So,' Vogel continued gently. 'Why didn't you make it with young Melanie Cooke?'

The other man's eyes narrowed.

'Because she was a vicious, knowing bitch,' he said, still sounding Scottish. 'She wasn't the way I like them at all. She was no child.'

Vogel almost had to physically gulp back his repulsion. He had worked with this man, lived out his professional life alongside him. Vogel wanted to attack him, just as the creature he had once known as Willis had attacked him, only more effectively. He controlled himself with difficulty.

'Come on,' he said. 'You can't ever do it with a woman, can you? Not really. Not the way they want. Not the way you want.'

The other man's eyelids flickered. He made no reply.

'You're all right as Leo though, aren't you? You can fuck a man all right. Can't you? That's no problem for you is it, Leo?'

Vogel felt Nobby Clarke's eyes upon him, burning into him. Had he really gone too far now? The man they had known as Willis took a huge intake of air, exerted his not inconsiderable strength, forced himself to his feet not withstanding the restraining hands of the two uniforms and stood, directly facing his four inquisitors.

'I am Aeolus,' he said, in that curious mix of English public school and classic Latin.

'I know not of what you speak. I am Aeolus.'

EPILOGUE

Prolonged further questioning brought about little change and next to no information from the multi-personalitied suspect. Leo, Al, Saul and Willis all seemed to have effectively disappeared beneath the wings of Aeolus. The CPS remained unsure whether a prosecution could be successfully brought in view of such extensive mental health issues.

Meanwhile, the Avon and Somerset Constabulary successfully applied to the courts to be allowed to remand their suspect in police custody without charging him for four days – the maximum period allowed except in cases of terrorism – whilst they continued their investigations into the case.

The Greater Manchester Police were asked to check out Willis's early life. They quickly found that the story he had told his ex-wife, although factually based, had strayed significantly from the truth.

Willis's father may well have been a wife-beating philanderer, who had yet to be found, but his stepfather, Peter Maxwell, was not as Willis had portrayed him. And he was dead. He'd killed himself soon after his daughter had been discovered drowned in her bath. Manchester Police had located Maxwell's brother, who told them that Peter Maxwell could not come to terms either with the death of his daughter or being suspected of involvement in it. The brother further maintained that Maxwell was a gentle man, who had never been violent or abusive to his wife, his stepson or his daughter.

But the brother said Maxwell always thought John Willis, whom he considered to be a highly disturbed child, may have attacked the little girl, even though he had only been twelve at the time. Maxwell's brother claimed that the young John had resented the presence of his stepfather from the start and been seriously jealous of his stepsister, whom he believed to have stolen the affections of the mother he adored.

It also transpired that Willis's mother was not dead. She'd

suffered from lifelong mental health problems, which she certainly seemed to have passed on to her only son. She remained in a secure hospital having been sectioned under the mental health act when Willis was twenty and at engineering college. Eighteen months later, Willis had suddenly decided to change his career choice and become a policeman, selling the Manchester family home and relocating to join the Avon and Somerset Constabulary.

Chillingly, there was more. At about the time Willis left Manchester, a fifteen-year-old girl, who lived nearby, had disappeared and never been found. Following the new information indicating that Willis was a multiple murderer, the Manchester Police organised a search of the house which had been the Willis family home. They dug up a concrete patio, which neighbours told them the young Willis had built and found the decaying body of a young female. Nobody had much doubt that she would prove to be the missing girl. It seemed that Willis had something of a fondness for concrete.

To an increasingly shocked Vogel, the greatest puzzle was why on earth Willis had decided to become a police officer. He wondered if it could have been a sick joke, but Willis had kept up a highly plausible act for an extraordinary thirteen years. Vogel supposed it was possible that, in his day-to-day identity, Willis had genuinely wanted to become a normal, everyday policeman. That he'd been subconsciously fighting off his other, highly disturbing identities, along with any memories of his already violent past. Freda Heath considered that could have been so.

Vogel wondered if Willis had ever actually succeeded in fighting off his other identities but, given the accumulating murders the police were finding, the DI had his doubts. So the terrible possibility remained that Willis had been responsible for more unknown deaths, and more bodies might be buried at his Bristol home – which was now being searched on a scale verging on virtual demolition. But none had been found yet.

All they could deal with was what they knew. Hemmings and Vogel pushed the Crown Prosecution Service as hard as they could. Ultimately, it was agreed that the suspect, now calling himself Aeolus, would be charged with the murders of Melanie

Cooke, Tim Southey and Manee Jainukul. The magistrates advised that further charges may be added at a later date.

The alternative would have been for Willis/Aeolus to be detained indefinitely, under the mental health act. Broadmoor and similar mental institutions served their purpose and were no picnic, but Vogel, along with Hemmings and Nobby Clarke, had been determined that the due process of law be pursued.

All three of them believed it vitally important, not only because of the nature of his crimes, but also because of Willis's position as a detective sergeant in the Avon and Somerset Constabulary, that justice should be seen to be done.

Having been duped himself, Vogel accepted that the creature genuinely suffered from dissociative personality disorder. Vogel was no expert on the health of the human mind, however he believed absolutely in the concept of evil. He'd seen too much of it in his police career not to. Vogel hoped Willis would be tried in a court that also recognised the concept of evil. A court which would judge him to be an evil man, with a number of twisted perversions which he indulged by the adoption of disparate personalities. He hoped the jury would follow the example of the one in the trial of the Yorkshire Ripper. In 1981, Peter Sutcliffe was charged with the murder of thirteen prostitutes and the attempted murder of seven more. No doubt on the advice of clever, but, in Vogel's opinion, unscrupulous counsel, Sutcliffe had pleaded not guilty to murder on grounds of diminished responsibility, owing to a diagnosis of paranoid schizophrenia. But, in court, the jury had rejected the plea.

On the fourth day after the arrest, Vogel formally charged the detained suspect under his birth name, John Henry Willis. Willis stood before the DI, vacant and glassy-eyed, as if not really aware of what was happening to him. He had a brief already muttering about him being unfit to stand trial. Vogel remained hopeful but not unduly optimistic.

However, Vogel was not hopeful about his own professional future. He'd already been told that he could face suspension, at least, on all manner of grounds. In a way, he didn't mind, because he felt he must have been guilty of some sort of dereliction of duty in failing to recognise the kind of man Willis was. He did mind being used as a scapegoat, though, as he certainly hadn't been the only one fooled by Willis, but there was little doubt that a scapegoat was what the Avon and Somerset Constabulary were desperately seeking.

Immediately after Willis was charged, Vogel left to visit Dawn Saslow at Southmead Hospital, where she had remained since being rescued from her underground prison. Saslow seemed to have perked up. When Vogel had visited the day after her admission, she'd still been tearful, disorientated and clearly in considerable pain. Now, she was sitting up in bed, in one of the smart, single rooms which Southmead provides. Her stripy, tracksuit-style pyjamas were clearly not hospital issue, someone must have brought her own in for her. She had also washed her hair.

Make-up, however, would be out of the question for some time. Saslow's face was still a mass of bruises and Vogel knew that her right cheek bone had been fractured. Her nose and lips were swollen and distorted. When she spoke, her voice was slightly slurred.

'Good to see you, boss,' she said. 'Sorry I'm not a prettier sight.'

Her voice and manner were cheerful, but Vogel could see that keeping them that way was a huge effort for the young DC. He told her that Willis had been charged and professed more confidence than he actually felt that the man would stand trial.

'That's great, boss,' said Saslow.

She seemed slightly awkward with him, however, which she had never been before. Perhaps, Vogel thought, she too held him responsible for what had happened. He didn't blame her. He only stayed a few minutes. He could see how tired Saslow was and he felt awkward with her too.

For once in his life, he reckoned he had worked enough twelve and even eighteen hour days.

He headed home, feeling as low as he ever had in his career.

Mary was at his side as soon as he walked through the door.

'Any news?' she asked.

'We've charged him.'

'Yes. You said you were going to. I meant, news about you, David.'

Vogel had told her that he might be suspended and shook his head.

'It'll be all right, you'll see,' he said.

'Yes, of course,' replied Mary, smiling brightly. It was a smile that was almost as forced as Dawn Saslow's attempt at cheeriness, thought Vogel. Mary's mobile, which was in her jacket pocket, rang. She took it out, glanced at the screen and put it back in her pocket.

'Aren't you going to answer it?'

Mary shook her head.

'Anyone I know?' Vogel asked.

Mary coloured slightly.

'I-I was going to tell, you,' she began hesitantly. 'Only you had so much on and then, what with Willis and Saslow, well . . .'

'Go on,' said Vogel flatly.

'Well, you did tell me to contact your sister myself, if I wanted to. You know – when we had that silly row. So I did. I phoned her. I explained that you were unsure what to do about it all, that you weren't quite ready. She had no idea you'd not even been told you were adopted. I explained how shocked you were and everything . . .'

Her voice tailed off.

'Did you, indeed?' Vogel murmured.

'I'm so sorry, David,' said Mary, 'I know I shouldn't have done it without talking to you again.'

'And that was her calling, the woman who says she is my sister?'

'Yes.' Mary paused.

'I don't think there is much doubt that she's your sister, David,' she continued boldly. 'Your half-sister.'

'Give me your phone,' said Vogel.

Mary removed it from her pocket again and handed it to him. He pushed return call.

A bright young-sounding female voice responded.

'Hello Mary, thanks for calling back.'

Vogel didn't speak for a few seconds.

'Hello?' queried the voice.

'It's David,' he replied quietly.

There was a pause at the other end of the line.

'Oh my God,' said the voice. 'It's just so good to speak to you.'

'It's good to speak to you, too,' replied Vogel and, rather to his surprise, he found that he meant it.

He reached out with his free arm for Mary and pulled her close.

ACKNOWLEDGEMENTS

I am incredibly grateful, for their expert advice and assistance, to: NHS Psychiatric Consultant Dr Billy Boland, and former Detective Sergeant Frank Waghorn of the Avon and Somerset Constabulary.

Lightning Source UK Ltd.
Milton Keynes UK
UKHW04f2039230718
326146UK00001B/1/P